Son of Skye

THÉRÈSE PILON

iUniverse, Inc.
Bloomington

Son of Skye

Typography and page composition by J. K. Eckert & Company, Inc.

iUniverse books may be ordered through booksellers or by contacting:

iUniverse
1663 Liberty Drive
Bloomington, IN 47403
www.iuniverse.com
1-800-Authors (1-800-288-4677)

ISBN: 978-1-4620-7061-9 (sc)
ISBN: 978-1-4620-7062-6 (hc)
ISBN: 978-1-4620-7063-3 (e)

Library of Congress Control Number: 2011961647

Printed in the United States of America

iUniverse rev. date: 11/23/2011

This book is dedicated to my dad,

Lorne Carmen Blake.

You were my light in the darkened places.

1

"So, what do you think?" The sun's light, reflected through the hall window, glanced off the painting Leah held delicately between thumb and forefinger. The colors had not set yet, but she couldn't wait to show the auburn-haired woman her work.

"It's beautiful." Slender hands reached out to pat Leah's shoulder in a gesture of unspoken fondness.

Leah came around to stand in front of her mother's easel. The painting was only partially finished, but even in its half-finished state, it was a thing of beauty. They were all there—not in their entirety, mind you, but they would be soon: all the old friends from that other place that was often thought of, but rarely spoken of, for fear the memories would vanish as a dream does after one awakens from a deep sleep. Looking at the painting, it was easy to see where Leah got her talent.

The sudden forlorn howling at the forest's edge shattered the morning's peaceful stillness.

"Chera!" Ignoring the overturned easel and the spilled paints, which ran and pooled across the ornately marbled floor, Leah raced to the window, her mother right behind her. The open space below them was empty.

"There's nothing there." Nickolous was peering into the morning's mist. If there had been something there in the shadows of the wooded area, there wasn't now.

"Wait!" Leah hissed between clenched teeth as she grabbed her brother's arm. "There. See?"

Nickolous followed her gaze. There was nothing. Nothing except the empty clearing rimmed at the outer edges with huge trees of oak and maple. To the left of this ran a narrow stream with tall grasses and a few aspen lining the bank. At night, long after the day was silenced, and the creatures that ruled the twilight emerged from their hidden sleeping places, Nickolous and Leah would lie in their beds, lulled to sleep by the musical, mystical sounds that entwined with the night.

"Well, whoever or whatever it was, it's gone now." Nickolous turned away from his sister, and for a moment he was standing alone beneath the tree from the mists of his dreams, and the nameless eternal being was beside him, silent, yet speaking of things not yet understood, nor seen.

"My son?"

Brown eyes met blue as Nickolous realized with a start where he was and hid his disappointment by placing an arm about his sister to draw her away from the window where she stood, straining for a glimpse of what was not there.

§ § § § § §

The day deepened into twilight, as all days do. Most of the day had been spent cleaning up the spilled paint from the marbled floor and repairing the canvas. No one spoke of the morning's events, least of all Nickolous, yet each knew the thoughts of the other.

Supper was quiet and uneventful, and when the rain began later that evening, it wasn't surprising that Nickolous threw on his raincoat and went for a walk to be alone with his thoughts. Neither mother nor daughter tried to stop him, for they knew he would not go far—they too, wanted to be alone with their memories.

Leah squinted in the fading light. It was almost too dark to paint, but she was determined to finish it before morning, and besides, she wasn't tired yet. The light cast shadows against the wall, which seemed to dance about as she turned her attention back to the easel to finish the last of the scenes depicted: that of a large silver-gray wolf running through a shaded glen, while above, in a blue sky tinged with gold, a beautiful white owl glided silently, keeping vigil over those it watched below.

So engrossed was Leah in her work that she barely heard the hall door slam shut of its own accord. It was the gust of wind which accompanied the slamming of the door that grabbed her attention— that, and the disheveled state of her brother as he leaned against the closed door, gasping for air as the rain ran in rivulets down his raincoat and pooled about his feet on the marbled hall floor.

"Nickolous!" Leah was out of her chair, halfway across the room, when she realized that there was a look about her brother that was of another place, and she knew what he was going to say even before he said it.

"Orith. There. In the rain. He was beckoning with his beaded staff. He looked as if he'd been ill."

Nickolous turned to look at Leah, his large blue eyes wide with excitement. He lowered himself into the chair his mother offered and buried his face in his hands. Feeling suddenly weary, he looked up.

"What are we going to do?" He looked beseechingly at the auburn-haired woman who stood silently gazing down at him, her dark eyes mirroring his concern.

"We wait."

§ § § § § §

Sometime during the night, the storm passed, while the moon, full and round, rose white and luminescent, her soft light reflecting against the rain-laden trees. The soft breeze that had arisen was enough to shake the heavy burden from their leaves, while the spattering of the water as it hit the sodden earth made little sound.

Nickolous wasn't sure what had awakened him, but the pale light streaming through the curtained window told him the storm had passed, the dawn still a few hours away. Throwing the covers aside, he stood at the now partially opened window, peering into the clearing below. It looked empty. He strained forward as a form detached itself from the shadows beneath the trees.

Orith.

Nickolous refrained from calling out, afraid that when next he looked, the form would have vanished.

Orith, his companion of adventures past, waved weakly as he brandished his beaded staff skyward. White wings unfurled slowly as the great owl pointed south. Then there was only the starry night—that, and the curtains, which curled lazily around Nickolous's legs as the soft breeze wafted carelessly through the half-opened window.

§ § § § § §

"Well? Did you get through?"

The heavily cloaked figure shrugged wearily as Sarah placed a steaming gourd of tea in front of him. Orith accepted the drink gratefully, for the journey "between" had been difficult, and he had not yet fully recovered from his illness. Sarah patted him gently on his shoulder, her large brown eyes full of concern.

"I think I got through both times, although, with the rain, it was difficult to tell. The second time for sure," Orith answered as he drew a warm blanket about his frail form.

The sudden gust of wind caused everyone in the small room to look up. Chera, soaked and dripping from the rain, trotted in. Careful to avoid those huddled about the fire, she resisted the urge to shake herself, knowing it would not be polite or appreciated.

"Chera." Gabriel moved to make room for his mate. He nuzzled her gently before turning his attention back to Orith.

Orith still held the hot drink tightly, as if to draw warmth from the hollowed-out gourd's contents. The cavern was eerily silent as everyone waited for him to speak. He trembled slightly as he set the gourd on the roughly hewn table. "If I got through, then others might; with that in mind, we must be prepared. A-Sharoon may be hidden from our view, but her handiwork is not."

Chera nodded in agreement, for even though the storm had peaked in its ferocity, it still carried with it a warning that none could mistake. She sighed deeply, for she knew what Orith meant. Her short foray into the forest this night had revealed much. She met Orith's gaze openly, yet said nothing. Beside her, Gabriel, his blue eyes missing little, spoke; the words were meant to reassure the others; still, there was an undertone of something more—something best left unsaid for now in the words. "It's been a long day. We all should get some rest," he said decidedly, and the other companions agreed.

Long after everyone had gone off to the comfort of their beds, Orith sat at the table, thinking, his mind seeking the answers to unknown things while the flickering flame from the single candle danced with the shadows upon the earthen walls.

§ § § § § §

"You look terrible." This from Leah as Nickolous sat down to breakfast.

"Thanks," Nickolous replied sarcastically, as he reached for a hot croissant.

Saying nothing, but observing her son's tired expression, Nickolous's mother wordlessly passed the strawberry jam, then sat down across the table from her son, her expression one of concern yet guarded in its intensity. She shrugged slender shoulders as she pushed her dark hair back from a face that had seen much. Dark circles shadowed her eyes, and her high cheekbones with their alabaster skin bespoke of an unknown ancestry that her son and daughter shared. She sat back, watchful.

Nickolous tried to eat but found the food tasteless. Exhausted from lack of sleep, and haunted by Orith's visit, he wanted nothing more than to find a way back to that place that pulled at him day and night without a moment's respite. The final battle was yet to be fought, and it was obvious that they were needed. It was also becoming clear that somehow the magic had followed them; or rather, it had always been there, waiting for them to find another door; another entrance. Sighing deeply, Nickolous rose from the table, determined to find a way back to Skye and those he had left behind.

Leah glanced at her mother as her brother left the room, yet neither said anything, for they knew what he was feeling.

§ § § § §

"How did the hunt go?" Chera asked, as Gabriel sent sentries to scout ahead of them. Confident that there was no immediate danger, Chera strolled leisurely beside her mate in the early morning's dawning.

"As well as can be expected," Gabriel replied, his voice low and throaty. "The vermin hide when they hear us coming, and for the few we find, there are hundreds more we don't see. Their hidden lairs run deep, and even the most stalwart of my pack hesitates at the dank tunnels when we come across them."

"And who can blame them?" Chera muttered beneath her breath, remembering all too well her own experiences from the not-too-distant past. She paused suddenly, her body taut, as a familiar sound reached her sensitive ears, her posture alerting her mate as he scented the air and that which was carried upon it.

The towering form, unexpected, was nonetheless a pleasant surprise, as Jerome, his round face beaming, lumbered out from the forest's depths to greet the two wolves.

Gabriel greeted the forest warrior warmly, glad that this fierce but gentle giant was on their side, for Jerome was of the old race. One of the most ancient of the forest clans, he and his kind held the ability to change their appearance when needed. Like the most revered of the forest guardians, the mighty oak, Jerome and his warriors could change at will and become like those mighty sentinels that watched over the forests that were ever changing. They and they alone remained the same while the world about them changed. They were the watchers of the forest; guardians of the smaller of the clans.

Yet Gabriel was also aware that Jerome, who could not possibly have had time to reach his home, could only have returned for one reason, and he wasn't entirely sure he wanted to hear it. "And the rest of your warriors?" Gabriel asked as Jerome fell into step beside him.

"The most trusted and fiercest of my warriors have been positioned at the gateways," Jerome answered, so softly that his companions weren't sure they had heard correctly.

"The gateways to the *Before* and *After?*" Gabriel asked incredulously.

"Yes."

"That cannot be!" Chera's voice was anguished as she stopped to stare up at the warrior of the forest.

The look on Jerome's craggy face said more than any words could ever say, and the wolves felt an unfamiliar panic at the news that the most sacred of the learnings were threatened by dark shadows.

"Not even A-Sharoon would dare such treachery," Gabriel growled, the sound deep and throaty, so that Chera, who knew her mate better than anyone else, glanced at him in concern.

"For the vengeance she craves, she would destroy all, even herself. That combined with the fact that she has aligned herself with a power that is darker and greedier than she..." Jerome motioned helplessly with his war club, unable to say more, the emotions flowing through him so great that he fell silent.

§ § § § §

Nickolous suddenly put his hands to his head, cradling it as if in great pain. The unseen watcher started forward as Nickolous crumpled to his knees, then stepped back just as quickly beneath the concealing shadows of the giant oak tree.

Nickolous had risen to his feet and was looking around, bewildered by what had just happened to him as the figure melded with the shadows, back into the forest depths.

Only the slight trembling of the tree's leaves caught Nickolous's attention as he gazed deep within the forest's depths, wondering...for it was a day of no wind.

It was that kind of day.

§ § § § §

Sarah was so busy gathering small pieces of driftwood for their morning fire that she failed to notice the hooded figure standing in the center of the path, watching her. "Old One!" Sarah dropped her arm-load of wood as she recognized the bent figure of her old friend.

The Old One, wizened and bent, her skin darkened by the sun to a leathery brown, was older than most; her turnings beyond count. She was one of the *"knowing"* clans. An old she rat, she saw what others could not or would not, and so she carried with her the unwritten knowledge of the before time deep within her memories.

As Sarah rushed to embrace the Old One, Timothy appeared at the forest's edge, his arms laden with fruit for their breakfast; while the Old One hugged Sarah to her fiercely, glad to be back among friends. Later, as Sarah retrieved the wood she had dropped in her haste ear-lier, the Old One fell into step beside Timothy, and for a time they walked companionably side by side; content to be in one another's company once again.

"Was your journey a good one?" Timothy asked as Sarah, arms once again laden with wood, hurried to catch up to them.

"First, let's eat some breakfast; then we can share our news," Sarah suggested, for she had noticed how tired the Old One looked. The shadows beneath the weathered eyes had deepened in the short time they had been apart. Something untoward had happened since last their paths had crossed, Sarah was sure of it.

It wasn't long before the cavern where they had taken shelter was filled with the aroma of flatbread, which had been baked on the hot stones placed over the coals of the fire pit, and tea, which had been steeped in a small earthen pot, resistant to the intense heat of the flames that struggled upward from the glowing coals in the very cen-ter of the pit. These were left uncovered so that the air circulating through the cavern could fan them into small flames from time to time, keeping the dampness out. Sarah also brought out some wild honeycomb she had been saving. This, along with the fresh berries that Timothy had gathered earlier, completed the simple meal.

All the unasked questions of earlier were put aside until the last crumbs had been eaten and the tea served. Then, as Sarah bustled about cleaning up, while at the same time reassuring the others that, yes, she was listening, the Old One began her tale.

2

After the battle between A-Sharoon and those of the forest clans, after Nickolous and Leah had returned to that far-off place they knew as home, the Old One and those of her clan who had survived decided to return to theirs. Along the way, their numbers had dwindled; as they happened upon others of their kind, where the prospect for resettlement looked good, many stayed on. By the time the remainder of them had made it home, most were so disheartened by the destruction that surrounded them, they had simply salvaged what remained of their possessions and dispersed to different areas where they could attempt to build new lives.

The Old One, against the advice of her friends, had made the return trip alone. Everything had gone well until she had been caught in the eye of the storm. Cold and wet, she had taken refuge beneath a stand of ancient oak trees, their thick, sturdy branches entwined so tightly that she was kept reasonably dry and protected. Then, as the thunder rolled, and the lightning flashed, a shadowy form had appeared and briefly took shape.

By now, Timothy and Sarah were holding their breath, waiting.

Was it?

Could it be?

Timothy leaned across the table to gaze into ageless eyes, and the question went unasked as the Old One shrugged her shoulders.

"Who? Nickolous? Or just the wishful imagining's of an Old One who was cold, wet, and weary?" She patted Timothy's hand in a silent gesture of understanding before leaning back against the padded backrest of fragrant cedar boughs that Timothy had made for her earlier. "Who knows?"

The sudden knocking at the entrance of the opening caused them all to jump. Startled, Sarah turned, then, recognizing their visitor, laughed in delight.

"Owen. We had not thought to see you so soon." Timothy greeted the white owl warmly.

Owen gratefully accepted the place at the hearth that was made available and leaned close, the warmth running through him. Glad to be back among his friends, he drank long and deep of the drink given him.

As he returned the nearly empty gourd to Sarah, Timothy answered the unasked question. "Orith fares well."

"That's good. I was worried about him, and the journey was hurried because of it." Visibly relaxed now and warm, Owen met the Old One's gaze evenly across the roughly hewn stump that served as a table.

"We have only won a reprieve—if that's what you're wondering."

Owen smiled; despite the sharpness in her voice, he, better than anyone, knew her true heart. Laughing softly, he reached out to gently pat her shoulder. "Old One, it is truly good to see you again." He leaned back, his expression now serious. "There's more to come. I'm afraid we've only won a reprieve at best, as our old friend says. If we had destroyed A-Sharoon when the opportunity presented itself...well, what comes our way now would be much easier to deal with."

Sarah sniffed audibly, her silky whiskers twitching back and forth in agitation. Placing the hollowed-out gourd that served as a drinking cup down carefully, she gestured through the open door toward the mist-shrouded mountains. "And what of the others?" she asked, her large brown eyes narrowing as she grew angry at the thought that the forest clans had to face yet another threat, this one totally foreign and unknown. "Are we to wait around like children so that what little we have left will be taken yet again? Why, within all the writings and hidden lore, can't one of the gatekeepers, or watchers, or whatever they are, find the daughter's lair and end this once and for all?"

"Because, little daughter, the time of the two centers to join the circle is not yet complete."

Sarah gasped as Timothy, sword drawn, leapt toward the open door, only to find Owen there ahead of him, barring the way.

3

Deep within the cavern, a blue-white light flickered, then sprang upward toward the ceiling where long, fragile fingers of ice fire explored its prison. Finally, with a shuddering sigh, it retreated back to the floor, receding into itself until it was once again no more than a glowing ember.

After a while, when the echoing sighs had fallen silent, what appeared to be nothing more than a shadow within the deepest depths of the cavern began to move toward the barely glowing embers. There were no cautionary moves, for the fire's keeper did not fear his reluctant prisoner; rather, he drew comfort from the creature's sorrow in its unwanted confinement. Drawing a deep breath of satisfaction, he turned from the Living Flame toward the woman who stood behind him.

A-Sharoon flung her heavy cloak carelessly on the earthen floor, heedless of the narrowed eyes which followed her movements with disdain.

"Woman, what do you want here, in this sacred place?" The rasping voice seemed to reverberate throughout the cavernous room where the two of them stood.

A-Sharoon looked disdainfully at the barely glowing embers, then at the scowling figure beside her. Her head raised defiantly, brows arched; she gazed down at the speaker, for she was a good deal taller than he was. Like two combatants, they stood thus for some moments, eyes locked, searching each other's depths for signs of hidden thoughts.

11

A-Sharoon broke the stifling silence; the words honeyed and soft. "I needed to speak to the master of the night. I need to know what progress had been made...that is, has there been any contact with our allies in the hidden places."

The red eyes that peered at her from beneath the hooded robe would have been enough to give anyone else pause, but not so the Daughter of Darkness. In her quest for vengeance, and by her birthright, all trace of humanity had been extinguished. Therefore, she was not about to fear a comrade of the darkness whom she secretly considered to be inferior, but nonetheless needful...for a time.

"What you have need to know of, you will know." The eyes that now glared at her were no more than slits and the answered reply little more than a snarl as the figure turned aside; the rustling of heavy robes were the only sound to be heard as the hunched form moved slowly out of sight.

A-Sharoon stood a moment longer before grabbing her cloak from off the earthen floor, and as she did, the blue-white flame, which had retreated into a small spark of near nothingness, flicked with the rapidity of an angered serpent toward her outstretched hand. Her reaction was nearly as quick—but not quite.

The freezing effect, even through the unseen barrier that separated them, was only momentary. The flicking tongue of the flame had barely grazed the upturned palm through the shield that held it captive. As A-Sharoon nursed her tingling hand, a self-satisfied smile played about her blood-red lips. Kneeling down, she gazed directly into the flame's flickering depths and was flung backward by the sudden blast of flame that shot upward, off the earthen floor, then just as quickly settled back within its center. Rising, A-Sharoon stood a moment longer, her pulse racing at the prospect of this new and unexpected ally.

Outside the cavern's entrance, the sentry on duty shivered in the damp humid air as the sounds of dark laughter crept upward from the hidden places, to seep into the outer world of the living.

§ § § § §

Timothy, sword drawn and already arcing upward, was flung backward, where he landed in a tangled heap at his sister's feet. The Old One had risen quickly as Owen had moved to guard the unexpected visitor, her old eyes hardly daring to believe what they were seeing. In all her years of studying and seeking the truth of the before time, she had never thought to see the believed weaver of legends with her own eyes. Sarah, too, was staring in disbelief at the opened door and that which filled the breadth and depth of it.

"Sorry, old friend," Owen apologized as he helped Timothy up from his sprawled position where he had landed against the jagged rock. Meanwhile, the unannounced visitor had moved further into the cramped room.

"Who—what—are you?" Sarah's whispered question was surprisingly loud in the sudden silence.

"I am that I am, just as you are who you are. I am that which is feared. I am that which is revered. I am. I am the keeper of dreams. The legends you weave within your deepest memories, I hold for you, so that when the time comes, you may fulfill your destiny. That is who I am." The regal head lowered so that they were eye level. The being spoke again as the hooded covering fell back, revealing a face so beautiful, yet so terrible, that it was hard to look upon without feeling joy and fear in the same breath. "I am who I am, but, like you, I am mortal."

"But the teachings..." The Old One was bewildered by this unexpected turn of events.

The laugh that resounded in the silence was low and melodious. "The teachings? Old One: we who guard the gates are not immortal. There are many things which go on seemingly forever, but nearly everything has its time under the heavens. Those who guard from above ensure the continuance of the teachings of light to those below." There was a gentle sighing sound as the being partially unfurled great black wings, and the next words were whispered.

"My time approaches. Another must be found worthy of the quest. For many turnings I, and those most trusted, have seen to it that the balance was kept even. It is a sad day that comes when the balance is tipped to favor the night. Yet all is not lost, for another has been chosen to learn the sacred teachings, and it is he who will lead the darkness to the destruction meant for those who entrust themselves to the keeping of the light—and betray that trust."

The golden head bowed lower so that Sarah saw what the others could not: great crystalline tears gathered then fell unheeded down a face that was ageless. For a brief moment, Sarah gazed into old-young eyes, and she saw.

Owen felt suddenly older than his turnings as an inexplicable sadness filled his being. The others felt it, too. The Old One sniffed loudly as she rummaged for a handkerchief amongst her tattered belongings. Sarah, her big brown eyes luminous with emotion, turned

away as she fought to keep her emotions under control, while Timothy coughed self-consciously. When next he looked, it was to discover what the others already had—

The visitor had vanished.

Silence, complete and overwhelming, threatened to suffocate
them as translucent tendrils of white mist rose up from the damp
earth to caress their weary bodies. As the companions brought their
emotions under control, a sudden understanding passed between
them, even as the eerie wailing sound reached them—even before
the wind, bitter and biting in its cold fury, swept through the little
abode as if searching.

§ § § § § §

"Mother?" Leah knocked gently on her mother's bedroom door,
waiting patiently for an answer. There was none.

Nickolous, having returned from an early morning walk, had just
removed his jacket and was closing the closet door when he heard his
sister's anguished cry. Taking the stairs three at a time, he reached the
landing where his mother's room was; the door leading to the bedroom was ajar. Inside the room, Leah stood, gazing in horrified fascination at the empty bed and the stain that lay dark and damp upon its
surface.

A-Sharoon—the word, unspoken, hung heavy between them as the
tension in the room deepened; while Nickolous felt a darkness rising
within him that was nearly overwhelming; for even as he centered his
thoughts, he tried to look into that other place, his senses seeking. He
blew out his breath slowly—there was nothing.

When at last a cooler head prevailed, it wasn't his, but Leah's.
"Nickolous?" Leah placed a hand on his shoulder, for she was determined to stay as calm as possible.

Long moments passed before Nickolous's breathing calmed
enough to give way to more lucid thoughts. Yet even when it did, the
anger was still there, along with the need to draw from deeper within.
Somehow, he knew his mother was alive. That knowledge served to
calm him further, but there was something wrong with the events that
had brought them here; to this place, this day. Their mother was powerful in her own right—protected by abilities even her son and daughter could not yet comprehend. How, then, could this have happened?

Drawing in a deep breath, Nickolous met his sister's questioning
gaze. They both sensed what the other wanted, as they had once
before, in that far away place of legends and dreams, and their pur-

pose was united. Within an hour, the bedroom was cleaned and all traces of any struggle erased.

Although not spoken of aloud, it was agreed that Aunt Erlin, as well as the household staff, all of whom were on vacation, must not know what had transpired in their absence. Even though the house would remain virtually empty for the next few months, it was important that, to outside appearances, everything remain the same.

The entire house had been searched from top to bottom for clues. The fact that nothing had been found further confirmed the suspicion that other-world forces had been responsible for the sudden disappearance of a mother who had just been getting to know her children, and they her. The recent happenings cast a pall over the old house and its two inhabitants who restlessly paced the width and breadth of the house's massive grounds, their minds seeking answers, their eyes searching.

The fine mist that heralded the night was falling damp and thick upon the earth long before Nickolous and Leah gave up their search to seek the warmth of the fireplace in the den of the well-lit house.

4

Intense and searching, icy tendrils reached out as the wind shrieked, seeking, while the forest warrior shuddered, his limbs twisted in agony.

The small, loathsome creature glared upward at the guardian of the gate. Yellow eyes narrowed to mere slits on the elongated face as the feral creature snarled a warning to those gathered about. With long strides, the woman swept through the snapping, howling throng, her staff sweeping in a wide arc, sending anything in its path scurrying for cover.

"So, great guardian, where is your power and strength now?" The silky soft voice purred as the bearer of the staff drew herself up to her full height, which was imposing, to say the least.

With a sharp intake of breath, the watcher in the woods withdrew further back into the dense foliage that concealed him—the woman turned her head, listening.

In the taut silence that followed, even the wind stilled its aimless wandering as the woman's piercing gaze swept the open spaces and probed the forest's depths. Finally, satisfied that no intruders lurked nearby, she returned her attention to the Ancient One; guardian of the Living Flame.

The guardian, one of the forest warriors from before the times of remembrances, sighed deeply; his large frame shuddering against the vicious attack while his trunk-like legs glistened, dark and wet with the tears of the elements of life.

The unseen watcher shuddered as A-Sharoon used her staff to bruise and tear; but still the forest warrior stood, tall and unwavering, while the unnatural wind swirled about, causing havoc wherever there was something to be tossed or thrown.

The light, brilliant white, temporarily blinded her as sudden heat seared the staff. Dropping it, A-Sharoon flung an arm up to shield her face as the wind whipped about her, hot and humid. Then, the white light vanished as quickly as it had appeared.

Unseen eyes watched in voiceless silence as A-Sharoon, coughing and choking from the nearly unbearable heat, recovered her composure and knelt to retrieve the intricately carved staff. Shaking the staff furiously skyward while muttering incantations, she withdrew back to the shadowy depths of the forest; her small army of loathsome things closing ranks to ensure none followed the secret path their mistress took back to her lair of darkness. The smell of that which is unclean lingered long after they had departed.

And still the watcher in the woods waited…waited in the stifling silence that precedes the passing of that which is evil. And when the forest birds tentatively began to sing, and the smallest of the four-footed clans began to scurry about, he approached the guardian of the gate. But even then, he did so cautiously. Gentle hands caressed the grievous wounds until the great limbs no longer shuddered in pain.

As the forest warrior, tall and proud, gazed down at the winged healer who had risked much by revealing himself, an unspoken understanding passed between them as the two stood, their thoughts now one, the parting no more than a silent acknowledgment. The winged one turned away, eager to be gone from this place of sorrow, for he felt in part responsible for some of it. He had arrived too late to thwart the dark one's plans.

The Living Flame was gone—stolen by a creature so low, once one of their own kind, that the guardians who watched from above had been caught off guard. Realizing their complacency, they had tried to intercept the ancient dweller of the earth's hidden places but had been too late.

With a last backward glance, the weary traveler drew his midnight wings about him as the hidden winds once again swirled from the sacred places, blowing that which is unclean away. When the dust settled, there was only silence—that, and the forest warrior who remained standing; a mighty sentinel still, guarding the broken gate, which lie scattered in pieces around him.

§ § § § § §

"All the more reason we have to go to the above world for the boy," Gabriel replied, his tone brooking no argument as he watched the small flickering fire; the flames reflected eerily in his cobalt-blue eyes as he turned to face Owen.

Owen looked thoughtfully at those gathered about in the hidden cavern. "We may not have to. There may be another way to bridge the two worlds and bring Nickolous to us, for he feels our presence here as well as there; in that other place. If A-Sharoon is not stopped, it could affect all the worlds that bridge the essence of being. We will not be the only ones affected by the perfidious acts of this Daughter of the Night."

Timothy paced the cavernous room angrily, his long silky whiskers twitching in agitation. "We can't let that happen. There must be a balance—"

A shriek rent the air as the shadowy form leapt toward the opening, straight into Chera, who was returning from her night's hunt. Wherever it had been heading, it never made the journey, for Chera was in no mood to show mercy this night. Her silvery-gray eyes narrowed as she tossed the thing aside carelessly, her gaze fixed upon her mate.

"Well, I guess there's no need to ask where that thing came from," Sarah commented dryly as she held a tattered piece of leather to her nose to mask the pungent odor that suddenly permeated the cavern. She wondered silently what the rest were wondering: why hadn't someone smelled the odious creature long before it was seen scrambling toward the entrance?

Gabriel knew by Chera's stance that not all had gone well on the hunt, and he waited silently, knowing that what must be spoken of between the friends this night would forever change how they looked upon one another. "And so?" Gabriel faced his mate across the fire; waiting.

Everyone turned to stare at Chera as a sudden chill pervaded the cavern, causing the fire to flicker wildly; while the shadows splayed against the earthen walls crept up and out seeking as Sarah crept closer to her brother, Timothy.

Owen, the eyes and wings of the night, shuddered violently, as if he had already heard the words that now tumbled forth from Chera's mouth.

"The Living Flame is gone. Stolen by one who dares to think he can use the light to aid the darkness."

Sarah sobbed uncontrollably as Gabriel and Chera, Owen, Orith, and the Old One stood, speechless, unable to say anything, except to marvel that their world still continued. It was Owen who caught the Old One as she fell. Carefully placing her inert form upon a makeshift bed, he touched her wizened face gently.

"Rest, Old One. Sleep the sleep of healing and dream the dream of renewal," Owen murmured softly, before turning to face the others who stood, silent and watchful.

"Is she..." Sarah hastily wiped at the moisture on her cheek as the tears continued to flow silently.

"No. She only sleeps the sleep of dreams. This is her kind's most powerful gift. Be thankful she is with us in this darkened time, for if her heart were black and full of misdeed, we would have even more to worry about." For the first time in a long time, Owen felt a renewed hope, for it was not often that the Old Ones could call upon their hidden gifts. Seeing that Sarah and Timothy did not understand, Owen hastened to explain that there were times when some of the Old Ones could journey to those beyond places of mist and imagery and draw those they needed back with them. This was such a time.

"So then, all is not lost. There is yet hope?" Sarah asked, her big brown eyes glistening.

"Yes, Sarah," Owen replied. "There is hope."

"What about the Flame of Living Breath? Has it been extinguished, or does it languish in some dark place surrounded by evil?" Gabriel asked Owen as he arose from his cramped position beside the Old One's inert form.

"The Flame survives, as it must. They cannot destroy that which they cannot understand," Owen replied, much to everyone's surprise. "However, we must prepare for the worst and hope for the best. The guardian of the gate must have help. Those of us who can must go to that sacred place and help guard against further damage. Once there, I am sure that we will learn more about the dark dwellers' intention."

"By dark dwellers, I assume you mean A-Sharoon and *He* who dwells beneath the earth in the darkened places?" Timothy asked as he moved quickly about the cavern, gathering supplies that would be needed for the journey.

"Yes. For many years, there were rumors of a dark one who practiced the dark secrets. But as we were never confronted with more than rumors, we never bothered with him. Believing that he was a harmless hermit, our concerns were for what A-Sharoon was up to."

"A mistake we intend to remedy," Gabriel growled in irritation, suddenly restless, the need to be on the hunt once again strong within him.

"What about the Old One?" Chera nudged her mate gently, sensing his concern and discontent. His compassion for an old friend and his need to protect the guardian's gate was nearly overwhelming.

"Do we move her?" Gabriel nodded toward Owen, waiting for the big owl to respond, for he had studied the old writings in his youth.

For long moments, Owen stood, staring down at his old friend thoughtfully. Although it pained him greatly to leave her behind, he knew it would slow them down to take her. Besides, wherever she was walking at this moment, her steps must be sure and the way back clear. Decisively, he made up his mind.

"Timothy?" Owen turned toward the two large mice that had been with them since the beginning.

Timothy stepped forward. "I'll stay and guard the Old One while she's on her journey." Timothy didn't hesitate in his reply, for he knew his mission was just as important as Owen's.

"I'll stay with my brother." Sarah had stepped forward to stand beside Timothy, her gaze fixed fondly on the Old One who lay so still beneath the shabby coverlet. They were all in this together, for better or for worse, and Sarah had resolved a long time ago to do what was necessary without complaint—even so, she shivered inexplicably as the wind blew through the myriad of connecting tunnels.

Everyone hurried to their tasks as the cool breeze caressed them with unseen fingers. Long after it had retreated, back up the tunnel, each one of them were left with sharp prickles running up and down their spine.

"I'm sorry that we must leave you here unprotected," Gabriel apologized to Timothy and Sarah. He didn't feel comfortable leaving them here, in this place, alone, but he knew he had no choice. Their journey could not wait, and if the Old One could not guide Nickolous to them, then they would have to find another way. Looking back now, Gabriel realized they had misinterpreted some of the old writings: that the battle in the clearing of light turnings past had not been the battle that had been foretold. Rather, it had been a test of their strength to face what was to come, and the boy, so quickly forced to become a young man in a time and place so foreign to him, was gifted with the "*knowing*."

Gabriel sighed; weary to the center of his being, as Timothy nodded, silently acknowledging the big wolf's concern for him and

Sarah. Strangely, he had no fear of being left here in this place. To him it was simply a resting spot, and as soon as the Old One awakened, they would continue their journey to whatever fate awaited them.

Sarah, on the other hand, did not share her brother's philosophy and had agreed to stay for different reasons; the foremost reason being her fondness for the prone figure before her. She had no wish to leave the Old One behind, unguarded; so with that in mind, she hugged Owen and wished him well. As the big owl stammered his surprise, Chera found herself suddenly enveloped in a hug and Sarah's large brown eyes peering into her own. "Safe journey, my friend." The big wolf nodded, acknowledging the whispered words as Sarah turned to face Gabriel, who stepped back warily, muttering something unintelligible beneath his breath. Sarah laughed, surprising them all, and saluted the great silver wolf.

"If it's possible, if we can, we'll send one of Jerome's warriors to guard the path and guide your footsteps to where we wait. Orith will already have heard the news, so he will not return here but will follow us." Gabriel stood a moment longer at the cavern's opening looking back; then, with a decisive nod, turned, and with Chera at his side, loped effortlessly into the deepening day. The beating of powerful wings could be heard as Owen took flight, his duty to search the darkened corners and pathways of the forest floor.

§ § § § § §

Timothy pushed the covering aside and stepped outside into the early morning's dawning. The sun had set, the moon had risen, and another day had dawned since they had been left. Still the Old One slept; her breathing even and undisturbed. Shielding his eyes, he peered into the damp mist that swirled about him. There. He was sure of it now—something was out there.

Sarah moved nervously about in the cavern as she waited for her brother to return. As she bent to place another log on the fire, she found herself staring into a pair of narrowed, yellow eyes.

Timothy wheeled about as Sarah's screams filled the air, the sheer terror in her voice unmistakable.

§ § § § § §

Sarah and the changeling stared at each other from opposite sides of the cot where the Old One lay, still in a deep sleep. Long, jagged teeth protruded from the creature's foam-flecked mouth as it clawed the air threateningly, its yellow eyes narrowed to mere slits as it prepared to change form.

It was in this state that it was most vulnerable, and Timothy, remembering all too well past experiences, took advantage and thrust his sword toward the thing. As it fell to the earthen floor, an eerie cry filled the air, as the changeling, not mortally wounded, but now enraged that it had been challenged, rose to its feet and charged yet again.

Sarah stood mesmerized as the glowing eyes held her in their embrace. Out of the corner of her eye, she saw her brother leaping toward her and something else; but it was all in slow motion, and she couldn't seem to move fast enough as the roaring beast flung itself toward her and the one she guarded.

5

Nickolous wakened with a start. Sweat dampened his brow as his heart thudded heavily within his chest. He'd been dreaming—again. He shook his head wearily as he threw back the bed coverings. It would be much later that he would look back on that awakening and think it odd that he had never noticed the unnatural cold that morning. Nor the distant howling which seemed to reach through the mists thin coat of concealment, so that the seen and yet unseen could observe and were observed by realms not yet known by most of living kind.

"Nickolous." The sound was barely a whisper.

Nickolous was halfway down the winding staircase when the first draft of cold air hit him. Shivering, he hurried down the stairs and grabbed a heavy woolen sweater, which had been draped haphazardly across the bottom railing the night before.

"Nickolous!" For a moment, Nickolous stood frozen in time as the voice, stronger this time, carried with it the owner's identity.

"Old One?" Nickolous hardly dared breathe the words as he started toward the opened door, only to find Leah there ahead of him. She, too, had awakened to the sound of someone softly calling her name.

Together they both stood, peering into what appeared to be the early morning's dawning but wasn't. The moon, incredibly full and round, hung like a giant obelisk in the jet-black sky, made even more so by the mist's frothing, swirling, semi-transparency. Nothing else could be seen but the unending white stuff—Nickolous turned his head slightly to one side, listening.

The soft keening of the wind swirled about the two as they stepped out of the house into the arms of the mist, which embraced them damply.

"Where are we?" Leah's voice was lost to the wind's sighing. Her brother leaned down so he could hear the barely audible words.

"I don't know." He had to cup his hands together and yell into his sister's ear. Leah looked up at him towering over her, his piercing blue eyes so like—

A vision of the huge wolf, his blue eyes flashing, appeared before her, and then it was Chera's voice calling her. There was an urgency to it that could not be mistaken or denied. Leah's heart thudded painfully within her chest as Nickolous's face came into focus.

"What?" Leah's voice cracked with emotion as she shook her head to clear it.

"I *said,*" Nickolous was nearly yelling as he gripped Leah's shoulders tightly. "I said, I think we're lost. I can't see the house or the river. We should have reached the fence that borders Aunt Erlin's property by now. Something's up, and I'm not sure we're going to like it."

"*Nickolous…*"

The voice was so clear and so close that Nickolous turned his head, expecting to see a pair of warm black eyes set in a familiar wizened face. There was nothing. Nothing except the frothing whirling fog that curled lazily about him, and when he looked back, his hands grasped empty air.

"Leah?" Nickolous spun around, his breathing ragged, his gaze searching.

There was only the thickening mist and the wind, with its high singsong sound as it blew through the foliage against his face, to answer him.

§ § § § § §

Emptiness. Wind. Rain. A fog-like shroud that surrounded him and clung to him like a living, breathing thing. Nickolous shivered in its grasp as he breathed on his ice-cold hands, trying to feel some warmth. He had no idea how much time had passed since he had stepped away from Aunt Erlin's house into this seemingly empty void he now found himself in, and surprisingly, he really didn't care. He did not fear this place, for he knew it well. Taking a deep breath, he strode ahead, toward a faint gleam of bright light shining in the distance.

§ § § § § §

Leah held her breath as the snuffling sound came closer. As thick as the fog was, something had been tracking her since she had been separated from Nickolous hours earlier. At first she had wandered aimlessly, afraid of the unfamiliar sounds that spun around her as the wind rushed about; at times nearly suffocating in its intensity, at other times carrying with it the distant howls that seemed to be guiding her. Now, she only wanted to escape the seemingly unending mist that chilled her, and the unknown thing that followed her.

§ § § § § §

Nickolous approached the cavern warily, every sense alert for danger. The crude leather covering at the entrance flapped gently as he paused, unsure as to whether the wind or someone inside was the cause. Too, he was suddenly aware that he was not even carrying a weapon with which to defend himself. Yet the indecision was fleeting, for the sudden scream tore at him with a remembrance of loyalty beyond thought of self. As he burst through the doorway into the darkened gloom, the shadowy form that threatened those within rose to its full height to face him.

Nickolous stood frozen as the thing wavered. Narrowed yellow eyes shifted from the intended victims to the newcomer, while the smell, which had begun to permeate the room, was incredible. Nickolous well remembered this kind of adversary, and a deep sense of foreboding and helplessness threatened to overwhelm him. He was unarmed, and this beast was nearly invincible.

Then a feeble groan from something beneath a tattered blanket caught his attention; that, and the brief glimpse of a beloved face pulled at something deep inside him; something forgotten, but apparently not lost. It was the ability to call for strength from the land of mists, high in the mountains covered in snow and cloud, a place of awe and wonderment; of mythical legends and dreams—the home of winged warriors, and a guardian that protected her own.

Nickolous drew himself upright to face the creature, which moved from its hunched position as it flexed razor-sharp claws. As it turned, it transformed, even as it leapt toward him.

Timothy threw himself across the cot, pulling Sarah with him in an effort to protect her. As he fell, he threw his sword at the outstretched hand that reached out and unerringly caught it.

In one fluid motion, the sword was grasped, and swung with deadly accuracy. Although not a killing blow, it was accurate enough to cripple, if only temporarily. "Get out!" Nickolous yelled as the creature shook itself, trying to rise from its fallen position on the cavern's floor. "Take the Old One with you. Run to the forest and hide!" Nickolous shouted as he advanced toward the beast, sword raised.

Timothy scooped the ragged bundle up in his arms, while Sarah, still dizzy from her fall and frightened nearly out of her wits, nonetheless managed to follow her brother outside. As they fled toward the relative safety of the forest, the weather-beaten leather flap covering the entrance fell haphazardly back in place; while the wind whirled about them, drowning out the sounds that emanated from deep within the depths of the cavern.

Panting with exertion, the creature reared back as Nickolous started forward, his own heart racing wildly.

§ § § § § §

Timothy laid his burden down gently in a moss-covered grove surrounded by towering oak trees. The mist, damp and clinging, still surrounded them, but it wasn't as dense here, for it was shortly after sunrise, and the light from the morning's soft dawning traced patterns through the fog, slowly dissipating it. As Timothy rose from his kneeling position, a thin, leathery paw shot out from beneath the torn and tattered blanket. Startled nearly out of his wits, he fell back; knocking over Sarah.

"Nickolous. You must help him." The Old One had risen to a sitting position; her talon-like nails digging painfully into Timothy's forearm. Brown eyes met black; having spent her strength, with a soft sigh, she laid back and slept.

"She sleeps the sleep of healing." Sarah placed her hand gently on her brother's shoulder as she spoke. "*Go.* We will be safe here, in this place."

Timothy ran, pulling the small dagger from its leather sheath, silently acknowledging to himself that it would be nearly useless against such an adversary, even as he withdrew it; nonetheless, it would be better than nothing.

§ § § § § §

Nickolous sidestepped as the creature lunged. Weakened and not yet able to shape-shift, the thing was enraged. It shook its head from side to side, bellowing its rage as frothy foam flew everywhere. Nickolous wiped the stuff disdainfully off his clothes; his eyes locked on the beast as it prepared to leap. Taking a deep breath, he stood, waiting.

6

"Lord Moshat, the boy calls."

Rising with some difficulty and aided by an ornately carved wooden staff, Lord Moshat removed a small, hand-carved, wooden box from a drawer. Placing it in the opened hand of the messenger, he commanded: "Go with all speed. Do not be seen by the forest dwellers if at all possible."

"And the bracelet?"

"Leave it with the boy. With the passage of time comes knowledge, and only the chosen one can unlock its secrets. Go now and protect the path he must walk, but let him discover the power within himself through his own means and experiences. *Go.*" The last words were whispered into the shadows cast by the mornings early light. *"May the shadows cloak you my friend."*

Long after the messenger had left, Lord Moshat sat, gazing into the fire's flickering depths; wondering.

§ § § § §

Thrown to the ground by the sheer force of the wind, Timothy struggled to rise. Coughing from the dust, blinded by flying debris, he bent forward into the wind's fury, determined to reach the cavern and Nickolous.

Nickolous staggered to his feet. Shaking his head, he wiped the wetness that ran from his forehead into his eyes.

The embers from the fire had been scattered during the scuffle, and the creature, still weakened from Nickolous's blow, lay panting in the darkened corner. Its yellow eyes glowed eerily, and the jagged tear that ran down its side was dark with a glossy wetness that deepened with each sudden movement. However, it was a deceiving wound, and Nickolous knew that it was only a matter of moments before the thing would be powerful enough to do what it had been sent to do. Rising slowly, cautiously, he edged toward the cavern's opening, hoping to make it outside into the light and fresh air before the changeling recovered its strength.

Snarling angrily, the creature reared upright, guessing Nickolous's intent as it studied him through narrowed eyes. Knowing its limitations, and that it was still too weak to turn into something more powerful, it leapt with surprising strength at the darting figure—and missed. Howls of rage filled the empty cavern as the creature raced after its prey.

Nickolous hit the ground rolling as an angry roaring filled his ears. In an instant, he was on his feet and running. The stand of majestic oak trees was straight ahead, and it was toward these that he fled. He could almost feel the heated breath of the thing behind him as he looked up at the sound of his name being called above the wind's wailing cry.

"Timothy!" The words were shouted out as he was forced to the ground by something unseen. The wind was like a funnel, encasing him momentarily in a cocoon of safety, as a blood-curdling shriek rent the air behind him.

§ § § § § §

Timothy, bent almost double against the wind's onslaught, was determined to reach the cavern and Nickolous. As the wind roared around him, he saw a form barreling toward him and the changeling not far behind. For a moment, everything seemed to stand still. Frozen, unable to move, battered by the wind, he could see what Nickolous could not. Then, there were only the two of them, and where the changeling had been, there was nothing—nothing save the imprints of its feet in the sodden earth, where it had reared upright as if to meet an enemy in battle.

It was as Timothy bent down to help Nickolous up that he spotted something glinting and partially buried in the clay like mix of soil. Warily, using the tip of his dagger, he picked up the ornately carved arm bracelet as Nickolous unerringly reached out and took it, placing it on his forearm where it nestled against his skin. It was a perfect fit.

"Timothy." Wordlessly they clasped forearms. Now that the danger was past, both gave in to the sheer pleasure of being reunited again.

"Sarah and the Old One—they are safe?"

"They're but a short distance from here; over there, just inside that stand of oaks." Timothy motioned toward the forest, all the while grinning delightedly.

Nickolous drew in his breath. His friend looked haggard, and there were shadows beneath his eyes that hadn't been there when Nickolous had left; with a start, he realized that his friend had aged in the short time he had been gone.

"How long?" Nickolous asked quietly, as Timothy sheathed his sword.

"Many turnings have passed; too many since the battle." Timothy reached out to touch Nickolous's shoulder gently, as if to assure himself that he was real; that he wasn't dreaming. "The peace lasted but a short time." His brow furrowed thoughtfully as he asked, "Leah, she is well?"

"She was fine the last time I saw her," Nickolous replied as he absently traced the intricate patterns of the bracelet with a forefinger. "Wait a minute, with everything that's happened, I nearly forgot—I can't be sure, mind you, but I think that she came through with me."

Timothy gasped, alarmed. Somehow, the Old One must have brought them both back; either that, or someone else had drawn her through. He shook his head in bewilderment, knowing that he would have to seek out someone with more knowledge than what he had in these matters.

"Come." Timothy turned toward the forest where Sarah and the Old One waited, motioning for Nickolous to follow. "Come," he said again. "Perhaps the Old One will have some answers," he muttered more to himself than anyone else as Nickolous strode to catch up.

§ § § § §

Chera crouched in the dense foliage, her keen sense of smell telling her that her quarry was close by—she grinned to herself—the youngest of the wood clans would have moved more quietly then this one. As the rustling in the underbrush grew louder, Chera pressed herself further back to wait.

§ § § § §

Leah had been startled to find herself suddenly alone in the thick mist. At first she thought her brother had gone back to the house, but as she walked further, she realized that she was nowhere near the house; and to make matters worse, she was sure that something or someone was following her. Determined not to bolt blindly into the unknown, she fixed her gaze on the faint pinprick of light off to her left, and keeping her gait at a leisurely pace, she began to move steadily toward it. Every now and then, she would pause to listen, certain that she could hear the soft pad-pad of footsteps behind her.

§ § § § § §

Owen flew low as he scanned the hidden places beneath for unwanted watchers, for it would be here, in this densely covered forest, that the unseen would be watching. He veered sharply to the left as a loping form caught his attention. The skinny, gray creature paused at the edge of the clearing, gazing furtively about before continuing on as Owen watched from his perch atop the ancient gnarled tree. The sudden silence was nearly unnerving; even for him.

Something was following the scraggly creature, something that triggered familiarity and loathing deep within his memories—memories that were within all beings; a gift from the elders of the before times, dormant in most, though some had been gifted with the ability to draw those memories from deep within. It was those beings who became the teachers and respected elders, who taught those who wanted and sought knowledge. But there were also those who used the gift of the *remembering* for darker things to further their own power, and it was to this end that Owen and others like him struggled to even the odds.

The heavily robed figure followed the lone sentinel at a distance—not because he feared there would be any resistance to his passage, for it was his presence that instilled fear, and it was that fear which gave him power. As he moved out into the open, he paused, aware that he was being watched and that the watcher did not fear him, but loathed him and his kind. Still...

With a half turn, he acknowledged the white owl's presence; then moved forward into the open, which afforded little protection. Aware that some of the smaller of the forest clans were peering from their burrows and dens, he drew himself up and, throwing a portion of his cloak over a shoulder, strode forward so that the distance between himself and the lone sentinel lessened.

Owen turned away in disgust. *Lord Nhon!* He had not expected to see that one in the pure light of day. Waiting to see no more, he flew westward while, on the ground below, the hooded one paused long enough to glance upward at the departing form, his thin lips parted in a grotesque grin.

"Enter." A-Sharoon barely looked up from her work as the creature sidled in, head down, feet shuffling nervously as it awaited its mistress's notice; it was some moments before she stopped what she was doing. Still, she never looked up from her work; deeming the one before her much too insignificant and therefore beneath her direct notice. "Well, what is it? What is so important you would interrupt me at my work?" She raised a midnight black brow questioningly.

"The veil was lifted. Even without the woman, they have somehow been pulled back." The messenger backed warily toward the door, ready to flee for its life. Its mistress's temper was legendary.

Drawing herself up to her full height, A-Sharoon dismissed the informant with a wave of her hand. As the creature scurried out of sight, she crossed the cavernous room in one swift fluid motion; pulling the thick hide covering across the doorway, she wedged the edges tightly into the crevice. The sentries on watch outside did not need to be told that no one would be allowed entrance until the covering was removed.

§ § § § § §

The cavern was damp, the musty smell permeating everything within while the small fire offered little warmth to the woman hunched over it. She placed another piece of green wood upon it, watching silently as it hissed against the flames that tried to consume it. Drawing the thin woolen blanket about her shoulders, she ignored the grating sound behind her as the heavy door, hewn from rock and moved by a cleverly hidden mechanism, creaked inward. Nor did she turn at the sound of footsteps as someone entered the room and moved toward her, choosing instead to gaze into the flickering flames as the heavily robed figure towered over her.

A-Sharoon glared at the woman's back and cursed her silently. She knew—had always known—that she would never break this one to her will. She smiled inwardly and chose her words carefully. She would let this captive know that it was only a matter of time before she and hers were defeated and destroyed. As she spoke, she noted with satisfaction the effect her words were having as the woman rose gracefully, and turning, faced her.

Slowly, the woman drew her hood back to reveal fine features and long, flowing auburn hair. Large brown eyes met black as a slender hand came up to touch the silver amulet that hung delicately about her throat. For long moments, she remained silent; her gaze locked with that of her captor; listening. Words, softly spoken, carried strength. "What you seek, you will not find. You will destroy yourself with this quest, and any who follow you, Daughter of the Night."

The fire, little more than glowing embers, flared suddenly against the wood, flames climbing up and over the logs to catch and hold. The sudden warmth seemed to envelop both women as A-Sharoon shifted her gaze to glance uneasily around the cavern. She felt the unseen presence watching but shook off the inner warning, confident in her own abilities. Once again, she fixed her gaze on her captive, only to find herself confronted instead with a frothy swirling mist that curled against her, the dampness seeking—

The woman she had sought to hold as ransom in her battle was gone. Only the tattered robe she had been given to ward off the never-ending dampness remained, crumpled in a heap at her feet.

7

Leah walked steadily, her gait unhurried, pausing now and then to examine the flowering honeysuckles that sprang up wild everywhere, their fragrance sweet and honeyed. The whir-whir of the tiny hummingbirds could be heard as they darted about from plant to plant, quarrelling over the contents within. Leah ducked as one of the small creatures, in a bid to escape an irate neighbor, whizzed past her head. As she turned to watch its acrobatics, she felt, rather than saw, the sudden furtive movement of something concealing itself within the forest's shadows.

§ § § § §

Chera waited patiently, thankful that she had caught Leah's scent before anything else had. The identity of the thing that followed doggedly behind her was unmistakable. She settled back to wait, her lips curled in a grimace of loathing.

As Leah hurried past the thicket where Chera lay concealed, she felt the *unseen* watching her; unaware that it was Chera who watched, she panicked and ran, the branches tearing at her arms and face as she stumbled over the rough ground. Unheeding of the gnarled limbs of ancient trees that reached out to embrace her passage amongst them, she never saw the deep leaf-covered pit that once had brimmed with water from an underground passage, and as the moldy leaves covering the edge, slippery from the night's frost, gave way beneath her weight, she disappeared into the ancient tunnel, too surprised to cry out.

§ § § § § §

"What is it? What's wrong?" Timothy had moved to stand in front of Nickolous; his small dagger unsheathed as he held it out of sight at his side. They had come to the edge of the clearing and were about to go into the dense underbrush to where Sarah and the Old One waited.

"It's Leah. Something's happened." Nickolous spoke softly, his attention riveted on the small grove of massive oak trees straight ahead. "I can't sense her. She's somewhere where our thoughts can't touch each other."

"She's safe—for now."

Old One, it's good to see you!" Nickolous lifted the Old One up and hugged her. "How do you know? Can you see her?" Nickolous asked as he gently set her down.

The elder looked up at him and marveled at how tall he had grown since the last time she had seen him. "I can't see her, but I can sense her, and I sense that she is not afraid; in fact, she seems to be quite calm. That's more than I can say for you!" The Old One laughed as Nickolous swept Sarah up and around as she squealed in delight at the return of the boy, now a young man, who was once again with them.

Timothy, watching the three of them, felt a fierce pride and an inner knowledge that they were no longer quite as alone as before. "Come, we must seek the safety of the forest; there are too many eyes here." Timothy knew better then to risk being in the open any longer. Hurriedly, the four friends gathered their belongings and pushed deeper into the forest's depths, the cool shade a welcome change from the stifling heat of the day.

§ § § § § §

The leaves had filled the passage where Leah had fallen, leaving a musty odor that masked her scent. Still, Chera's senses told her that this was where the trail ended. Not knowing what awaited her in the darkness below her feet, and unsure whether others followed the path of A-Sharoon's most recently dispatched sentinel, Chera wasted no time in returning to where Gabriel and the others waited. By the time Gabriel and the others returned with her, the day's shadows had lengthened into the quickening of the night. In silence, they stood above the rim of the pit, each deep in thought, until finally Jerome spoke, his voice rumbling from deep within his chest as he tapped his war club against a trunk-like leg.

"This is an ancient place of knowing, where the Old Ones gathered long ago to share their knowledge, hopes, and dreams. In this place there was safety and peace; nothing evil could penetrate the caverns below." Jerome paused as he looked at the anxious faces gathered about him; his own thoughts were racing ahead, trying to figure out what to do. It was a hard thing, this knowing what others did not; for a part of him knew Leah was safe, but another part of him felt the breath of evil following their passage. A huge hand thoughtfully stroked a craggy face as he made up his mind. They could not risk any more delays and, as important as Leah was, for now, she was safe. One of them would stay to guard the entrance, while the rest would traverse the path that would take them to the guardian.

It was no surprise then that, a little while later, it was Chera who remained behind to guard the place that hid Leah within its unknown depths.

§ § § § § §

"That was delicious." Nickolous leaned back against the giant tree trunk that shaded him, as well as those gathered about him. Sarah nodded her thanks for the compliment as she tidied up the remains of their simple meal.

The Old One had attempted to help but had gently been told to rest, which she had without argument. As she settled herself beside Nickolous, she sighed deeply. Her aging body was telling her it was time to slow down. Everyone laughed when she mentioned it, for it was hard to believe that the Old One could ever just sit back and observe without being in the midst of everything.

Even Nickolous laughed, much to the Old Lady's chagrin. She reached out and patted him gently, her black eyes searching his light blue ones, and he sobered; for he saw and he knew what the others did not: what had begun turnings ago as an adventure was now a quest.

§ § § § § §

Sarah and the Old One had fallen asleep earlier, and Timothy was hunched over the small fire, stirring the embers absently with a stick while Nickolous watched him thoughtfully; his own thoughts wandering, and so it was that the sudden appearance of the warrior before them, wraithlike, startled them.

Timothy leapt to his feet, at the same time drawing his sword. He felt a hand on his shoulder holding him back.

"Wait, my friend," Nickolous spoke gently, as he peered at the shimmering vision that slowly beckoned them, a long slim finger pointing eastward. With a turn, dark wings unfurled, and the visitor vanished, leaving behind only the scented breeze in the deepening twilight.

Timothy turned toward Nickolous, his expression puzzled as he slowly sheathed his sword. But Nickolous wasn't looking at him. His arm was tingling as if a thousand pins were pressing upon him; and it was the worst where the bracelet was, clasped around his upper arm.

Nickolous and Timothy both stared as the bracelet almost became transparent, the silver shimmering in the shadows cast by the fire's eerie glow mesmerizing them; pulling at their senses as the metal changed in appearance. Nearly translucent now, it changed yet again, and when next they looked, a silver bracelet glinted back.

Timothy reached out to touch the bracelet, only to find himself being flung backward by an unseen force. Shaking himself, he rose quickly to his feet and stood staring down at the intricate silver armlet that encircled his friend's arm.

Nickolous forgot about the sensations prickling along his arm as he watched the apparition of the warrior fade—or was it an apparition? He wasn't sure, but something familiar was tugging at him: a memory of misty places and an ancient warrior telling him of things meant to be, a timeless enchantment of legends that were more than legends, and winged warriors that were silent guardians.

Both Nickolous and Timothy were brought back to the present by the overwhelming silence that suddenly surrounded them.

Sarah, awakened out of a deep sleep, stumbled to her feet, grumbling irritably. The Old One, however, was awake instantly; her inner senses warning her of trouble. Grabbing her staff, she moved with surprising agility to where Nickolous stood, her eyes widening as she recognized that which rested upon his arm.

Nickolous turned at the soft touch on his shoulder. The Old One nodded, her black eyes unfathomable, for there were some things that one didn't openly acknowledge, and so it was she turned away before he could see her face. She sighed deeply as she drew her staff back beneath the folds of her heavy cloak. Had the others been watching, they would have seen the slight glow before it was hidden from view. As it was, the Old One knew the staff would have to be kept out of sight until the time was right, for not even she knew how to unlock the bracelet's secrets. What she did know, however, was that the staff, which had been passed down from the before times to her kind, had slept—until today.

Nickolous turned away, his thoughts now back to the present. For a moment it had been as if he could see a far-off place reflected in the silvery engraved depths of the bracelet that now seemed as if it had always been his. He had also seen what Timothy had not: the ornately carved staff the Old One carried was connected somehow to that which he wore about his arm. The Old One had moved away so swiftly that he was sure she knew more than she was willing to share just yet. Nickolous sighed deeply, wishing the others were here.

Jerome. Owen. Orith. Where were they when he needed their combined wisdom?

8

"Where's Owen? He should have returned by now." Jerome paced impatiently back and forth in front of the fire which had been lit earlier. In truth, he wasn't as worried as he was eager to be gone from the place they had chosen to spend the night. There was a feel about this place he didn't like. It was as if they were being watched, and as the moon rose, a great white luminescent globe in the star-studded sky, the feeling grew. He glanced to where the others were. If they felt what he felt, they weren't showing it. Still…

He tried to relax; perhaps it was just his imagination. Everywhere they went, there seemed to be traces of A-Sharoon's having been there before them.

§ § § § §

Owen flew swiftly, gliding silently on the warm air currents as the dusk deepened; only using his wings when he had to. Even the slightest sound could be heard from below, where thin, bedraggled things gazed upward with drooling mouths and elongated faces, their narrowed eyes ever watchful for danger. Owen drew in a deep breath as the large shadowy creature on the ground below scuttled out of sight. He did not pursue it, knowing that it would be long gone by the time he swooped down to intercept it. Instead, he veered sharply eastward, the sudden unease nearly overwhelming him as Jerome's whispered voice came to him.

"To us," it said.

Owen flapped his wings against the night wind, all pretence of silence gone. The smell of something putrid came to him; then vanished. Not knowing what his friends faced, he gained height until he was hidden within the mists of the dark clouds that scudded across the sky, periodically blotting out the moon's pale light.

§ § § § § §

Gabriel, his head high, scented the breeze that wended its way around him. He had slept but a short time, his senses awakening him, and although he did not sense what the big warrior sensed, he knew Jerome well enough to trust the forest warrior's abilities to reach beyond where most others could not. Whether the danger had been there before them, or whether it was still to come, it did not matter. They would be ready. He moved cautiously to where the warrior of the forest stood. "What is it, old friend? What walks through the night?" Gabriel spoke softly so as not to awaken Orith, but there was no need, for the great white owl had awakened, sensing the unseen.

He blinked in the half light. There was danger. It was carried on the back of the wind to him along with the elders who spoke, their voices unheard by others. They were warning him. "We must leave this place. *Now.*"

Orith and Gabriel nodded in agreement. As they headed southward, they did not look back, which was a good thing, for the small clearing was suddenly filled with scurrying things, and narrowed slitted eyes watched their departure hungrily.

§ § § § § §

"Out of my way!" A-Sharoon wielded her staff as squeals of protest echoed through the night. Drawing her heavy woolen cloak about her, she stood at the top of the knoll, looking down. "You!" She pointed her staff at her first officer. The crowd drew back, lest the creature had displeased their mistress; in which case, the further back, the better.

The officer stepped toward her but was careful not to get too close. Its association with A-Sharoon had been longer than most; simply because it had learned to choose the right moment to reveal certain things. "Your Ladyship," the thing said as it bowed low in front of its mistress.

A-Sharoon waited, her white hands clasping the wooden walking staff. Her black eyes bored into those of her officer, looking behind their depths for deception; a fact her subordinate was well aware of and prepared for.

"There has been nothing untoward reported." The sentry paused, gauging the woman's mood. It stepped back, looking furtively about; ready if the need arose to flee. Then: "We are still waiting for the changeling to report back." Its black eyes with their soulless depth managed to look up, its gaze now locked with the woman's as it waited.

A-Sharoon remained where she was; silent. Her gaze never left the creature's face, and the narrowed eyes that gazed back at her revealed nothing more than the words that had been spoken. A-Sharoon turned away, her long garments flowing about her like a living thing.

§ § § § § §

"So, what are we to do now."

It wasn't even a question. Lord Nhon said nothing, and A-Sharoon felt her anger rising. In the flickering light of the dimly lit cavern, Lord Nhon smirked in satisfaction at his ability to hold this haughty woman before him in her place. He turned his back to her, ignoring her, knowing she fought to control the urge to strike out at him.

"Well, are you going to answer me, or are your abilities grown so weak that I must take over?"

Lord Nhon's whole body went rigid as he turned slowly around to glare at A-Sharoon.

Black eyes met his gaze evenly. Lord Nhon let his breath out slowly, determined to put this Daughter of Darkness in her place. "We wait."

A-Sharoon stared at Lord Nhon's retreating form, so angry she could not speak. In the long silence that followed, her breathing slowed, and her thoughts turned inward to a time before remembering, a time of growing and learning. She smiled to herself in the semi-darkness, and the half-formed words she was tempted to throw at the retreating form remained unspoken. Instead, she turned and retreated to her quarters, where she worked far into the night preparing.

Lord Nhon waited a little while before calling the sentries to him. "Watch her."

The wolf-like creature nodded assent and disappeared into the darkened corridors.

§ § § § § §

"So, he thinks to undermine me, does he?" A-Sharoon flung her long hair over her shoulder as she knelt down to stir the embers of the fire. Taking some powder from a small flask, she threw it onto the glowing embers. A sickly sweet odor permeated the room as she fanned the embers into tiny flames, while her first officer edged closer to the door's opening, unsure of what to expect. A-Sharoon straightened slowly and turned toward him, her expression unreadable. "Go," she said, then added, "but not too far. I may have need of you this night."

§ § § § §

"Timothy?" Nickolous felt the wind brush his cheek, but it was more than that. It was a sighing that touched him from deep within; and he drew in his breath sharply.

Timothy turned to face him, at the same time inhaling deeply of the scents carried by the night's breeze. "Shh." Timothy touched the scabbard on his side, grasping the handle of the sword, ready to pull it out, but there was no need. The sudden appearance of Owen, gliding wraithlike and silent against the velvety backdrop of the starlit sky, was a welcome sight indeed to the weary travelers.

"Owen."

"Nickolous."

Silently they gazed at one another, glad to be in each other's presence once again.

"So, the Old One drew you back. We thought so," Owen said as he acknowledged the others who crowded close, their thoughts unspoken but heard. "We found Leah's trail; Chera guards the entrance. Jerome, Gabriel, and Orith are on their way to the guardian's gate. There is no time to lose."

"And Leah?" Nickolous gazed deep into Owens's eyes; then nodded. The others looked at each other curiously but asked no questions. It was obvious Leah was on her own quest. "Well, then," Nickolous said decisively, rising to face Sarah, who was about to say something. He put out a hand to silence her. "Ask nothing, for there are no answers right now. Our paths will cross with that of my sister, of that I am sure. She is safe. Do not worry." He put an arm about her to assure her. He didn't understand how he knew it, but he sensed that Leah was about to have her own adventure, and that they wouldn't be sharing this one, but would come together again when this was all over. He smiled down at Sarah to reassure her as he looked at the others; he knew she was fond of Leah. They all were.

"Nickolous." Owen was peering upward, into the morning's early dawning. The stars were still visible but less bright, and the wind was picking up. The sudden cold gust of wind caused everyone to shiver.

"I think," Nickolous said, his gaze meeting that of Owen, "that we had better leave—"

The big owl nodded assent; moments later, they were on their way, moving silently through the forest's depths.

The watcher, well concealed from prying eyes, observed their departure, noting with satisfaction that Nickolous wore the armlet, but had the sense to conceal it as well. With the wind to aid him, the unseen warrior took flight.

Owen heard the whispering sound, but only the swaying branches, caught by the growing wind, greeted his gaze as he looked back. The Old One, however, glanced up in time to see the winged form high overhead. Then there was nothing. Grasping her walking stick firmly, she moved steadily forward, her mind more at ease now that she knew they weren't alone.

Nickolous drew in a deep breath of fresh air, glad to be on the move again. He was anxious to see Gabriel and Jerome, for there was much he had to tell, as well as ask. Although he had made no mention of his mother, she was, nonetheless, not far from his thoughts. In the few months that they had been together, there were still so many things that were left unsaid and unasked. Nickolous sighed deeply as he remembered all that had passed between them; so much, yet so little in such a short space of time. Even as his mind went back to that day she had disappeared, he somehow knew that she was safe. Somehow, she had escaped A-Sharoon...

The shadowy form that stepped into his path drew him from his thoughts, and the loping silvery gray form was a welcome sight that almost overwhelmed him.

"Gabriel!"

The huge wolf nearly knocked him down as he rushed to greet his friend of adventures past. "Nickolous. My friend, it is good to see you." The great wolf said no more, for he could not. Not one to show emotion, except to his mate, Chera, who even now guarded this young one's sister, he was overwhelmed momentarily by emotions. He stood in front of Nickolous, marveling at how much he had grown since their last meeting as he looked deep into the startling blue eyes, so much like his own, wondering at what he saw there. But before he could say anything more, Jerome had lumbered up, his gait slow but steady, and Nickolous was being gripped in a bear hug that left him breathless.

Nickolous could not believe they were here. In his dreams, he had seen them—felt their presence—and wished he were here with them.

As Orith approached, his gait unhurried, his back hunched a little more then what Nickolous remembered, he drew in his breath sharply. It had been too long. Turning from Jerome and the others, he grasped Orith in a hug. He had missed them all and none more than the rest. Standing with them gathered about him, he felt the exhaustion wash away. And as he looked at each one, he knew there would be much to tell around the fire's flickering light this coming night.

§§§§§§

It would be much later before they would have a chance to stop. The day had deepened into the inky blackness of the night before Owen, tired and exhausted, returned with news that they were close to their destination. It would be wise, he said, to stop here, in this place, to rest and leave by the dawning's first light. Later, as everyone rested by the fire, comfortable and content from the hot meal and warm drinks, Nickolous began his tale.

Jerome stroked his chin thoughtfully as he stared into the blue-white flame. Reaching for a charred stick, he stirred the coals until they caught at the dry wood that had been gathered earlier. For as many turnings as he could remember, he had studied the teachings of the before times, when the worlds were growing, and the doors were constantly opening and closing. Some of those who visited those far-off places never came back, while the few who did return walked between the two worlds, trying to discover where they belonged. He closed his eyes against the vision. The path that Nickolous had been thrust onto was fraught with danger, and even though the winged warriors watched over him...

Sighing deeply, he turned his attention toward Gabriel.

The big wolf was standing beside Nickolous, his expression unreadable. He, too, was wondering about the relationship between the warriors of Skye and the young man who now stood before him. That Nickolous and his sister were not of the forest clans was clear enough. That their mother was of Skye was merely theory. The guardian protected her own; so obviously, there was a relationship between the two, but what? Gabriel peered into the fire's flickering shadows, trying to find an answer.

Orith sat close to the fire, glad for its warmth. He, too, was thinking on the words that had been spoken as he glanced from beneath his heavy woolen hood at the Old One. She was older than them all by countless turnings. Her knowledge, layered deep within the wizened but still vital body, could say much about this night's telling, but her face remained unchanged. He smiled to himself, knowing that for all their wondering, things would have to unfold as they were meant to.

"Well?"

Everyone turned their attention to Nickolous, for it was he who had spoken. Sarah had cleared away the remains of the simple meal, and as steaming gourds of tea appeared, everyone drew close to the fire, for the night had become chilly, and the fine white mist it drew with its presence permeated everything within its grasp.

"Jerome?" The voice was questioning.

The giant warrior shifted his position so that he was facing Nickolous; his green eyes gazed past him into the forest beyond. "I think," he said, as he reached for another piece of wood, "that there are no answers for some things. That A-Sharoon bridged the two worlds, and that your mother was abducted, is very disturbing; however, I think there is more to this. A daughter of Skye would not be taken so easily, unless there is a reason for it."

"What do you mean? Is it possible that the Daughter allowed this so that the Old One could call Nickolous safely here?" Timothy asked as he leaned forward into the fire's faint glow.

Jerome nodded his head slowly although, deep down, he wasn't sure if it was true. He glanced over to where Gabriel sat.

The big wolf was about to say something; then, thinking better of it, he remained silent. There would be time enough to wonder after they reached their destination. He rose decidedly to his feet. "The hour grows late. We must rest a little, for we do not know what awaits us on the morrow." Gabriel nudged Nickolous gently. Although he wasn't showing it, Gabriel knew that he was worried. "Have no fear, my young friend."

Nickolous looked down into eyes that seemed as old as time itself. Nodding but saying nothing, he reached out to stroke the thick, silvery fur. "Thank you," he replied, as the big wolf settled close to him.

Later, as Nickolous drifted off into a restless sleep, visions of mist-shrouded places in long-ago dreams haunted his sleep, while a young woman, his mother, stood, arms raised, calling the Eagle to her, long auburn hair flowing behind her, caught within the wind's gentle grasp.

§ § § § §

"Nickolous." The words were whispered and urgent. "Awaken; time grows short." Orith leaned close and shook him gently. Even as

Nickolous was rising to his feet, Jerome and Gabriel were rousing the others.

Nickolous gazed upward into the predawn, and it was a moment before he realized the reason for the urgent awakening. The stillness that surrounded him was absolute. Nothing stirred on a morning that should have been alive with movement. Nickolous turned at the sound of approaching footsteps, their gait slow and unhurried. The Old One stood there, watching.

"Old One?" Nickolous knelt down so that he was at eye level.

The Old One said nothing, her gaze turning to the shadows within the wooded forest. "Come," she said.

Nickolous turned to follow, his senses tingling.

9

A-Sharoon strode angrily through the corridors of the cavern, toward the distant light—toward Lord Nhon.

Scurrying out of her path was indeed a task, as the staff she carried reached far into the darkened corners, and those who cowered there would feel the bruises for many days to come.

"Well?" A-Sharoon said no more. Her black eyes glowed with an unnatural intensity as she stood, tall and proud before the hunched form.

Lord Nhon straightened slowly, his hooded cloak concealing the features beneath. A-Sharoon could feel the suppressed rage of the being before her but chose to ignore it. In fact, it didn't bother her in the least. Lord Nhon pulled back his hood, revealing red-rimmed eyes in a skeletal face ravaged by the evil that consumed him. Like many of those who practiced the arts of darkness, he appeared savage, his facial expression terrifying and unreadable. His eyes, narrow lidded and nearly closed against even the dim light in the cave, were mere pinpricks of black within the redness that surrounded them. In the dancing shadows, he looked almost feral as he smirked at the black-haired woman who paced angrily in front of him. "They are nearly to the gate. Your 'best' have obviously failed their tasks they were set to do!"

The words were spat with a vehemence that even A-Sharoon could not miss. She glared at Lord Nhon as she swallowed the retort that threatened to burst forth.

"What. You have nothing to say?" The long bony fingers pointed accusingly at A-Sharoon as she glared defiantly back at Lord Nhon.

"Woman, what have you to say? You have failed. Your minions, although they are legion, are apparently impotent against even the weakest of the wood clans, while a boy not yet a man strikes the changelings down like the wind breaks trees before its wrath. Speak!" The voice barked as A-Sharoon remained motionless, her black eyes blazing.

"The fault lies not with me," A-Sharoon replied, her dark eyes flashing. "You were supposed to prevent them from entering through the veil." Her voice rose accusingly.

"Yes, but it was you who entered their world to take the woman. By your own folly, it was you who left the door open!" Lord Nhon hissed as he turned his back on her. He was angry with himself as well for not having seen this coming. The old teachings with their hidden meanings were sometimes difficult to translate, the ancient script known only to a few. And even then, who knew what had been lost in the translation? Lord Nhon turned around to face A-Sharoon, his expression unreadable as he calmed himself. It was pointless to argue with her. He shrugged his shoulders in resignation. "What's done is done."

"What do you mean, what's done is done?"

"I mean exactly that." Lord Nhon removed a powdery substance from a leather pouch tied to his belted waist. "Let's see…" He held the stuff in front of his mouth and blew gently. A sickly-sweet aroma filled the air as the shadows cast by the flickering fire danced and grew upon themselves until there was just one writhing form.

A-Sharoon watched in silence as the thing swirled and darted about the dimly lit cavern as if seeking entrance to the outside world, all the while drawing on the power that emanated from the being that had formed it. She turned away in disgust. "Child's play!" The words were drowned in the sudden roaring that filled her ears as she was flung unceremoniously to the floor.

"Child's play? I think not." Lord Nhon's voice held a hint of smug satisfaction as he watched A-Sharoon hastily rise, her expression as dark as her robes.

"So, you think to frighten the Clans with a shadowy being that has no substance?" A-Sharoon's black eyes glittered even in the dim light, her breathing shallow. "Pah!" She spat the words in disgust, no longer trying to hide her anger. "You." She pointed a long slim finger at Lord Nhon. "Are nothing more than a novice, if that is your best." She pulled herself up regally and smoothed her rumpled cloak. Removing a crystal vial from within its depths, she removed the stopper and, stepping to the dying embers, poured the contents into their smoldering depths.

§ § § § § §

"By all that is sacred!" Timothy exclaimed, grabbing the nearest tree for support as the earth shuddered and trembled beneath him. He looked wildly around, trying to locate the others. The ground beneath his feet rolled and heaved as spasm after spasm wracked it, while a low moaning rippled through the trees as he twisted anxiously about, searching for the others.

Nickolous found himself face first on the ground, the backpack he carried thrown some feet away, the contents scattered carelessly about. The Old One was beside him, her leathery paws grasping his arm tightly as Sarah crouched nearby, her heart thudding in fear. Only Jerome remained standing, his great bulk keeping him upright as the earth heaved around him.

"Are you all right?" Nickolous asked as he helped the Old One up. Sarah scrambled to her feet, shaken but unhurt, her large brown eyes searching the clearing for her brother, Timothy. She was relieved to see him a few yards away, brushing the debris off himself.

Grimacing, he pulled something sticky from his fur and wiped it on the dried grass at his feet as Owen glided soundlessly above the little group; watching. Being airborne, he had felt the change in the wind currents and had fought to stay aloft. Now, he remained alert, his keen eyesight seeking out that which was unwanted within the shaded places below.

The earth tremors had stopped by the time that everyone had found their scattered belongings. Quickly now, they gathered silently together, and, after assuring himself that everyone was okay, Gabriel scouted ahead, only to find nothing amiss. Puzzled, he returned to where the rest waited, and together, the little band hurried toward their destination.

§ § § § § §

"The moon rises. The time is near." Although the fire that burned in the center of the cavern was warm and welcoming, the messenger approached no nearer, choosing instead to wait in the shadows.

"How close?"

"They are but a short distance from the gate."

"Nickolous?"

"He walks with the companions." The messenger inclined his head slightly—"They guard him with the strength given to those pure of heart."

"Ahh, it is as I had hoped." Lord Moshat turned to the woman who had risen from her place at the fire. Blue eyes met brown in unspoken understanding.

The warrior who had delivered the news stepped back in surprise, for he had been unaware of another's presence.

Lord Moshat, aware of the other's discomfort, motioned the warrior closer. "You are a trusted friend," he said, as he laid a hand on the other's shoulder. "However," the grip tightened as he tried to convey the importance of what he was about to say. "However, only myself, and of course, now you, know of the Daughter's presence here." Lord Moshat's piercing blue eyes peered into the warrior's own.

It was only for a moment, but the warrior nodded a short, curt nod, nearly indiscernible. Lord Moshat relaxed his grip on the other and then turned toward the woman, visibly relieved.

"None must know of this. None." The elder sat down wearily. The news was good; better than he had hoped for, and yet it had not been easy. The battle for the Living Flame had come at a terrible cost to both sides. Lord Moshat rubbed his chin thoughtfully as he stared into the fire. Aware that the warrior waited silently at the fringe of the shadows, he dismissed him for the night; knowing that he would remain close lest he was needed, before turning his attention back toward the woman who stood silently watching him.

"Will he be safe? Is he strong enough for what is to come?" The woman turned anxiously toward Lord Moshat, her eyes on his face, searching.

"Aleta." Lord Moshat spoke softly, his hand on the woman's shoulder. He had known her since she was born. He had mourned when he had thought her lost and had been overjoyed when she had returned. Now, he knew, her heart was aching for the son she had known such a short time. Sighing deeply, he sought the words that would bring her comfort. Finding none, he drew her close and together they sat, each one silent, lost within their own thoughts.

§ § § § § §

The clearing was much as the winged warrior had left it. To the friends, it was a scene of desolation. Sarah wept unashamedly as Jerome, his face somber, spoke in hushed tones to the guardian—he who had guarded the Living Flame since the beginning. The warrior, weakened from his ordeal, was relieved that the others had come to this sacred place of knowing. In pain, but no longer mortally wounded, he noted Nickolous's presence and wondered if he would remember.

"Hush now," the Old One whispered sternly as she grasped Sarah by the shoulder; then hugged her gently.

Sarah sniffed, trying to stifle the sobs as she brushed the wetness away, but it didn't help. "I don't understand how this could have happened," Sarah sobbed as she tried to stop the tears. Timothy was clearly just as distressed but showed little emotion as he helped the others. There was much to do, and not enough time to do it in.

"Gabriel?"

The big wolf turned as Nickolous reached him. "Look." It took a moment for Gabriel to recognize the small, shimmering object nestled within Nickolous's partially closed hand. The big wolf drew back his lips in a snarl. The diamond vial, glittering in the sunlight, had a familiarity about it. It was one of A-Sharoon's.

"I think we need to summon Chera."

Gabriel looked at Nickolous in surprise as he threw the vial down in disgust. Even here, in this sacred place, the evil emanated from it.

"Don't worry my friend; my sister is safe." Nickolous placed his hand on Gabriel's shoulder, kneeling down so that his gaze was level with that of the wolf's, he gazed into eyes as blue as his own "It's all right. Leah will be okay. We need Chera here with us."

It took only a moment for Gabriel to make up his mind. Ordinarily, he would have hesitated, but his inner sense urged him to listen to Nickolous as his mind flashed back to their first meeting on that clear moonlit night so many turnings ago. Only Nickolous was no longer the young boy he had been that night in the clearing. The journey between the two worlds had accelerated his maturity somehow. And the armband—only it was much more than that, and Gabriel knew it. It was no ordinary piece of worked silver. If the ancient scripts were true, it had been forged by one of the elders of Skye, one of those winged ones who dwelled among the mountains of myth and legend. A new awareness surged through the wolf as he nudged Nickolous affectionately before calling Owen to him.

§ § § § §

"It's past midday. Owen should be back by now." Gabriel paced anxiously back and forth as Jerome repaired the gate that once had barred the way to outsiders. The big warrior turned from what he was doing, his gaze sweeping the forest's edge. It was hard to see beyond the outer fringes that guarded the darkness within, even for him, with his acute sense of knowing; finally, exasperated, he turned toward Gabriel.

"Don't worry," Jerome said as he turned back to his task. He wasn't worried about Owen, but he felt uneasy nonetheless. He paused to wipe the sweat from his forehead with a large forearm. Yes, it would be a relief when Owen returned, hopefully with Chera not far behind.

§ § § § §

Chera followed Owen, her stride almost matching that of his winged flight. She hadn't argued when he had appeared, startling her, his appearance unexpected but certainly not unwelcome. She knew she couldn't breach the cavern below, for it welcomed only those who were chosen and she doubted that Leah was close by, for she would have sensed her. The forest about her had grown so silent it was unnerving. So it had been with barely a backward glance that she had left the hidden place where once the guardians of light had held their sacred council.

The lone watcher, cloaked heavily despite the stifling heat of mid-day, watched the wolf's departure from its hidden place among the giant ferns and softly scented flowers. When the great owl had passed from sight, the wolf following steadily in its wake, the figure moved silently, so silently that not even the leaves on the bushes moved to mark its passing.

Long moments passed as the robed figure stood gazing down at the spot where leaves and twigs had fallen and settled to nestle naturally into the shallow pit. A slender hand appeared from beneath a tattered sleeve, and the oblong crystal stone held within the holder's palm caught the sun's light and held the golden beams that traced across its surface, while the wind, warm and inviting, grew.

Sodden leaves, heavy with dampness, mold, and mildew, slowly began to rise as the breeze, softly blowing, yet silent in its flight, turned the leaves over and over until they spun upward into the canopy of trees overhead. The robed figure raised a hooded head to watch their passage beyond the living trees and then gazed down at the crystal, which now lay cold and silent in the small white hand. Still holding it tightly, the figure descended the crude stairs, which had been cut out of the rocks at the beginning, and carefully felt along the cold gray rock wall with one hand while sliding the crystal over the ancient script, which once had been deeply embedded and was now all but rubbed away by the elements.

Carefully, so as not to tear away the fragile moss that clung to the crevices of the etched writings and thereby reveal to others what lay deep within, the figure avoided touching the fragile things that guarded the door. For indeed, this was the door to the *Beneath,* the place of enlightenment and truth.

Drawing in a deep breath, the figure passed the stone in front of the door, as once again the light caught and held within its fiery depths. A hand shot up to shield a face as the white light burst forth. Whether from the stone itself, or from the rock, or both, it mattered not, for the result achieved was the desired one.

A smile touched the haggard face as the robed figure disappeared into the black depths that beckoned, while the forest remained silent long after the door had closed and the brown decaying leaves, suspended by the whirring breeze above the trees, had fallen to earth once again, there to nestle softly within the hollow that cradled them so gently.

§ § § § §

"Owen." Gabriel looked past the white owl as he landed gracefully in the ruined courtyard, while Chera's pace quickened as the forest was left behind, for she saw her mate waiting within the forest's shadows.

Although Nickolous was happy to see her, he, along with the rest of the friends, busied themselves with various chores so that Gabriel and Chera could be alone for a while. Everyone knew how much the big wolf had missed his mate, and the day had lengthened into early afternoon before Gabriel and Chera turned from their private conversation and joined the others.

Sarah, pleased that everyone was together again, prepared tea and made flatbread to go with the wild honeycomb she had brought. She had cheese but was saving that for supper. They had chanced a small fire for cooking, certain that, for now, they were safe. Even so, Jerome kept his heavy war club beside him, reaching out every so often to heft it, bouncing it slightly off the hard earth as if to test its strength, so that if there were any unseen eyes watching, they would know he was prepared.

"So, what is our next move?" Nickolous asked as he absently turned the drinking gourd over and over in his hands. "Do we wait for

A-Sharoon to find us, or do we find her? And how do we go about locating this Living Flame? Doesn't anyone know if it still burns?"

"It burns, my young friend. It lives, as it must," Gabriel replied.

"How do you know? How can you be so certain?" The gourd broke as it hit the ground, shattering in half as Nickolous stood up; the prickling that ran the length of his spine warning him; they were being watched.

"It lives," Gabriel replied, his voice low and throaty. As he turned, the air above him exploded into shrieks as Owen, talons tearing, brought the spy to earth.

10

Jerome sighed deeply as he prodded the thing with his war club. It was a lone scout, its duty to follow and listen. Fortunately for them, it wouldn't be missed for a while.

"These things stink with a foulness that deepens even after they are dispatched," Timothy snorted disdainfully as he balanced the inert form on his sword, careful not to touch it, for it reeked of untold darkness.

Gabriel watched as he went through the gate to the forest's edge, before turning his attention back to Owen. "Was that the only one?"

"As far as I could see," Owen replied as he stretched his snowy wings wide before folding them back, close to his sides. He was tired, and even though he had scanned the garden with eyes that missed little, he feared that there were others close behind the first. He turned to Jerome. "How close are your warriors?"

The big warrior stroked his chin thoughtfully as he gazed into the distance to a place only he could see. "They should have been here by now; that they are not means something has happened." He turned to Gabriel. "I will pass the night with you, and by lights dawning, the guardian should be strong enough to take my place. If I cannot reach my warriors in our old way of communication before the sun rises, I will go and search for them."

"Then I will go with you."

Jerome turned, startled, for he had thought Gabriel, Owen, and he were the only ones in the clearing.

Nickolous's resolve did not falter under Gabriel and Jerome's intense gaze. Indeed, it seemed that his eyes were even bluer, and even as Jerome was about to say no, he changed his mind. As his gaze met that of the Nickolous's, he glimpsed a little of what lay in the hidden places behind those blue eyes. It was a birthright to those chosen for something good—Jerome stood for long moments, stroking his chin thoughtfully.

"I'm going with you." With that, Nickolous turned away, for he had seen the Old One, hunched over, carrying a heavy bundle of wood. Gabriel and Jerome stared after his retreating form, and as he reached the Old One to take her burden from her, Gabriel turned back to his friend of battles past. There was laughter behind the fringes of his blue eyes; that and something more. "The boy swiftly becomes a man."

"Yes," Jerome agreed softly, his expression thoughtful, his voice nearly a whisper so that Nickolous would not hear. "I hope for all our sakes that tomorrow will bring my warriors." He sighed deeply as he headed toward the forest's edge; Gabriel watched him go, his own thoughts troubled. Throughout the long afternoon, even after the evening shadows had deepened into the dusk that brings the blackness of night, the peculiar whistles echoed throughout the wood until that was all the travelers could hear within their own minds.

§ § § § §

Nickolous had fallen into a restless sleep while the fire had burned low, leaving only a few glowing embers, as Sarah, curled against the Old One, slept fitfully; while Timothy and Gabriel kept watch, although both doubted that anything untoward would occur. As Gabriel watched the moon rise, his thoughts returned to a more primordial time, when the night wind had brought with it the scent of the prey and the pack had hunted as one. He sighed deeply. The only one constant these days was Chera. He nuzzled her gently; glad for her presence, thankful that at least this one thing had not changed.

As the night deepened and passed, the white gray of dawn brought with it the rolling mist that crept along the ground, seeking, its damp tendrils curling lazily around anything that stood in its path. Jerome ignored the cloying dampness; well aware that time was running out. As morning's dawn washed away the night, a faint answering cry responded.

§ § § § §

Caught in between the two places, neither awake nor asleep, Nickolous reached out to touch the fragile, white, bell-shaped flowers that hung heavy with perfume; their thick vines wrapped tightly around the ancient trees. He drew his hand back, aware that something wasn't right as the wind blew softly from the high places, passing over the gullies and valleys in between, the whisper of the wind as it fanned his cheek warning him.

The winged warrior watched, aware that another pair of eyes watched also.

§ § § § §

Nickolous awoke covered in sweat. Rolling to his feet, he leaned against a tree for support, his heart beating wildly. He pulled back, startled at the touch on his arm. "Old One." He let his breath out softly, relieved.

"Come," she said. "Come along with me. These old bones need to get some exercise, and besides—" Her grip tightened as she steered him toward the forest's edge. "Jerome has heard from his warriors." Dark eyes peered up at him, and her nails dug into his arm as she pulled him down toward her so that she was looking directly at him. "You must be careful, Nickolous. You are not the young boy you were on that moonlit night so many turnings ago. There is a power deep within you." She lowered her voice so that Nickolous had to strain to hear her next words. "Go with your heart. Trust no one."

Nickolous looked at the Old One in surprise as she released her grip, as Sarah, excited and out of breath, rushed toward them, bursting with news.

"Gabriel says to come quick." Sarah pulled Nickolous along while the Old One hurried behind. Once, she stopped and looked behind her, the hair on the back of her neck bristling. Tilting her head slightly to one side, she listened, stilling her own heartbeat so that she could focus. There was nothing—nothing except Sarah's chatter as she pulled Nickolous further ahead, and after a few moments of waiting, she hurried on, clutching the staff beneath her robe tightly, for even though she had seen nothing, and the birds that flitted from tree to tree were going about their morning business as usual, her keen senses warned her they were being watched.

"Gabriel?"

The big wolf, glad that the morning's dawning was not seeing Nickolous leave with the warrior of the forest, greeted him warmly. "Jerome returns with good news: his warriors are but two days march from here. They will be positioning themselves along the way, for there are those who must guard other gates." Gabriel paused, his nostrils flaring as the breeze fanned him; the scent was fleeting however; then it was gone altogether. He shrugged, knowing it would be a useless thing to send Chera out. Whatever it was would be long gone by now.

"The others?"

Gabriel turned to face Nickolous, his blue eyes fathomless; he sighed inwardly. So much to tell, but the telling? Would it be understood? "There are many doors to other places. You yourself have come through two of them." Gabriel lowered his voice as Nickolous fought the prickling sensation that crept up along his arm.

He knew that if he raised his sleeve, the armband would be nearly translucent in its wild beauty—that if he looked more closely, he would be lost in the depths that swirled within the intricate carvings that covered the silver metal.

He chose not to look.

"The guardians of the gates are many. They guard these places with not only their physical strength but with their hearts as well." Gabriel drew in a deep breath, careful to mask his emotions. He did not want Nickolous to know how perilous their situation was. "If a guardian loses himself to the darkness, if he betrays the sacred trust of those Ancients who chose him from the beginning, the strength and purity that guarded against the darkness of the heart will become a thing of blackness. The guardian, a son of the light, will himself become a thing of ugliness. No one will want to look upon this being without fear and loathing."

"These beings—how are they different from A-Sharoon and her scurrying things?" Nickolous asked.

"A-Sharoon was born to the darkness. She has never known the good. She has never known love, kindness, or compassion. She *is*. The good of the world has always…will always…be at odds with her kind." Gabriel nudged Nickolous gently.

"What of the 'Fallen'?"

"The Fallen? Let's just say that the difference between the two is opposite."

"Opposite? I don't understand." Nickolous gripped his arm where the band rested to still the burning sensation that was creeping up along his shoulder into his neck.

"Whereas the battle between good and evil has been fought since the dawn of time, even before the beginning, the outcome was always the same. Either we win or A-Sharoon wins. Either way, it's only for a time, and then it begins again. When a guardian falls, it's different.

All the knowledge, all the light that protected the weak and the innocent, becomes a power within the power." Gabriel's voice trailed off
as Nickolous watched him thoughtfully.

The tingling sensation was lessening now, and he removed his
hand slowly from the armband. Gabriel watched him through narrowed lids, the big wolf glad that the boy kept the bracelet hidden
from prying eyes. Nickolous stared beyond Gabriel to the forest, his
thoughts racing ahead. Something was bothering him. Gabriel
watched him intently; waiting for the question he knew was to come.

"Lord Nhon was once more than what he is now, wasn't he?"

"Yes."

"Which gate did he guard?" Even as he asked the question, Nickolous dreaded the answer he knew was to come.

Gabriel looked at him with sorrow-filled eyes. Even though he
himself had not yet come into being at the time of the telling, he knew
the story well. He and others like him had been chosen before they
had even drawn breath to protect against the day that the unspeakable
would occur. Gabriel sighed deeply. "The gate to the Light of Truth.
The gate of the Living Flame." Gabriel turned aside, his sorrow
clearly visible.

"There are those among us, older than the others, who remember
Lord Nhon when he was a being of truth." The Old One spoke quietly, taking up the thread of the story, her face upturned in the day's
bright light.

Nickolous looked into her eyes, but she wasn't looking at him; she
was seeing something else. As she began to speak again, her voice
low and melodious, Nickolous found himself walking with her, back
to a far away time of her youth. As the story unfolded, a woman, long
auburn hair blowing gently in the wind, watched from a mist-
shrouded place where none below could see.

"Lord Nhon was a being of pure light, there, from the high places."
The Old One motioned toward the towering mountains, their tops
obscured by thick white clouds. "Anyway, even though I was very
young, I remember when the darkness came and settled over the land
for a time. There was no day, just the endless night as we huddled,
frightened, in our homes, as the storms raged all about and the lightning flashed in the mountains beyond."

"How long did the darkness last?" Nickolous asked as he peered
thoughtfully into the distance, studying the far away twin peaks nestled together; yet even from this great distance towering over the
inhabitants in the valley below.

"How long?" The Old One's brows furrowed thoughtfully as she rubbed her forehead gently, remembering when she was a youngling and the details of that terrifying time. "Let's see—" She closed her eyes against the memories that threatened to pour forth. There were too many—and so she went to that still small place within herself that was the gift of her kind: to sort through and chose.

She opened her eyes, squinting upward into the bright light; grateful for the warmth that it brought to her aging body. "Yes, now I remember. The storms raged over the valley for twelve risings and settings of the sun. In all that time, we ate by candlelight, the food cold, nothing hot to warm us, only our parents' arms about us to help us go to sleep." The Old One's voice was barely a whisper.

"Why couldn't you build a fire?" Nickolous asked.

"It was summer, a time when we gathered the wood from the forest as we needed it. It was so sodden from the heavy rain and mud that washed down from the high places, it wouldn't light. Even after, when the light came back to us, it was many sleeps before the chill left from all that rain dissipated from our bodies and our homes."

"What happened then?"

"Lord Nhon had been defeated by those who guard from above. From that day forward, only those born to the forest guarded its secrets. The Flame remained, and Lord Nhon was exiled in the caverns below, the entrance guarded by the forest warriors and the Living Flame. But even in exile, Lord Nhon worked his dark magic. As A-Sharoon, spawned during the long darkness, drew her first breath in a cave far away, the once-great warrior planned his vengeance. It took many turnings, and we grew from younglings to what we are today."

The Old One paused, her breathing uneven, as if the remembering was becoming too much. It was some moments before she let out her breath slowly, calming herself, before continuing. "As we battled A-Sharoon those few short turnings ago, the storm she caused with her own darkness acted as a catalyst to free *him* from the protected place where he had been entombed."

"How was he able to capture the Living Flame? I mean, couldn't it have consumed him or something?" Nickolous asked, at the same time feeling foolish for having asked the obvious.

The Old One turned to look at the young man that walked with her, his brilliant blue eyes questioning and eager. She suddenly felt even frailer, thinking of the turnings that had passed. She shook her head as images of her childhood, followed by her youth and the place where she was now, crowded her thoughts. All that time. All spent on preparing for the possibility that two evils, each one unaware that without the other they would not exist, would come together, setting in motion a set of circumstances that could possibly turn the worlds of knowledge back into themselves.

The Old One paused, suddenly aware that Nickolous was standing still, watching her. Those eyes. There was something familiar... She shook the feeling off. Impulsively, she reached out to grasp his hand. Whatever it was, she would remember when she was supposed to. Of one thing she was certain: there was no darkness in this young man. She thought of the question so innocently asked and laughed softly, for indeed, hadn't they all wondered the same thing? Even she herself, a clan elder, one of the *"knowing races,"* had pondered that one. The answers she received frightened even her. However, the answer was one they all had to face.

"For more turnings than we can imagine, the Flame has existed, the power within the power, protected by the pure. Lord Nhon was ageless, near immortality, a gift to those who protected the light. The Ancients, in their wisdom, decided that this gift of near immortality would ensure the most trusted of the guardian warriors would protect the Flame with their very being. The turnings passed and the world changed. The guardians, concerned for the future, sought to commune with the Flame, but most failed in their attempt, except Lord Nhon. The warrior's thoughts, once only concerned with keeping the truth, turned back to a time before the darkness, before the light, and the seeds of discontent grew. He and he alone now knew of things long unspoken of—protected." The Old One's voice trailed off; she covered her mouth to stifle the sob as Nickolous drew her to him to comfort her, sorry now that he asked the question.

The Old One pulled away. Wiping the moisture from her face, she patted Nickolous's arm reassuringly. "It's all right. Even though some things are painful to speak of, they must be told." She wiped her face again, trying to stop the silent flow of tears that coursed unheeded, down her leathery cheeks. "The Flame is many things. At different times, when the worlds are in distress, it changes. No. No." The Old One had already perceived the question Nickolous was about to ask. "Fire and ice are akin. The form of the Flame remained, buried deep within the heart of it, and that is what the warrior waited for: the change. When the worlds shifted in their needs yet once again, Lord Nhon took the heart and imprisoned it in the darkness before it could consume him."

Nickolous hugged the Old One to him, feeling as if he had caused her distress.

She patted his cheek gently with a leathery paw as if reading his mind. "I'm just getting too old and cranky for all this wandering about." She smiled up at him, a thin, weary smile. "Come. I do believe that's breakfast I smell. Sarah and the others will be wondering where we have gotten ourselves off to."

The others were waiting when they got back. Orith moved over to make room for the Old One as Nickolous eased her gently down on the mossy ground while Sarah, seeming to know what was needed, placed a padded pillow made of fragrant cedar boughs behind her back. Everyone sniffed the air appreciatively as the aroma of the hot breakfast wafted around them. Even Gabriel and Chera joined them, politely refusing the food offered, their company nonetheless appreciated while the clearing rang with laughter and small talk, something that everyone needed to take their minds off the last few days.

Sarah had just finished tidying up and was about to serve tea when Owen returned from patrolling the forest, his long white wings folding gracefully at his side as he landed soundlessly beside Sarah, startling her, so that she very nearly dropped the tea she was carrying. "Owen!"

"Sorry, Sarah. Ahh, something smells good," Owen said as he drew in the scents around him.

"Go on with you; there are leftovers there on the ledge." Sarah hurried away as Owen inclined his head and took his leave, noting that Gabriel and Chera, accompanied by Jerome, were headed his way. Sighing deeply, he headed toward them. Breakfast would have to wait.

11

A-Sharoon paced angrily back and forth, her robes twining about her body as she turned this way and that, her black eyes glittering. In a fit of rage, she threw the vial of amber liquid at the cavern's wall; then watched as the contents spattered the earthen floor. A putrid odor, like that of decaying refuse, filled the room, but she didn't care; she was tired of being watched, her every move monitored and reported. They were supposed to be partners, she and Lord Nhon. She laughed into the gloom. The partnership was becoming more one-sided with each passing moment. She was no longer in charge, and she hated it.

Moments passed, but the shadowy figure remained where it was, its size and breadth filling the doorway's opening. It had arrived as the vial had shattered, shards of glass flying everywhere, and had paused at the doorway to admire the black-haired woman's cold beauty.

A-Sharoon spun around, expecting to see Lord Nhon's smirking features peering at her from beneath moldy-smelling robes. But it wasn't Lord Nhon who stood there; it was someone as yet unknown to her. Cold, bloodless fingers found the other vial hidden with the folds of her robe; and ever so slowly, it was withdrawn.

"Stop." The figure moved into the room. Ducking to clear the doorway, one hand threw the heavy woolen cloak over a shoulder, while the other gripped the hand that contained the vial.

A-Sharoon gasped as the vial was wrenched from her grasp. "How dare you!" The words were hissed through clenched teeth.

The heavily robed figure threw back his head and laughed; the hood slipped back, revealing his face to the shadows that surrounded them, darkly vaporous shadows crowding upon one another as if to see this newcomer. A-Sharoon stepped back in surprise. She knew this man; there was a familiarity about him...

§ § § § §

Jerome felt it first. The forest warrior trembled as if from a sudden chill, while the wolves looked uneasily about, instinctively knowing that there was something evil close by. Sarah, her eyes wide with undisclosed fear, grasped Timothy's arm, while the Old One gripped her walking stick tightly to her. But it was Nickolous who felt it most keenly; the tingling sensation started at his fingertips and raced up his arm, only it didn't stop there. As he moved away from the others, his whole body felt on fire, and as Gabriel rose to go to him, Orith stopped him. Like the Old One and Jerome, much of what he had learned had come from experience. A feathered wing brushed his scarred face ruefully. "Leave him be," he whispered hoarsely, filled with emotion. "It begins."

"What? What begins that we already don't know about, Orith," Sarah asked. They had to strain to hear the answer.

"Darkness," Orith replied. "Darkness within the darkness. The One. Lost to the worlds beneath; hidden by the breath of the night— nurtured by the shadows."

"*The forgotten.*"

"Gabriel." The words were barely a whisper, but the big wolf heard. They all had heard.

§ § § § §

A memory of childhood, of running through deep underground caverns. Running. Always running. Memories of something. Someone. A-Sharoon shook her head. The man before her—she knew him. "You," she whispered into the darkness.

"It is I." There was amusement in the voice as the hand that imprisoned hers slowly released its grip. "*Remember.*" The man's breath was hot upon her face as he lightly caressed her cheek. A-Sharoon pulled back, away from his touch, as a thousand memories flooded her being.

"How did you get past Lord Nhon's watchers? He'll be furious if he knows there is *another.*" A-Sharoon glanced uneasily about as she became aware of the silence. There were no scurrying sounds. Nothing. She smiled a cold approving smile. The teachings—

Words, inaudible to the cloaked figure before her, but nonetheless familiar, formed from bloodless lips as a hand, cold as winter's frost, reached beneath her robes and withdrew a yellowed piece of parchment.

The man smiled in approval.

§ § § § § §

"How long before the potion's effects wear off?" A-Sharoon leaned across the table, anxious that the visitor be gone before Lord Nhon returned and the watchers awakened.

"Patience was never one of your virtues. Don't worry; it'll last long enough." The robed figure laughed, then went back to studying the paper before him.

"Well, can you translate the writing?"

An exasperated sigh was the only reply.

§ § § § § §

Jerome paused, a silent sentinel within the heart of the forest. Sweat beaded his brow. He didn't bother to wipe it, for he was concentrating on the echoes within the forest's depths. The Unseen One. The *Other*, once more legend than fact, had threaded his way through sacred paths to the darkened places. Jerome turned away, unable to sense anything else. The small ones, the tiny inhabitants of the forest, shrew and vole, the earth diggers, had turned from their task of watching and gone to earth.

The big forest warrior did not wish to intrude on their thoughts, for he knew they wept. He knew he must find the others. He was concerned for Nickolous, for he knew what he wore on his arm. Once, when he was a young one, he had gotten lost in the forest. Frightened and alone, he had been found by one of the beings from above. For him, there had passed a short but happy time, for he had been an apt pupil, and Lord Moshat an excellent teacher. The bracelet, a sacred object of power and knowledge, had been there from the beginning. Only one who walked between the two worlds could wear it—or so the legends told.

The elders, those who had been gifted with the blood memories of the ancestors, had told of a night when there had been a great battle between the beings who lived above and one of their own. As the great one had fallen and darkness overshadowed the land, the Daughter of the Night had drawn her first breath, and it had been the breath of evil that nurtured her. As the turnings passed, it became evident that only A-Sharoon walked the depths of the deep places with the night, and there was no other—or so they had believed, and the little watchers had breathed more easily and relaxed their vigil.

Jerome knew he must get to Nickolous and the others. The whispered words of the Ancients, the unwritten thoughts of the elders; Jerome berated himself for not having paid more attention to the obvious facts. They had prepared for what they could see, not for what they could not.

Three.

Jerome shook his head trying to think. What was the significance of The Three? He must ask the Old One. She would know. As he hurried toward where the others waited, sentinels, ever alert, closed the path behind him, for where he had been was a sacred place.

§ § § § §

Nickolous felt as if he were on fire. Images of a forgotten time crowded upon him as the swirling mist surrounded him. Dimly, he could hear the others calling him. He tried to turn, to see, but could not. So he gave it over and allowed himself to be consumed by the white tendrils that reached out to caress him.

§ § § § §

A-Sharoon watched as the man carefully re-rolled the parchment that he had been studying. "Well?" When there was no answer, she sighed in exasperation. "Come now, you didn't study the writings all that time and not learn anything." Her voice was full of reproach.

The man replaced the hood so that his features were concealed before answering her. "Your rash actions have nearly destroyed those that live in the beneath." He held a gloved hand up to silence the words he knew she was about to speak before continuing. "However, all is not lost. Lord Nhon, though powerful, is not undefeatable." The voice lowered, but A-Sharoon felt the suppressed anger within the next words that were spoken. "To partner with the Fallen One was a very stupid thing to do. In all things, there must be a balance. Remember, we are not like those who dwell in the high places. Not even the Fallen. We were not made through greed and deceit, nor did we have to manipulate to be. We have always been." The man leaned forward so that his face was mere inches from A-Sharoon's, the words spoken in an ancient dialect of a forgotten race. *"We are."*

"Then why did you not reveal yourself? All these turnings, you were but a faint memory. Together, we could have been one!" A-Sharoon was almost shouting as, turning, she paced the cavern's length. When there was no reply, she turned angrily about to find herself alone.

Lord Nhon was just entering the cavern when the shrieks of rage reached him. Not wanting to deal with whatever had set the woman off this time, he turned aside and went straight to his chambers, closing the heavy wooden door behind him. Because he did not go further into the cavern's depths, he did not see the myriad of sentries slowly awakening from their drugged sleep. Nor did he see how quickly they drew themselves to attention, their feral faces peering into the darkness for things unwanted, not wanting their lord to know they had fallen asleep at their posts.

§ § § § §

"Nickolous!" Sarah struggled against the arms that held her.

"No. Leave him. Don't try to touch him; it might do more harm than good." Gabriel stood; his feet set wide apart, his strength wavering against the wind's onslaught. Orith and the Old One, their ragged cloaks little protection against the fury of the storm that surrounded them, remained where they were, waiting.

"Jerome!" Chera's shouted call against the wind was all but lost to the howling elements.

But the warrior of the forest had heard the call; as did the others. As they moved forward against the wind's wrath, heads lowered, war shields up, they managed to encircle the companions that surrounded Nickolous.

As one, the warriors entwined themselves together and stood straight, shields placed to the front to block the wind's tearing force. Orith relaxed his grip on the Old One as he drew what was left of his robes about him, as the wind raged up and over the little group, while the warriors formed a solid, impenetrable wall to protect those inside.

Gabriel remained where he was, alert for any danger. Although the warriors guarded without, he was taking no chances. It was obvious that Nickolous was in a place they could not reach, and right now, he was vulnerable; so, until he could be reached, or until he returned to them, Gabriel would stand guard.

"Old One." Jerome pushed his way through the nearly solid wall of forest warriors. Chera, sensing that something was terribly wrong, immediately joined Gabriel.

"What is it? What's wrong?" Her growled question was nearly lost to the wind's howling. Sarah clutched Timothy's arm so hard that her brother winced as the Old One withdrew her staff from beneath her robe and drew a circle in front of her. Orith, too, withdrew his staff and placing it in front of him, also began to draw in the sand. The others watched in silence as a picture began to form, along with ancient writings that were of a script that none recognized except those who made the marks.

§ § § § §

Nickolous looked around himself; he was in a high place of rolling hills covered with scented flowers. There was a familiarity about this place. He realized that this was the place from his dreaming time when he had been caught in between the two worlds. Neither awake nor asleep, neither here nor there but on the bridge in between. But this—this was different. This time he was here; completely here, and beyond him, the distant mist shrouded hills beckoned. He did not need to look behind him, nor below, for he knew he was protected. The sudden pull of the bracelet against his arm drew him toward the hidden places where Lord Moshat waited.

§ § § § §

"He comes." The winged warrior stood just inside the doorway.

"We don't have much time; we must prepare. The forces that allow him to be here will soon weaken, and he will be pulled back. Hurry!"

The messenger stepped back in surprise at the sudden agility of his master as Lord Moshat crossed the room and threw open the doors. "Come," he said. Then, seeing the shocked look upon the sentinel's face, he spoke more softly. "Come, my friend. Nickolous cannot stay long. He walks a forbidden path for a mortal."

"But he is part of one, part of another." The messenger turned toward Lord Moshat; one sleek brow rose questioningly.

"Ahh," Lord Moshat replied. "But therein lies the key; the problem being that he, himself, doesn't know that, so therefore he is not aware that his powers, not ours, got him here. He has much to learn. The three paths await his choice." Lord Moshat had turned back into the room and stirred the small fire in the hearth as he spoke.

"And if he chooses the wrong path?" the messenger asked as he moved forward into the room, his senses telling him that their visitor was almost at his destination.

Lord Moshat turned to face him, his presence seeming to fill the room. His cobalt-blue eyes bored into those of the other. "He won't," was all he said, his gaze now on the open doorway and the one who stood there.

Saying nothing, Nickolous moved into the room, his gaze meeting that of Lord Moshat's, a flicker of recognition deep within him fanning the need for answers. He knew that he didn't have much time. As the messenger closed the door behind him, his duty now to protect those within, Lord Moshat's voice began speaking, low and melodious, in the language of the elders of Skye.

12

"There is a never-ending circle of life."

"It can be broken."

The Old One looked up at the speaker and scowled. "Yes, it can, but it always returns, back to its center, then out again." The Old One shook her cane at the speaker.

Sarah turned away, embarrassed. She ought, she thought, to have known better.

Orith smiled beneath his hood. "Sarah, it's okay; not many of us have the years of knowing as does the Old One."

"Hmph. You're as many turnings as I, if not more," the Old One retorted as she bent back to her drawing.

"Old One?" Jerome asked, his wide, craggy face creased with lines of exhaustion. "What can you tell us of the Unseen One?"

"A legend of the Ancient Ones from the before times," the Old One replied as she straightened up, her expression wary. "What makes you ask such a question?"

"Why, the little ones. The clans of the earth dwellers who live beneath; those who live their lives burrowing, who seek the unseen." The forest warrior was puzzled as to why the Old One was acting as if she did not already know this.

The Old One gripped her staff tightly as she stood, unflinching beneath everyone's gaze. Then, as if the knowing was too much, her shoulders rounded and a high-pitched keening, like that of something mortally wounded, sounded throughout the wood.

The sound was everywhere. Beneath. Above. Beside. And the forest replied in kind, the answering echo deafening.

§ § § § §

Far below the companions, deep within the earth where caverns opened then closed nearly upon themselves into small narrowed passages, tiny creatures moved about, their long noses, their eyes, snuffling. Finding the bright light of day nearly unbearable, they had taken the task to themselves of guarding the places beneath. So it was that, as the cries from the world above reached down to touch their senses, they found the one they sought.

§ § § § §

"We had hoped that this day would never come." The Old One sat, surrounded by her concerned friends, as Sarah placed a gourd of hot tea in front of her. They rested a little apart from the place where Nickolous stood, unmoving, Gabriel at his side. Jerome, his heavy war club beside him, stood near enough to hear what the Old One was saying, yet close enough to aid Gabriel if need be.

"The Unseen One, tell us about him," Jerome urged gently. "How is it he has remained hidden these many turnings? Our watchers are everywhere."

"The watchers' eyes cannot see everything that melds with the night." The Old One's tone was regretful. "For more seasons than I care to remember, the little ones have kept vigil, waiting for that one to show himself, if, indeed, he even existed. You see, the Ancients foretold of the two: one born to the darkness; the other, the light. The Unseen One was a supposition of old warriors who dreamed of a different time. A powerful time...it was the dreaming time." The Old One fell silent.

Jerome felt the Old One's anguish. As she had talked, he had seen the images of that long-ago time, and as with all of his kind, the telling triggered a remembering within himself: images of a long cavern filled with soot and smoke from a fire that was never allowed to burn out, its center burning white hot, then red. It felt as if the forest warrior had been punched as the realization of what he saw hit him.

Slowly, he reached out to grasp the Old One's shoulder in understanding. He should have known. Those Ancients who dreamed, who guarded the secrets of life, who had been more then what they had appeared to be; they had spent their entire existence dreaming. It was they who had never let the fire diminish, they who had kept the circle whole; complete. Jerome turned the Old One so that she was facing him. Black eyes looked into green.

Shadow warriors. Warriors of Skye. Both descendants of a mystic race. The Living Flame.

Jerome understood. All the friends did. They had seen the images exactly as Jerome had. Somehow, something had caused the dreamers to separate themselves from the circle and the Flame. Both continued to exist, gaining in power, helping each other. Once the two had acted as one.

"They couldn't have known that evil would come to one of their own, pure since his first drawing of breath." The voice, unexpected, startled them all.

"Nickolous, are you all right?" Gabriel stood close, alert for anything untoward, his concern for his young charge evident.

"Where were you? Can you talk about it?" Sarah touched his arm gently, her eyes wide and questioning.

Everyone fell silent, watching, as Nickolous moved forward staggering slightly, obviously exhausted from his journey. Jerome put out a limb-like arm to steady him as Sarah rushed to get him a hot drink, while the Old One, concerned because she noticed how cold Nickolous looked, rummaged in her belongings until she found a tattered wool blanket.

Nickolous pulled the heavy woolen blanket about his shoulders, glad for the sudden warmth. He had been cold before, but this—this was different.

"You have traveled far, the way long and dangerous. You had to find your way there and back as well as protect yourself along the way. The chill will pass, but be careful," the Old One warned. Her eyes watched him carefully; afraid he had come to some inward harm from his journeying. She reached out to grasp his cold hand as the other reached up to secure the blanket about his shoulders. Her whisper of, "You must not go there again, alone, for the path is now watched. They will be waiting," was lost to the other companions as the wind swirled about them.

Nickolous squeezed her gently to let her know he had heard. He felt a little warmer; the tea was hot, and he drank it quickly, feeling its warmth as it coursed through him. He had barely finished when Sarah was there with more. "I cannot tell you where I have been, or what I have done." Nickolous looked around the little group, feeling as if he was betraying them, but he knew that to share anything could bring harm to them if they were ever captured. A shudder passed through him as he thought the unthinkable.

"The shadows of the day bring the night, and with the night, the eyes of the unseen," Nickolous spoke softly, as he rose wearily to his feet. He turned to Jerome. Words formed in his mind but went unspoken. Nonetheless, the forest warrior heard.

Gabriel moved closer; his body was taut with expectation as Chera, fur bristling, remained close. From outside the protective circle, a shout of warning rose as the sky darkened with untold numbers of winged things. A chill, unnatural on such a warm day, remained in the air long after their passage.

"What were those things?" Sarah asked as she looked fearfully at her feet, as if expecting to find one there.

"I don't know, but it looks as if they were heading somewhere," Timothy replied. "One thing's for sure; they weren't interested in us—this time."

"They'll return, make no mistake about that," Owen muttered, his expression taut and drawn. "They're spies for Lord Nhon."

"Oh, great, just when we get used to A-Sharoon's chattering, chittering, smelly things lurking underfoot, something new pops up!" Sarah exclaimed.

Owen hid a grin as he watched Sarah toss their belongings into a pile; checking as she did so for anything unwanted.

§ § § § §

"Here, take this." Nickolous turned to see Orith holding out a leather-bound book.

"Orith, I can't take that; it's yours." Nickolous, overwhelmed that Orith would offer him his most treasured belonging, tried to give the book back, but Orith refused, his tone insistent.

"It never was mine to keep," he said, his tone gentle. "Take it."

Nickolous carefully opened the book, noting as he did so the ancient script. At first glance, the writing was indecipherable. He tried to hand the book back; "Orith, it's no use to me, I can't read the sc—" he began, and then stopped as Orith spoke; his tone broking no argument.

"Look at the script again."

Glancing down at the opened book, Nickolous was surprised to see words where before there had only been markings he hadn't understood.

"What you need to understand shall be provided when the time comes. Use the knowledge well." Orith had let the hood that nearly always hid his face slide back over his shoulders.

Nickolous found himself looking into eyes the color of dark amber, and for a moment their gazes held; each one trying to communicate things unspoken in words. Slowly, Nickolous turned away, his heart heavy; for each had heard the other, and Nickolous felt Orith's weariness... The great white snowy owl was older than most of them had guessed and he was tired.

"There is learning for every step that is taken through the turnings of one's life, young one."

Nickolous turned toward the speaker. The guardian of the gate stared thoughtfully after Orith's retreating form. Nickolous nodded, acknowledging the other's presence; glad to see that the wounds that had looked so terrible but a few days past were nearly healed.

"I remember that day," he spoke quietly so that the others wouldn't hear. "In fact, if I remember correctly, there were two of you: alike—yet not alike." He took a deep breath; exhaling slowly. "You know, I dreamed of that place for months; it still haunts me."

The guardian didn't turn to look at Nickolous, but each knew the other was listening. "The heart that burns deep within the Flame weeps," the guardian spoke slowly. It was hard for him, this thing called talking. His turnings had been spent guarding the eternal; there had been no need to speak. Then the unthinkable had occurred... He bowed his head sadly; the Flame was no longer his to keep. He was glad Nickolous remembered that day when he had helped him safely through the mists that guarded the high places; he turned to look at this stripling who offered his world an unseen light to burn away the darkness. Blue eyes looked into his soul. Emerald eyes as old as the forest itself looked startled as a knowing surged through the guardian. With a sharp intake of breath, he stepped back. *The Ancients Knew...* Exhaling slowly, he moved away, satisfied.

Still unsure of what had just taken place, Nickolous watched as the departing figure sought out Jerome, and taking him aside, said something. The big warrior looked thoughtful for a moment, as if he were weighing the words that had been spoken. Having made up his mind, he nodded assent; while a series of whistles, low and melodious, filled the air. A slight opening appeared in the circle, and before anyone could stop him, the guardian of the gate slipped through.

§ § § § §

"What do you have to report? Speak!" A-Sharoon whirled around, catching the guard as well as the messenger by surprise. Her staff sent them both flying. "Speak!" Towering over them both, A-Sharoon's eyes glittered with a coldness that made the guard sidle sideways and the messenger cower beneath her glare.

"They are still at the gate; protected by the warriors of the forest." The words that poured forth were hurried as the creature bent lower until its face was level with the earthen floor; not daring to look up until it was given permission to do so.

"And the Other—"

Lord Nhon stood within the doorway, his red eyes glittering. "Yes, what of the *Other?*"

A-Sharoon turned at the sound of the hated voice; while the guard tried to shrink even further into the shadows, away from its cowering comrade, as Lord Nhon entered the cavern. A-Sharoon faced him in the gloom and dankness, made even more so by the Fallen One's presence.

"Did you hope to deceive me, woman?" Lord Nhon growled, his voice feral as he glared at her from beneath his hooded cloak.

A-Sharoon stood, tall and proud; unflinching beneath the other's gaze. "I think, my Lord—" She bowed her head slightly, her tone mocking. "Our association is at an end." Turning, she strode purposefully away, her movements self-assured and graceful.

Lord Nhon watched her go, aware that with every step she took, she expected opposition to her blatant betrayal of their partnership. Red eyes glinted like small coals as his mouth twisted into a grin. He watched, amused, as her two cowering followers scuttled sideways, thinking to evade him and follow their mistress back to her lair. Had he been in a giving mood, he might have let them pass. But he wasn't…

§ § § § § §

A-Sharoon kept walking. She hated the daylight, preferring instead the cover of night. Shielding her eyes with part of her cloak against the glare of the sun, she made her way into the deeper parts of the forest that had once been hers to rule. She knew she could not tire, for there were many hours of travel ahead. She drew in a deep breath; her coal-black eyes shone unnaturally as she walked faster, now and then reaching out to twist an obstinate branch out of her way. She'd been sent to earth, and earth was where she would stay.

Lord Nhon? She'd wait 'til that one was destroyed; then, and only then, would she return to the world above.

A-Sharoon paused at the bottom of a moss-covered ravine, glad for some familiarity. This place she remembered well, for it was unusually steep, with large jutting rocks overshadowing the narrow gully where she stood. She inhaled deeply of the scents that rested here, and a part of her was glad she had returned home.

Whispers of things hidden in crevice and burrow, above and below, followed the passage of the Dark Daughter. Reaching the top of a knoll, she paused long enough to draw her heavy cloak about her slender shoulders; fastening it about her throat with an ornately worked pin. It was dark and dreary here. The canopy of trees was so thick overhead that neither sun nor rain seeped through, leaving only mold and rotting vegetation upon the ground. Most would have avoided such a place—A-Sharoon reveled in it.

§ § § § §

"I want all the entrances sealed. No one is to leave without my permission. No one." Lord Nhon threw more wood into the fire as he spoke, his thoughts on what was in the adjoining cavern. He knew A-Sharoon had somehow touched the thoughts of the Flame, and it surprised him that she had left while it remained in his possession. Then again, she alone could not wrest the Flame from him, for not even her changelings and shadow creatures were a match for him.

Lord Nhon stared into the fire, determined that even if what his spies were saying was true, it would make no difference. Rising, he summoned the captain of the guard…

"Do you understand?" Lord Nhon wanted no misunderstanding. The wolf-like creature standing before him nodded its head in answer, foam spewing from a mouth that couldn't—or wouldn't—stay closed.

"Loathsome creature," Lord Nhon muttered beneath his rancid breath as he turned away.

§ § § § §

"What are we to do now?" Sarah asked; resigned to the fact that they would be on the move again, she had already begun packing.

"We find Lord Nhon," Gabriel replied.

"And then what? We just walk in and get the *Flame,* just like that, I suppose." Sarah's voice dripped with sarcasm.

Timothy tried to give her that "look" so she would be quiet, but it was no use. She would have ignored him anyway. She turned to Gabriel, her brown eyes flashing. "Why don't we just wait here? If we send everybody away and leave ourselves defenseless, those smelly little growy things will come right away and attack us. No muss, no fuss. Lord Nhon will probably be right behind them."

The Old One choked on her tea, trying not to laugh. Orith, too, hid a smile beneath his cloaked hood, as Jerome looked on, amused.

Gabriel, as usual, registered no emotion. Chera, unsure of his reaction, stood between Sarah and her mate, for she had developed a fondness for her over the turnings that they had spent together.

Aware that she had spoken out of turn, Sarah nonetheless met Gabriel's gaze unflinchingly. "Well," she said, arching a dark brow as she crossed her arms. "I'm waiting."

A low rumble came from deep within the great wolf's chest. "Little one," he said, using a low throaty tone that Chera rarely heard. With a start, she realized he was trying not to laugh. "Little one," he said again, his voice more like that of the old Gabriel's. "If all had your fire, there would be no need for warriors and battle." He paused as his gaze held hers for a long moment. "They would return to their dark places to hide from the sting of your tongue!"

Chagrined, Sarah's gaze fell to her feet. Knowing she shouldn't have spoken so, she stood, drawing circles in the sand, for once at a loss for words.

"It's all right, you know." Sarah looked up. The Old One was there, her wizened face bent close so that what passed between them would be unheard by the others. "Never mind child; you had every right to voice what the rest of us were thinking. Besides," she sniffed loudly, her gaze directed at Gabriel, who was watching her, his expression now one of open amusement. "Sometimes we need to be reminded we aren't the only ones with an opinion."

Gabriel drew back his lips in what everyone supposed was a wolf's grin. "Point taken." He bowed his head slightly in deference to the Old One. "I'm sorry. It's just that these are dark times. To stay would serve no purpose. It's unprotected here, and we must find shelter before night comes. Trust me, little one." He was now standing directly in front of Sarah, looking down at her. "You would not want to face those '*smelly little growy things,*' especially during the hours between the darkness and the dawn."

13

"There are still a few hours of daylight left." Gabriel and Nickolous were standing a little apart from the others; watching as the guardians of the forest fanned out in the four directions; their duty to protect those following in their wake.

"Yes, but we need to reach a protected place that the eyes of the night cannot so easily see into," Gabriel replied as the last of the forest warriors disappeared from view. He didn't acknowledge the hand on his shoulder. He didn't have to. Too-taut muscles rippled beneath his fur as he turned to face Nickolous. Inhaling deeply of the scents surrounding them, the knowing that tugged at him was almost too much. "You must stay close to Chera and the others. Jerome and I will stay slightly behind in case we are followed, although I think the opposition will block the path ahead to prevent us from finding the Fallen One's lair."

"*Three.*"

"What?" Gabriel stared at Nickolous, not sure he had heard correctly.

"*Three. Three stones face three fallen forest warriors; their resting place the entrance to the Fallen One's lair that leads to the 'Beneath.'*"

"Wait. Speak no more of this yet. There are eyes everywhere. Come." Gabriel pushed Nickolous ahead of him, the fur along his back bristling as he signaled Chera to him. Sensing the sudden urgency growing within her mate, she moved quickly to his side, the others following suit as Timothy quietly unsheathed his sword.

Silently the little group moved forward; each one suddenly aware that this day was not safe, and that silence was their only protection.

§ § § § § §

Owen glided silently above his friends, his eyes searching the shadowed places for hidden things. Airborne as he was, he had no fear for himself—something evil moved through the sunshine on a day that held little warmth, and it was those who walked below for which he was concerned. Veering southward, he glimpsed something scuttling along a well trodden path; as he plunged to earth, he missed the large shadowy form closing in behind him.

§ § § § § §

Nickolous fell to his knees as screams not his own ripped through him. He felt, rather than saw, the unnamed thing closing in on Owen, the big owl unaware that death rode behind him on ashen wings; its purpose to destroy.

"Leave him be."

"Old One, he is in pain." Timothy's sword remained unsheathed, but he felt powerless against a foe he could not see.

"Leave him be. Do not touch him. Protect him so he can protect our own," the Old One rasped; her heart thudding wildly as she saw what the others hadn't yet.

"Orith. Help me." The commanding tone of her voice made Orith look up.

"Owen, behind you!"

Owen neither heard nor saw the frantic motions of those below. The creature was in the open, and he was headed straight for it.

"Oh, do something, please," Sarah pleaded, her voice barely audible, but it was enough—Nickolous focused on the scene before him, his mind carrying him to the place above Owen, who was plummeting earthward, his concentration on the creature now trying to evade his outstretched talons.

§ § § § § §

"*Careful,*" the voice whispered, and Nickolous understood. The bracelet must remain hidden.

The cloud creature was much the same as the one that had spirited A-Sharoon away turnings ago, but it wasn't one of hers. Power from a thousand turnings coursed through the entity that dwelt within.

"*Help us,*" the voices whispered.

Owen, sensing movement behind him, veered sharply, his talons narrowly missing his intended prey. Caught off balance, he plummeted to the ground, his fall broken by a mossy incline. As he tumbled over and over, he was vaguely aware of thunder roaring overhead and thought it odd that such a thing would occur on such a sunny day.

Nickolous knew instinctively that the creature was in a lot of pain; forced to do a bidding that was beyond its control, lashing out, hoping the agony would lessen if it did as it was commanded. But it never happened, and it remained a prisoner within itself.

He raised his arms and threw his head back. "Tell me what to do." The plea, unspoken, echoed and was heard.

"Guide him." Lord Moshat commanded from his high place, concealed from the clans who lived below.

The warrior of Skye, who watched, unseen, listened to the elder's words and nodded assent.

§ § § § § §

Silvery splinters of light shot through the gloom as the cloud creature writhed in pain. Again and again, the silver bolts hit it, passing through it, leaving silver threads in their wake, until they were interspersed throughout the shadowy mass.

Nickolous fell back, exhausted, not quite sure what had just happened, but Jerome knew. The forest warrior had sensed the change and had been prepared for the sudden darkening about them. Only he had seen the winged warrior, enveloped in the shadows it had created as it soared skyward, the slight trembling of the leaves on the nearby trees the only indication of his passage amongst them.

"Thank you." Nickolous bowed his head, his hands clasped in front of him. He was trembling from the sheer power racing through him, and he was cold—so cold.

"Owen. Where's Owen?" Sarah's voice roused the little group. Shielding her face with her cloak to protect against the swirling wind, she made her way to where she had seen him fall. Timothy, realizing what she was doing, raced after her, his sword still drawn as the Old One rose stiffly from her kneeling position, her black eyes searching.

"Look," she said, peering upward into the sky.

Nickolous rose unsteadily to his feet, his senses slowly returning to normal. The sky had cleared, and the cloud creature was no longer writhing and twisting like a thing gone mad. The silver threads had thickened, and it looked more like the kind of cloud you would see on a balmy mid-summer's eve when the sun was setting, her rays glinting like a child's prism turned to the light.

"It's at peace with itself. You have freed it." Jerome fell silent and, as he watched, the creature began to move slowly away.

"There was another. I felt his power aiding me; guiding me—" Nickolous turned his attention to Jerome. "What will happen to it? Will Lord Nhon be able to force it back to the way it was?" Nickolous asked as they stood watching it move gracefully eastward.

"I doubt it. Lord Nhon's promises turned it dark; then, when it wanted to turn back, it was too late, and he held it fast with a power that threatened to tear it apart." Jerome turned to face Nickolous, amazed that he didn't realize what he had done. The gifts he possessed could restore what was, or destroy the darkest heart, and he didn't even realize he held the key.

"Where will it go? Are there others like it?"

"Yes, they once belonged to one of the races of Skye' rarely seen by those of us below except when they have become dark warriors for the likes of A-Sharoon and the Fallen One. Why?" Jerome had turned to look at Nickolous, sensing something he had missed before.

"It was screaming. I could hear it. In here," Nickolous said, pointing to his head. "And here," he continued, pointing to his heart. He stood staring thoughtfully at the departing creature. "It was as if a thousand voices were calling, asking for help. I wonder," he mused, more to himself then to the warrior of the forest.

"What is it? What were you wondering?" Jerome prompted gently.

"It was as if there were others calling, asking for help." Nickolous turned to face Jerome, his blue eyes searching. "Are there others, like that one, asking to be freed from the darkness? Jerome, answer me!" He reached out and grasped the warrior's trunk-like arm. Just as quickly letting go. He had seen.

There was no need for them to speak words. In one moment Nickolous had seen those lost to the shadows. They were legion. Jerome knew—had always known. Nickolous looked into green eyes that reflected the emerald color of the forest back at him.

Wondering...

§ § § § § §

"We found Owen, he's a little shaken but unhurt." Sarah came running, her brown eyes bright. Trailing behind her came Timothy and Owen, the white owl shaking off the dead leaves and broken twigs that clung to him as he walked stiffly toward them, grumbling something inaudible.

"There are still a few hours 'til dusk."

"I know, but at this rate we will still be in the open, unprotected."

"And the night will still have eyes regardless of where we shelter." Chera spoke sharply as Gabriel looked at her in surprise.

"What's wrong?" He knew her better than anyone…

She was worried about something. Instead of answering him, she strode ahead. Gabriel had to hurry to catch up; a backward glance at Jerome assured him the others were being guarded as he followed Chera to a small gully where they could have a few moments alone.

They stood facing each other as the voices of the others drifted to them, barely audible above the softly whispering wind that followed them as they made their way warily to their destination.

Gabriel, lowering his head, nudged Chera gently. "What is it Chera, tell me. The others cannot hear." He nudged her yet again; then stood back, puzzled by her behavior. She was looking past him, as if he were not there. When she spoke, he hardly heard her, and when he did, he wished he hadn't.

"What did you say?" Gabriel shook his head, not believing what his ears had heard.

"The Daughter of the Night has returned to her lair. Alone." Chera turned to look at her mate.

"How did you come by this information?"

"Those of the earth. The little ones. The earth diggers."

Gabriel stood thoughtfully for some moments; his mind now on another thought that had been troubling him. "Chera, what about the others, those we sent ahead to clear the way?"

"Nothing. There has been nothing." Chera lowered her head. She was so tired; there was no end in sight. They were traveling blind, each step a guess, each clearing they entered a potential trap, and now this…

A-Sharoon.

At least when she was with Lord Nhon, the two were together. Separated, the two were even more dangerous, for they would never know from which direction the evil would come. Chera looked up as Gabriel stood over her, nuzzling her gently.

"We were born to this. It is our destiny. Together we will stand, or fall, as the fates would have it." Gabriel looked into her eyes. They had walked the same path for countless turnings, so attuned to each other that one often knew what the other was thinking. Chera rubbed her mate's cheek affectionately, feeling foolish that she had let her emotions get the better of her. She sighed deeply. She must, she thought, have seen too many turnings, to be getting this sentimental.

"We had better go, the others will be wondering where we've went."

"Yes, we'd better get back." Chera gave Gabriel a playful nuzzle; glad they had taken some time alone.

§ § § § §

"What is it? What do you hear?" Nickolous could feel the hairs standing up along the back of his neck.

Jerome placed a finger to his lips so as not to alarm the others who were now moving steadily, silently, along the forest's edge. He peered down at Nickolous from his great height, his green eyes searching for something. A moment later, Nickolous was shoved roughly to the ground as Jerome swung his club in a wide arc, the dull thud as whatever it was, hit the ground a telling thing—

"I guess I should be used to this by now," Nickolous muttered aloud as he brushed at the moldy leaves and twigs that still clung to his clothing. Gabriel and Chera had caught up to them and Chera went on ahead to scout while Gabriel fell into step with the forest warrior and Nickolous.

"Do you think there are more?" Gabriel asked as Jerome wiped his war club on the fresh grass, cleaning it before looping it loosely back at his side.

"Who knows? There are probably others lurking about, trying to get close enough to hear, so they can report back to their master," Jerome answered, then, rubbing his chin thoughtfully, said, "I find it strange that these are only Lord Nhon's creatures that we have seen as of late; I can't say as I've seen any of A-Sharoon's loyal legions in a while…" He arched a black brow in Gabriel's direction.

And so it was he learned that the mistress of the night was back where she had been spawned, and grown into what she was now. Jerome shuddered at the thought.

"If she has taken refuge in the 'Beneath,' she is unreachable. Not even my warriors can cross the chasm that joins the two worlds safely. Oh, would that the warriors of Skye could aid us in this quest." Jerome shook his head sadly at the thought of what lay ahead for them.

"This is our battle. If we don't fight for ourselves, we will never grow into anything more then what we are now." Gabriel looked at his friend as he spoke. What he said sounded good, but was it the truth, or was it merely an interpretation of their own needs and wants? He paused thoughtfully for a few moments and then asked, "What do you suppose drove her to ground? Certainly not us."

The answer was simple, but not what the great silver wolf wanted to hear.

The '*Other.*'

Legend becomes truth. Truth becomes a hard thing to bear.

14

Whispers in the dark. Frightening eerie voices. Shadows, dancing on the wall.

The little girl looked behind her, tripping over a rock and falling. Rising swiftly, she fled, oblivious to the pain for she had been taught to ignore such things. Running—always running, but she didn't know from what—she felt wetness on her lashes; angrily she brushed at it; wiping it away. She rounded a bend in the darkened forest; ahead of her a rock wall loomed, ancient and forbidding. Sighing in relief, she ran toward it, disappearing into the tiny opening in its center; she felt the protective embrace of the earth beneath and welcomed the power that surged through her.

A-Sharoon rose stiffly from her bed, her body aching from the exertion. As she splashed ice-cold water on her face, she suppressed the urge to throw something; angry she could not control the distant memories of a little girl who was always fleeing from something she could not see.

Hours later, staff in hand, A-Sharoon strode purposefully toward the center of the forest; a host of small skittering things following behind her. As she passed beneath the low-hanging boughs of the ancient fir trees, she paused, her up-swung hand demanding silence as her dark eyes swept the open places for things unseen. Finding nothing, she continued on, unaware that the little ones—the earth diggers—beat out a steady tattoo beneath the earth, the soft thrumming carrying to those who guarded from above.

§ § § § §

Lord Nhon stood watching the Flame as it threw itself against its prison; long tendrils of ice fire reaching out and up, to seek an escape. There was none. As the Flame sank back to the center of its prison, a soft keening could be heard. Rising to a wail, the cavern's walls shook as the being rose up; finger-like tendrils splayed across the top of the ceiling seeking entrance to the world above as Lord Nhon watched, his expression devoid of emotion.

§ § § § §

"There. Hear that?" Nickolous shielded his eyes with his hand as he looked upward.

Gabriel stood, nostrils flared, scenting the wind. "Whatever it was, it's gone now."

"No, wait." Nickolous could feel the heat coursing through him. He closed his eyes, and just as quickly opened them. He had seen. He turned to find Jerome next to him. Words, unspoken but heard, passed between them; Jerome knew the place well, for not even his warriors ventured into that forest's depths. The high-pitched calls brought his warriors to him, and as the circle closed about them, Orith and the Old One made their way inside along with the rest while Owen winged his way upward; his wings beating in silent unison, as golden eyes scanned the ground below for things unseen.

§ § § § §

"Are you sure?" Chera stood next to Gabriel, looking at Jerome in amazement. The dark forests depths held things best not met by the living. They would be defenseless in there.

"You know there are some things best left alone." The fur on her back bristled at the thought of entering such a place.

"We have no choice." The Old One stood beside Nickolous as she faced the others.

Orith, his face once again hidden beneath the hood that covered his scarred features, spoke softly. "Old One," he said gently, his heart heavy, for he knew that where they were going was a place of dark deeds. Few who entered ever returned the same. He knew, for he had been there. Had seen, and still carried the scars upon his body. He sighed in resignation, knowing that to argue would serve no purpose.

The Old One hurried to catch up; her thoughts reaching out to touch his. She felt his pain and knew of the ancient telling of that unknown place where evil had been spawned in that long ago time.

Shuddering at the thought of entering such a dark place did not appeal to her, but she knew that if that was where the Flame was, then that is where they would go. She gripped her staff tightly beneath her robes, drawing upon the strength that dwelt within the carved wood, hoping that when the time came, there would be enough of them to break the ring that imprisoned the Flame.

§ § § § § §

"I do not think that it would be wise to spend the night within the circle that guards the darkened forests depths." Jerome had pulled Gabriel to one side, slightly away from the others. His dark brow furrowed thoughtfully as he peered upward into the early evening sky. The pinks and gold's mixing with the more subtle hues that came together as the sun, tinged red, nestled softly within their midst.

"There's still a few hours before the moon rises. If memory serves, there should be a cave concealed in the side of that sloping gully, there, in the distance. If we can reach it, we will be well protected 'til morning's light."

"And what of Lord Nhon and those who do their dark lords bidding?" Gabriel asked, his voice little more than a throaty growl at the thought of being that close to Lord Nhon and his legion of followers.

"Once there, we will be protected against the prying eyes that seek. It will be the one night we can rest in safety, for it is a sacred place. Protected by the guardian, it was used as a sanctuary in time of need," Jerome replied.

"I know the place. It will serve us well this night." Orith said no more as Jerome moved to make room for him. As they returned to the circle of friends that awaited them, a companionable silence hung between them; each one of them reflecting on the memories of the past and how they knew of the place that awaited them.

§ § § § § §

A-Sharoon pressed herself in between the crevice cut deep within the rock and felt her way through the inky darkness until she reached a deeper, more spacious room. The smell of rotting fungus permeated the dank air that seeped in from outside. Feeling her way along the wall, A-Sharoon ignored the slime that came away on her hands as she sought, then found, a lever built into the jagged rock. Uttering a curse, she flung the crumbling pieces of rock to the floor and, using her long fingernails, turned the small piece that was left until it clicked against an ancient mechanism placed there countless turnings before.

The room was as she remembered it. For long moments she stood, drawing deeply on the fragrance of lingering scents that reminded her of things past. As her dark brooding gaze swept the length of the room, she smiled. Nothing had been touched. Everything was as it had been left so long ago. Finally, content that none had discovered this place in her absence, she begun what was necessary.

The fire burned for a long time in the dampness of the earth beneath. Yet even with the dampness, it fanned itself out and grew— growing until the shadows splayed across the walls and ceiling as if in wonderment of their freedom; after having been confined for so long a time beneath the nothingness of the cold gray ash of a forgotten fire pit, encircled with forbidding stone.

A-Sharoon stood, watching, pleased with herself beyond measure. When the flame had reached its peak, she removed a vial containing a silvery liquid from her belongings. Stirring the contents into the round iron pot, her voice, clear and cutting as the crystal vial she held, rose to a shivering trill as the cavern reverberated with new life.

§ § § § § §

The small sentinel stirred, its long sleep disturbed after countless turnings by something thought long gone. As it moved cautiously through the maze of underground tunnels, the sound became louder, the words being spoken, clearer. The fur bristled along the little one's back as it gained entry to the dimly lit cavern and observed the woman; intent upon her work, her long black hair flung carelessly over her shoulder as she bent to her task. The incantation cast; one dark brow arched questioningly as she glanced around the cavern, the slow drip-drip of the water trickling down the slime covered rocks the only sound that echoed against her senses.

Later, back within the safety of its own burrow, the little watcher began to beat its own message against the hardened ground.

§ § § § § §

The fire had long ago died down, and not even embers remained, yet A-Sharoon stayed where she was, her thoughts far away. She had been aware of the ground dweller's presence but had ignored it, knowing that before the sun set the whole forest would be alerted to her presence amongst them. She didn't care. Let the fear rise and grow. It mattered not. She was home. Let Lord Nhon think he had won and that the Living Flame was his.

A-Sharoon knew better—she had touched its heart, and for one fleeting moment had heard the voice from within the center speak. Words spoken for her alone to think on and decide their worth...

As she sank wearily upon her bed, sleep came swiftly, and for once the dreams did not haunt her.

§ § § § § §

The steady drumming against the hardened ground beneath his feet crept upward to the world above and burst forth like thunder, echoing against the driving wind. Lord Nhon caught himself, whirling about to stare at the Flame as it tore forcefully at its prison, comprehension dawning as his eyes narrowed, glinting blood red.

Spreading his arms in an arc, he muttered an incantation and watched as the Flame slowly settled, back to the center it held within itself. A soft fluttering sound, like the beating of hundreds of tiny wings filled the air as he turned toward the caverns opening.

"*Away.*" The words were whispered into the darkness. Then Lord Nhon flung his arms open, shouting into the emptiness that surrounded him.

"Away."

§ § § § § §

Owen flew against the updraft of wind that threatened to pull him off course, away from his intended destination. Powerful wings stroked in unison as he pulled slowly forward, every wing beat bringing him closer to the others who waited somewhere below.

Even as the great owl struggled to reach the others, there were those who made their way toward another destination. Hidden within the shadows that moved naturally throughout the day, they inched slowly forward; ever mindful their presence must not be detected. Those who were able to moved underground, the caverns used long ago by their kind a safe haven to breed the darkness that made them feared. Aware of this, Owen pushed himself to the limit. It was just before dusk that he spotted Jerome and the others a short distance away.

§ § § § § §

"Is it much further?"

Jerome stroked his chin thoughtfully as he looked down at Nickolous. "Soon," he replied; his emerald eyes narrowed as he studied his charge from beneath deeply furrowed brows "What is it? What troubles you?" He knew Nickolous well enough to know he sensed something, else he wouldn't have sought him out, away from the others. Or rather, the warrior thought wryly to himself, the Old One would not have motioned the others back. It always amazed him that her senses were so acute, that she knew before he himself did when Nickolous needed him.

"Something moves beneath the earth; something dark and terrible." Nickolous spoke so softly that the warrior had to strain to catch the nearly inaudible words; Nickolous wasn't looking at him; his unusual blue eyes were riveted on something in the distance—as if he could not bear to let the warrior see what he was seeing.

Jerome stopped mid stride to look at his companion; placing a big bronzed hand on Nickolous's shoulder, he turned him so that they were facing one another. Lowering his voice so that the others could not hear, he asked, "What is it? Are we in danger?"

"I don't think so, at least not yet," Nickolous replied; his voice trailed off as he once more looked away, unable to meet the warrior's intense gaze.

Jerome felt a sudden pain and realized that he was feeling what Nickolous was feeling. Pain. Intense. Hurting. Not for himself, but for the little ground dwellers; those of the smallest of the earthen clans who dwelled beneath them in the hidden places. Jerome reached out to once more to touch Nickolous thoughts and was nearly blinded by the intensity of the emotions that rushed through him.

"*Are they…?*" The rest of the question went unasked as Jerome saw what Nickolous saw. The knowing was almost too much to bear. Hundreds—thousands—Jerome turned his face away so that no one would see his distress.

"What do we do, Jerome, how do we stop this?" Nickolous asked as he tried to banish the images from his mind, at least temporarily.

Jerome looked down at him sadly, his warrior's heart heavy with the knowledge that there was nothing he alone could do, or for that matter, was there anything Nickolous could do. He looked away, toward the distant horizon, the forests shadows hiding the sacred place.

"Come," he said to Nickolous. "There are eyes and ears all about us. Come to the sacred place. It is there we will talk of these things." He paused for a moment. The words were breathed out softly, as if they were for him alone.

"*And More.*"

Nickolous nodded his head; understanding; his blue eyes scanning the area ahead of them, his thoughts guarded within himself for the time being.

The Old One slowed her pace, waiting for Nickolous. Glad for his company on this journey, she argued silently with herself that they were in no danger here. The power of the three combined would surely hold the darkness at bay. Nevertheless, she felt the sudden bristling at the nape of her neck as she threw her ragged cloak back over her shoulder.

Nickolous wondered at the Old One's stance as he approached. Her staff, which was usually obscured beneath a voluminous robe, was now in full view. And it was, to say the least, a thing of beauty, having been hand carved by a knowing hand. As he drew close, the gnarled fingers loosened their grip and the staff went flying through the air as if it had a life of its own. Nickolous ducked as it went by him, its aim running true. Dark wings folded in unnatural death as the creature plummeted to the earth, its form collapsing upon itself as it crumpled to nothingness.

By the time Jerome reached them, cursing himself because he hadn't seen the thing, Gabriel and Chera had arrived, their senses tingling. As the Old One bent down to retrieve her staff, Nickolous wondered why the armlet he wore had not given any warning of the creatures' presence. As he wondered at its silence, he felt the Old One's gentle touch upon his arm, her words echoing within his mind.

"*Not yet,*" they said.

"*Not yet…*"

15

"Well, do we chance having a fire?"

Everyone had turned to look at Sarah. Knowing she wanted to prepare a hot meal, Gabriel looked at Jerome questioningly, wondering if they could risk it. After all, it had been a long day, he thought, noting that they were well protected here, in this place.

"We need not worry, my friend. This night, at least, we are safe."

Jerome turned at the sound of the familiar voice, his gaze travelling downward. Orith, leaning heavily on his staff stood before him; looking up. The warrior pulled back, startled, for he saw the exhaustion within the golden depths of the eyes that gazed up at him—

Weary, Orith gratefully accepted the arm that Jerome offered for support.

§ § § § §

"Is everyone in position?" Jerome hefted his war club, once again testing its strength against one massive thigh.

Chera nodded curtly as she emerged from the forests edge. Jerome's warriors had blended in with their surroundings and could not be detected, and little was said as Owen glided soundlessly into their midst. Folding his wings to his side, he made himself comfortable, gratefully accepting the hot drink Sarah placed before him.

It wouldn't be until later—much later—when the dampness with its fine white mist that proceeds the night, curled about the forest floor; seeping even into the shadowy places that Owen would put the still partially filled drink down.

Looking at the faces he had come to know so well, he began to speak of what he had seen and heard that day.

§ § § § §

The lone sentinel rose up on his haunches; sniffing. He hadn't been to the lower places for untold turnings. There had been no need, for the dark one had left their depths a long time ago, returning briefly before leaving again. And yet—he turned his head at the sound, unexpected, but there. Pressing himself into the small crevice, he drew in his breath and waited for them to pass.

§ § § § §

Lord Nhon had sent the rest ahead. If there was trouble waiting, he wanted to be prepared. The caverns he had found were immense; their passageways reaching deep within the earth. Lord Nhon paused in the room where the bed with its tattered bedding was. It was obvious that if A-Sharoon had passed this way, her stay had been brief.

The sentinel waited in the darkness long after the snuffling and snorting had ceased. His skin prickling at the remembrance of the things he had seen passing by, mere inches from where he stood. In the silence that followed their retreat, back to the outer world, he had remained hidden; hardly daring to breath as the footsteps of the two-legged neared his secret place and paused, their owner's breath ragged and loud.

Lord Nhon remained still, listening. Finally, when he could detect no sound, he raised his head, nostrils flared, trying to scent the unwanted intruder. *He knew there was a watcher.* He also knew there were many hiding places for one so small. With an exasperated sigh, he gave it over and began following the tunnel that would lead him from A-Sharoon's lair to the outer world.

The little sentinel let his breath out slowly, thankful he had not been discovered. Easing his way through the small opening in the rock, he was well away long before Lord Nhon turned the corner that would take him to the ground above.

§ § § § §

Nickolous listened as Owen told of the survivors' struggle to reach the world above. Their tunnels, once a haven, had been filled with acrid smoke that strangled most of them where it found them. Those who managed to flee sounded the alarm—most, however, had found themselves trapped by the fumes and only a handful had made it safely to the outer places, scurrying to find cover from something they could not see; seeking out those who guarded the above places so that they might give aid. Once, during the telling, he had closed his eyes, trying to shut out the images from earlier that kept flashing through his mind. Jerome watched him closely; wanting to help, but knowing that he couldn't until Nickolous sought him out.

Nickolous opened his eyes to find the Old One watching him intently, her gaze unwavering as she reached out to touch his arm. Reaching out, he grasped her shoulder, squeezing it gently, his eyes searching her face. He knew there was something more to the telling, for a deed, dark and evil had been committed against the smallest of the innocents.

"Look to the center," the words were whispered. Nickolous pulled away from the Old One, realizing it wasn't she who had spoken—his gaze raked the circle of friends; searching...

§ § § § §

The earth smelled of dried flowers and rare incense, a smell which was not altogether unappealing to the senses. The heavily robed figure moved further into the earthen room that contained a circle of stones placed carefully there turnings ago, while the long tapered candle held in the small hand was used to light the others placed in iron holders wedged tightly into the rock. Carefully, so as not to disturb the placement of the stones, a small bundle of dry wood was set in the center and lit. The flames fanned quickly into a fire that dispelled the dampness and warmed the cavern, so that the woolen cloak the woman wore was soon discarded in a corner, her slight form now bent to the task at hand.

§ § § § §

"Lord Moshat." The messenger rose quickly as the elder entered the room.

"Nickolous?"

"He and the others are at the sacred place." "Excellent." Lord Moshat's brows furrowed, deep in thought. He turned to face the messenger. "Is there any sign of the *Other?*"

"None, my Lord."

"The sentries we placed in the hidden places, they've seen nothing?"

"There has been no sign of the dark one since he revealed himself to the Daughter—she is somewhere within the Dark Forest." The messenger lowered his voice. "There are those who watch and wait."

Lord Moshat sighed wearily, suddenly feeling older than his turnings. Dismissing the messenger, he settled himself into a chair and, opening the documents that were before him, studied the words written in the ancient language of the Ancients.

§ § § § §

Letting his breath out slowly, Nickolous relaxed, wondering if he would ever get used to this. He wasn't sure *who* had spoken, or, for that matter, *what*—what he did know was that his senses were tingling—that he was becoming more aware with each passing moment of other things that before had escaped his notice.

The Old One was sitting propped against a rock, her eyes half closed, watching. There were things at work here that were beyond her abilities to interpret or understand, and so she waited.

§ § § § §

Jerome shifted his weight carefully, not wanting to alert any of the *unseen* to his presence. Standing outside the entrance of the sacred place, he straightened to his full height; stretching his cramped limbs. As much as he enjoyed the others company, it felt good to be outside where he could feel the breath of the forest upon his brow and hear the little ones—those who were left—as they treaded their way through the forest. Leaning forward, he tensed, alerted to the strange sounds that suddenly pervaded his senses. Something else walked the night—something long forgotten—something not within the confines of his memories but the blood memories of his forbears.

A quick glance toward the fringe of the forest confirmed that his warriors were in place, their presence invisible to most but not all. The sudden piercing cry cut through the night's inky blackness and within moments the warning calls had changed to a trilling that warned of danger.

Brandishing his war club, Jerome started toward the shadow beast. Intent on diverting the thing from the cavern, he didn't see the other one creeping up behind him until it was almost too late; the movement, caught out of the corner of his eye as he turned, one massive arm swinging at the thing to divert it.

With a scream that echoed through the forest, the beast lunged sideways and in an instant had darted toward the opening, only to be met by Gabriel, his roars of rage drowning out the creature's own strangled screams of frustration.

As Chera leapt past her mate, the high-pitched keening cry with its wail of emptiness drew her inexplicably forward; while the night beasts, cloaked within the safety of the shadows, closed about Jerome and his warriors.

§ § § § § §

"No." One word. The speaker was tired and weary, but the tone brooked no opposition.

"But Jerome and the others, they need help," Nickolous protested, his hand on the dagger that Timothy had given him.

Orith's gaze never wavered; his voice had a hard edge to it as he replied. "There is no need for any others to risk themselves this night. The warriors of the forest have walked these woods longer than us all; they know what they deal with in the darkened places." His voice was tinged with regret. "We cannot help. We would only hinder the others who protect us, and you." He paused, weighing his words carefully. "You cannot risk yourself; you are inexperienced; too new to the gifts you have. We are protected here. The dark ones, it is said, cannot gain physical entrance, no matter what happens out there."

"Then why are the others out there, risking themselves if we are safe in here?" Nickolous asked, angry because he felt so helpless in the face of something he didn't understand.

"Some things must remain unchanged."

"And that's the answer. That's all?" Nickolous asked, his gaze locked on that of Orith's.

"There are few sacred places left; so few that they must be protected from those who walk with the dark ones, those who dwell beneath, protected by the shadows. The legends say darkness cannot dwell here, but if something with a dark heart were to slip through—if a watcher were distracted for one moment—there is always the possibility the sacred place could be breached." Orith paused, then:

"I have learned through the turnings to take nothing for granted. There is a delicate balance to everything, and I believe that if the circumstances are just right, one moment of negligence can cause the balance to tip, and not always in the direction we would like things to go."

Nickolous remained thoughtful for long minutes as he thought upon the words that had been spoken.

§ § § § § §

Jerome flung the last of the shadow beasts away from him while Gabriel, winded but unhurt, stood guard at the entrance to the inner cavern. As Jerome turned toward him, his brow heavy with sweat, Chera returned; her muzzle stained red; a deep gash ran from her shoulder and across her ribs, where she had been clawed. Seeing the concern in her mate's eyes, she motioned him back as she headed toward Jerome, the look in her eyes unmistakable.

"What is it, Chera, what's out there?"

"I don't know, but whoever, or whatever, it was has strength to be reckoned with," Chera replied.

Gabriel's fur bristled along his back as he cast a long, searching look toward the forest beyond, so cloaked in shadow it was almost impossible to see beyond the first line of trees. Even the moon, seemingly nestled as it was between the treetops, failed to disperse any of the dark shadows that dwelt beneath its soft caress. He sighed deeply, his warrior's heart weary from this long journey into what could only be a deeper night.

"Was it the *Other,* Chera?" Jerome asked, hoping the answer would be no, even as the words tumbled out.

"I don't know." Chera moved her head from side to side, still trying to penetrate the depths of the forest beyond. Sighing, she gave it up. Even her night vision was useless here in this darkened place of unknown things.

"There is something out there...watching—waiting." Chera was tense, the fur along her back bristling as the prickling sensation traveled up her spine. Gabriel moved closer, his senses picking up the unknown watcher, while Jerome gripped his war club, positioning himself in a warrior's stance. Immobile, the three stood, unmoving, waiting in the eerie silence that beckoned the watcher to come closer and be recognized.

§ § § § §

Hidden within the darkness that surrounded him, the tall, heavily robed figure observed the three who guarded the entrance to the sacred place. It had been merely curiosity that had drawn him here, that, and the wails of those unclean beasts that followed the Fallen. He had been surprised when the she-wolf had sensed his presence; her strength remarkable for what he considered a mere creature of the forest. The encounter had been brief and luckily the shadow beast had crossed his path, leaving its sickly sweet odor behind, else the outcome could have been entirely different for her.

Knowing the forest warriors reputation, he had no desire to engage one of these mighty guardians in battle, for this was not his realm—

not his fight—not yet. Drawing his woolen cloak tightly about him, he retreated to a safe distance.

It was of little consequence to him, this battle, for he would not interfere. Let the Clans destroy themselves. There had to be a balance in all things, and when it was over, and the balance was restored, then, and only then, would the decision be made if it were enough.

§ § § § § §

"Chera?" Jerome leaned down to touch the silvery-white shoulder. "Chera, whatever it was, it's gone now. The night deepens; we should go inside."

Chera nodded wearily, just now beginning to feel the aching, throbbing pain that coursed through her. Jerome was right. There was nothing there, and therefore no need for her to stay outside, for the night had a clinging, cloying, dampness to it that made her bones ache.

"Oh, my," Sarah said as she bustled about preparing water and searching for the healing moss that grew in the rock crevices to use on Chera's wound. As Nickolous watched Sarah fuss, he became aware of something else. It was a knowing that he hadn't had before. The Old One watched through hooded eyelids as he reached down, into her bag of herbs and deftly withdrew a small container of salve, its contents and healing properties known only to a few. Wordlessly, she watched as he went to Chera; his hands gentle and sure, he cleaned the gash and applied the salve.

Nodding perceptively to Jerome, the Old One closed her eyes, holding her thoughts to herself; for she hadn't reached the age she had by assuming the obvious was always correct.

"That's a nasty gash," Sarah said; the stress in her tone unmistakable as she hovered over her patient; something she would not have done, nor would Chera have allowed, but mere turnings past.

Chera shrugged, amused at the Sarah's concern for her well-being. The salve Nickolous had applied was soothing; the moss acting as a cushion against any undue pressure. She could feel the edges drawing together already. She spared a glance at the Old One, wondering what other magical potions she carried in her tattered leather bag. Stretching carefully, she laid down beside the fire, easing her wounded side to the glowing warmth. She sighed contentedly and closed her eyes.

§ § § § § §

Nickolous leaned forward, drawing warmth from the flicking flames of the fire; his mind on things unasked. Accepting the gourd

Sarah offered him, he stirred its contents absently; Jerome, guessing his thoughts, reached out and touched him gently. Lowering his voice so that the others could not hear, he asked, "What is it you wish to know?"

The blue eyes that looked back at him were startling in their intensity. "I wouldn't think that you would have to ask," Nickolous replied, rubbing the sides of the gourd he held as if to draw warmth from the hot contents inside.

"You're wondering how we got here—to this place—when but a few short turnings past you were in your world with your sister doing things that now seem but a distant memory." Jerome paused, drawing in a deep breath before continuing. "When you found yourself in a strange place with strange companions, you were a mere child, just beginning your journey into manhood—look at you now." He leaned back to appraise Nickolous.

"Yes. Look at me." Nickolous raised his arm to reveal the silver armlet that lay nestled against his skin. He rubbed it gently, feeling as if it had become a part of him—had always been.

"Something happened. I don't know what, but it does seem like I was always here; the other place I walked as a child but a distant memory." Nickolous leaned forward into the fires shadowy light, grabbing Jerome's arm with a grip that startled the big warrior. Looking up into moss-green eyes, he seemed to be searching for something, anything, that would help him to understand the feeling's that had begun to crowd in upon him.

"Nickolous," Jerome began, and then paused, his expression thoughtful. The big warrior laid his war club across his legs, caressing it as he spoke. Somehow it helped him to find the words that were there; deep within. Not the best orator at times when he felt stressed, he found that it helped to touch something that had saved him more than once, because he was skilled in its use. His gaze fell on it as he spoke, aware that Nickolous was studying him with those eyes that were so much like the others...

The winged warriors of Skye.

"I don't know a lot about your world; the world you grew up in, but I think time flows differently, depending on where you are. Coming here somehow accelerated your growth, making you mature beyond your years then if you had remained there—in that other place—" Jerome rubbed his hands together; sparing a glance toward the Old One. She smiled at him, her look one of amusement. The big warrior sighed resignedly. It was obvious he was on his own on this one. Silently he hoped that the answers he drew forth from within himself were the right ones.

"And?"

Jerome swung his gaze back to that of Nickolous, who was watching him, waiting, gauging what he heard and comparing it with what he felt.

"You feel you have always been here. In a sense you have." Nickolous raised a brow, his look questioning. "Is it possible to be in two places at once then?"

"That, I cannot answer. In my own thoughts, if I were to be in a place where I felt familiarity with everything I saw, then I would assume there was a connection that drew me there."

"What of the warriors of Skye? What of the winged guardian? How many places can a being walk?" Nickolous stirred the dying embers and put more wood on; watching as the flames flickered, caught, licking their way upward. Holding his hands up to the warmth now offered he stretched, and then leaned back, waiting.

"Anything is possible. The Old Ones believed that all living things were born with a knowing. Some ignore what they have been given; doing nothing with it, while others nourish it and let it grow. Some use their gifts for good, while others…" Jerome's voice trailed off as he stared thoughtfully into the fires flickering depths.

"While others become what they become." Nickolous finished, clasping his hands in front of him as he studied Jerome intently.

"Exactly." The big warrior bowed his head, lost in his own thoughts.

§ § § § § §

"*How long?*" A-Sharoon had turned to face the lone messenger, her tone merely curious. The creature let out a deep breath as it moved further into the dimly lit room, the soft breeze that wended its way through the tunnel was cool, bringing with it the pungent odors of things best left unknown.

"Lord Nhon prepares. His sentries guard the gate."

"The others, what about them?"

"They are at the sacred place, waiting."

A-Sharoon nodded; she was not surprised that the wolves and the forest warriors would find the cave of the Old One's and use it as sanctuary. They would remain there until morning's dawning and then? With a sharp intake of breath she dismissed the creature before returning to her work.

§ § § § § §

Lord Nhon moved his hands carefully, almost lovingly, over the runes that were embedded deeply in the rock face. He had once thought to spend most of his existence here; his turnings spent in learning and growing. A still small part of him longed to enter the secret chamber that lay beneath his fingertips and stand within the circle of the seven. His fingers curled into fists as he suddenly turned aside. Sighing deeply, he drew himself up, his red eyes glinting strangely as he moved a short distance away, undecided.

§ § § § § §

The woman stood, her back to a fire that offered little warmth. The chill had passed through her. It had come out of nowhere, taking her by surprise. She had sensed the Fallen One; even through the many feet of rock, his touch upon the sacred writings an insult to the Old Ones who had painstakingly carved them there in the time before time. Her heart thudded wildly within her chest as she waited, not knowing what she would do if that "*One*" tried to enter. She pushed down the sensation of panic that threatened to overwhelm her; then sighed in relief as the cold chill passed.

The ground upon which she stood was sacred. The rock that surrounded her was the living essence of all that *was*—had ever been— from the beginning. She turned as the slight fluttering sound reached her. Moving carefully, she peered into the darkness that shrouded the long corridor that stretched before her in whirling shadow. The movements ceased as she breathed shallowly lest she disturb those who slept beyond her in their sacred chamber. Drawing her woolen cloak tightly to her, she slipped into its welcomed warmth and returned to the fire. Kneeling down, she held her hands over the flickering flames that lapped slowly against the nearly consumed wood, which had begun to turn into blackened coal.

§ § § § § §

For long moments, the Fallen One remained where he was, watching; waiting. In the distance he could hear the sounds of battle. Still, he did not turn aside from his thoughts as he tried to penetrate the chambers below, his gift of perceiving without physically being there coming to the fore as he concentrated. So much energy was being spent on this one task that he wasn't aware of the one who observed him moving with a stealth that would have impressed even Chera;

until the being was upon him and he was turned, suddenly, sharply, his arms pinioned behind him in a vice-like grip that made him gasp.

§ § § § § §

"Gabriel!"

Even before the shouted words died to a whispering sigh, the big wolf was there. Leaping over the fire, barely missing the flames that flicked upward as the chill draft snaked its way through the room, he settled on the young man that stood upright, one hand clenched tightly against a forearm that felt as if it were on fire.

Gabriel's roar filled the cavernous room as the wind shrieked about Nickolous, leaving in its wake an overpowering sensation of the unknown.

Fighting against an invisible force that nearly threw her backward, the Old One rose to her feet, gripping the staff that had been hers from the beginning. Raising her head slowly, she looked up into Orith's eyes even as he drew her to him, his gaze protective as he threw his hood back, at the same time revealing his staff. With a gesture that was unmistakable to the others huddled about, he stood, once again straight and proud, the years rolling away as he gazed into the Old One's eyes.

Sarah and the others watched in awe as the two staffs came together with a thundering sound that caused the roaring to cease until only the silence enveloped them within its embrace.

Through a haze of numbing pain, Nickolous, bent nearly double, fought to maintain control as the staffs twined about one another as if they had a life of their own. And indeed, they did. For to those who were close enough to witness it, the low sighing was the joining of something that had a power of its own.

From the time of the dreamers—

The Seven.

Nickolous shook his head to clear it; the words familiar, echoing over and over, so that he knew he would carry them with him for the rest of his days.

Jerome stood close by, the big warrior recognizing the words from his own teachings—*they were from the forgotten time*—crossing his arms across his broad chest he stood, as solid and as unmoving as the sacred oak tree; his warriors stance warning the others away.

16

Time before time
Time of dreamers
Time of legends
Enchantments
Time of the sacred circle
The seven
Grandfathers of Legends
The seers
Guardians of the lost race
The weavers of hope
In their dreams I walk
The circle closes...
I dream.

"What's happening? Is he all right?" Sarah, her voice trembling, stood beside her brother, her big brown eyes bright as she watched Jerome and Gabriel.

Jerome waited patiently while Gabriel tried to absorb the whispered words that were not their own. The air about them had returned to normal, but it was obvious that Nickolous was still caught in the throes of something unseen. The Old One stood with Orith, her back straight, still clutching the staff tightly, while Orith stood beside the Old One, not at all surprised at the events which had unfolded. His grip tightened on his own staff, for the two had separated and were no longer entwined. Whatever had drawn the staffs together, once again had returned to its center.

"*Wait.*"

The Old One looked at her companion; Orith nodded slightly, but not before drawing the hood up so that his features were once again concealed. Frowning, the Old One stood with furrowed brow but within herself, silently weeping. Orith, knowing what thoughts were coursing through his companion, held her tightly; darkness enveloping them like a shroud, while a short distance away the Fallen One battled an advisory that was as good as he was dark.

§ § § § §

Great heaving breaths shook the warrior's body as he hurled Lord Nhon from him; the warrior, knowing his strength was nearly spent, restrained himself so that exhaustion would not completely overtake his senses as Lord Nhon, recovering quickly, lunged at the huge shadowy form that towered above him; unmindful of the fact that the warrior was three times his height.

This one he knew!

His palms turned outward—fireballs—forming at the tips of fingers that had held the essence of the beginning within their grasp—tilting his head back he looked up, his eyes red, gleaming with an inner darkness that most, seeing, would have feared for their own being. The fireballs, burned with an unnatural heat as they moved of their own accord upward, toward the heart of the forest warrior who had once guarded the Living Flame and now guarded the caverns that lay deep beneath their feet.

The night remained silent as the exploding balls of light illuminated the sky above the sacred place.

Seared by the intense heat, the forest warrior turned aside; one gigantic arm shielding his face, while the other reached out to grasp *this one* who had turned to the darkness. Trying to duck out of his grasp, Lord Nhon turned to flee, tripping on his robes as he did so, the result being the warrior missed him by scant inches. At the same time, swept by a need to avenge the theft of the Living Flame, the warrior leaned down to grab the fleeing form only to himself trip over an unseen boulder and in so doing, wrenched one of his trunk-like legs. Still weakened by the damage A-Sharoon had caused, he fell sideways, striking his side on the rocks that protruded from the moss-covered ground.

Lord Nhon pushed himself up, moving out of reach of the warrior's grasp. At any other time, he would have stayed to finish the fallen guardian, but his senses had picked up something that he was not prepared to face this night. Bowing slightly, he mockingly saluted the warrior, then he was gone. The darkened places offering him sanctuary as the huge bird of prey plummeted earthward, the keening cries echoing through the night.

Struggling to his feet, the warrior steadied himself as the sighing sound of something long unseen passed overhead. Unconcerned for himself, he bent to the task of making sure the ancient runes had not been disturbed.

It mattered little that the Fallen One had escaped, for the warrior knew their paths would cross again, and it did not occur to him to give chase, for he knew his quarry.

§ § § § §

Cautiously, the auburn-haired woman removed her hands from the thick slab of rock that guarded the entrance to the caverns beneath her feet. She would not—could not—enter their depths; for it was forbidden. Only a Son of Skye could traverse the places below to unlock the hidden things that could heal the darkest turnings.

Satisfied that nothing had been disturbed, the woman returned to the rocks that rimmed the fire pit, her thoughts with those who walked above. Carefully placing a piece of wood on the glowing red embers, she stood back and watched—watched as the flames slowly curled their way upward until the whole piece was engulfed in a glowing redness that pulsated with a life of its own. Then, and only then, did she turn aside and, going to the far side of the cavern, withdrew a yellowed parchment from a pile of ancient objects. Returning to the center of the room, she knelt down, spreading the document on the flattened ground, then, lighting a candle, she began to study the writing's before her.

§ § § § §

Nickolous leaned forward into the wind, motioning Jerome to him and at a predetermined signal from Gabriel the two exchanged places; while the warrior drew closer; his green eyes studying the stripling who stood before him.

Nickolous returned Jerome's gaze in kind; his blue eyes intent. Even before the words were spoken, they had already been heard.

"Wait!" Orith gripped the Old One's arm a little too tightly as his gaze searched the room, making sure there were no intruders—none to see or eavesdrop. Beneath his robes, he clutched the staff to him, knowing the Old One had done the same; finally, assured that only the companions were present, he leaned back, still watchful.

The Old One drew in her breath sharply, her senses reeling. Turnings without number had passed since this place they were in had been used. Yet something still lingered. She leaned slowly forward, her eyes not quite daring to believe what they saw; but hoping...

§ § § § § §

Wending its way through crevice and earth, the creature came. Gathering form and substance, the white frothing thing groped its way to the above place; the center of it remembering the before times when it had dwelled amongst those who had made their home in the darkened forest.

Twisting and turning, it followed the corridor's path until the passageway ended. Lord Nhon turned slowly, his red eyes glinting strangely.

"Welcome."

The words echoed hollowly throughout the damp cavern.

§ § § § § §

"Wait." Jerome rose to his feet; his war club clutched tightly to his side, his warrior's sense's warning him. The Old One watched through half closed lids as Orith began to rise from his seated position, his heavy woolen cloak parting slightly to reveal the staff. Still, the Old One did not move from her position, but Orith knew she watched and waited.

The silence was nearly overwhelming.

"What is it? What's wrong?" Sarah started forward but was stopped by her brother. Timothy shook his head warningly as he gently pushed her back, at the same time reaching for his sword.

The soft sighing sound grew louder.

Chera rose stiffly from her place beside the fire, aware that something was approaching the sacred place in which they now rested. As her gaze sought that of her mate's, she paused mid-turn, nostrils flaring, scenting the cavern for the unseen and shuddered in the flickering firelight as the sighing grew louder.

Nickolous leaned forward, instinctively baring his forearm to the shadows as he faced the cavern's opening while Jerome brought his club forward to the front of his chest; the wind whipping about them as the companions closed their minds against the onslaught of sound, while the sparks and debris caught within the grasp of the unknown swirled about them. Sarah opened her eyes and then shut them tight. Grey swirling things were taking form within the fire's shadow, while the soft sighing had become a deafening roar. Orith started forward, only to be flung backward against the Old One. Together they crumpled into a tangled heap upon the cold earthen floor.

Jerome rushed forward, swinging his club in an arc as soot and sparks flew through the air, making it nearly unbearable to be within the confines of the cavern. Amidst the howling, voices whispering ancient words could be heard. Nickolous raised his arms toward the ceiling, and from deep within, the words poured forth; unbidden, from a forgotten time as the intricately carved silver armband began to glow; the etchings upon its surface writhing, changing, then returning to their center as the hidden voices stilled and the howling ceased. From deep within the fire's depths, a blue flame flickered then grew; as the companions watched in awe, a form took shape.

Kneeling down on one knee, Jerome bowed his head to the apparition that had risen from the flames, suspended between earthen floor and ceiling. Nickolous, lowering his arms, moved slowly forward, his will not his own as the form beckoned him.

The silver armband glowed blue-white.

"Rise." The voice was gentle and soothing to the companions' senses. Sarah shook herself, the tiredness washing through her like a wave, to be replaced with a feeling of renewed energy.

"What is it you wish of us?" Jerome asked as he moved slowly forward, into the flames flickering light.

Timothy blinked, but when he opened his eyes, she was still there.

Gabriel and Chera moved cautiously, never taking their gaze off Nickolous. As Clans of the forest who felt the world's presence within their innermost being, they were not as shocked. Still, they were slightly awed to be in the presence of the fabled protectress.

Woman of the Flame.

Jerome moved closer. There was no fear within him, for his kind had protected the forest and those who had dwelt there for turnings beyond thought. It was this protectress that they served; his warriors protecting the earth that gave them life and substance; the little ones, the earth diggers being closest to the center, their eyes and ears relaying their thoughts and fears to those of the forest warriors. Jerome and his kind, gifted with the ability to see within the heart of those who were of the knowing clans, protected those who honored the living things around them.

§ § § § § §

Long hair flowed into the flames but did not burn, while white robes billowed gracefully about the slender form, curling about slender ankles and tiny feet that were partially hidden by the blue-white flames that shot upward. Fanned by an invisible breeze, the woman appeared to be suspended in mid air. Sarah watched in awe as the figure turned slowly around; arms raised, her gaze searching.

Nickolous felt the pull from within and without. The armband was now nearly transparent; the intricate carvings once again moving within the center of the silver metal. Nickolous raised a hand to cover it, then, just as quickly pulled it away.

The armlet recognized its own.

He stood just in front of the suspended figure, his head bowed respectfully. The woman turned slowly and stopped in front of him; her hair fanning out behind her like a living thing. The red and gold interlaced through her hair reminded Nickolous of spun gold. He pulled back; startled, as blue eyes peered into his own, and in that moment he understood.

Trembling, he drew in a deep breath; his gaze searching for Gabriel as the big wolf leaned against him, understanding his need to have someone familiar near him.

"*Come closer, wearer of the armband,*" the voice whispered. Nickolous looked up; the woman's lips had not moved, but her blue eyes studied him intently; their depths unfathomable.

"*You wear that which is of the Old Race.*" The figure was still turning slowly within the fire that did not consume, yet gave off welcomed warmth to those huddled about. Nickolous moved closer, a little wary, yet unafraid of the being before him.

"*Only one who is of Skye can wear such a thing. You have a grave responsibility; for you walk between two places, and the choices you make will not be easy.*"

Nickolous reached up to touch the cool metal with the intricate carvings that swirled, ever changing, within the silver metal.

"Who are you?"

The question asked was heard by all; Jerome sucked in his breath, waiting for the answer.

Nickolous looked into eyes that reminded him of the warriors of Skye as the form before him wavered, becoming nearly transparent.

"No. Wait!" he reached out to the figure and found himself suddenly caught up within the circle of blue-white flame.

The figure within the cool flames grasped his hand and he heard the words for him alone to hear.

"I am the keeper of the earth, and it is I who guard the sacred places." The figure bowed its head.

"I weep." A single tear rolled down an alabaster cheek.

Nickolous felt a great sadness well up within him. Jerome and the others watched from outside the circle, hardly daring to breathe as the pair within the flames spun slowly round and round, their words not heard by those outside the circle of fire. Nickolous drew in his breath; waiting, for what he wasn't sure. The flames licked upward, concealing him, and his world as he knew it, for a time was no more.

§ § § § § §

The cavern was warm, the fire within the center of the stone circle burned bright red, the embers so hot they were nearly transparent. The sweetish smell of burning grass was everywhere. Nickolous inhaled deeply, finding the odor not entirely unpleasant. The woman from the flame stood beside him, her face nearly hidden by her long fiery hair. She did not touch him but pointed a long tapered finger toward a corridor that stretched as far as the eye could see. Looking down along its length, Nickolous saw it was well lit with torches. Knowing without being told that this path was for him alone to walk, he moved cautiously into the semidarkness.

The dampness was nearly overwhelming; Nickolous blew on his hands to warm them, wishing he had worn something heavier. He had followed the corridor, the long underground passage going deep within the earth. Stone steps, cut painstakingly where necessary, blended in with the natural stone and the shadows, encouraged by the flickering flame of the torches, played eerily on the steps before him.

Voices.

Whispered words of legends and songs...

The steps ended, and Nickolous found himself standing in an enormous cavern lit by torches placed strategically within the crevices along the jagged rock wall. It was here where lichen and mushrooms grew, nurtured from the dampness that seeped from the fissures within the rock, cascading downward to touch the floor. A large fire burned in a central pit, and around this sat what appeared to be, at first glance, ancient warriors. There were seven; their frames hunched with the burdens they carried for the world within worlds.

Nickolous remained where he was, his head bowed in respect; waiting. The chanting grew louder; then an unseen voice was urging him forward, down the steps toward the circle where the elders waited. As he approached, one of the warriors rose from his seated position while the others remained where they were; watching, gauging, and waiting.

"Welcome, Son of Skye. We have waited many turnings for someone to go where we cannot." The warrior seemed to change as he spoke and Nickolous realized with a start that the person before him was ageless. Although the face was unlined, the eyes belonged to someone who had seen the world at its beginning and sorrowed for what it could not change.

Unbidden, but knowing that he must, Nickolous entered the circle of elders; the faint drumming beneath his feet growing louder as the circle closed; once more complete.

§ § § § §

Wind. Rain. Sun. Water pouring over a precipice into a basin polished as smooth as marble and white quartz that glistened in the morning's dawning.

All of these things assailed Nickolous on a level that was hard to absorb, but somehow the images that flashed before him slowed down and became something that was separate, each from the other. The smell of burning incense became stronger as the chanting became louder and the flames from the fire flicked at the ceiling of the cavern in places long forgotten in ritual.

The warrior who had greeted Nickolous at the bottom of the stone steps threw off the tattered leather robe that had been his from the beginning and, picking up the shell that was in the center of the circle, lit the contents within. Carefully placing the bowl on the ground in front of Nickolous, he watched with satisfaction as the smoke curled about those in the room, the smell soothing to the senses; the sense of well-being a welcoming thing.

17

Earth
Wind
Fire
Water
The elements of life.

So say the Old Ones; the Ancients of the forgotten time.

Within the memories of a dying race, a thread of thought was passed to another, and another; the memories not lost, but sleeping...

And now comes the awakening.

18

Nickolous opened his eyes to find himself alone in the cavern, and where the warriors had once sat within the circle, there was nothing. Leaning over, he ran his hands through the cold ashes of a fire that seemed long extinguished; the ashes sliding between his fingers like fine powder. Half rising, he leaned back, balancing himself on his heels as memories flowed through him of the things he had heard and seen; the memories now his to sort through at his choosing. He turned toward the steps that had brought him to this place, his intent to ascend them and return to the Woman of the Flame.

He was halfway up the steps when something made him pause, the hair on the back of his neck rising as he turned slowly around, his gaze sliding back down the stairs. There was nothing—Nickolous cautiously moved back down one step at a time. His senses alert, he stood once again inside the warriors' circle, his gaze sweeping the large cavern as he sought out whatever it was that watched.

§ § § § §

Jerome stood by the fire that burned to the ceiling, concealing the circle within. Knowing that the circle was but a gateway to the "*Beneath,*" the big warrior kept close, his war club ready, for he knew that the door must not be disturbed.

Gabriel stood across from the warrior of the forest, his blue eyes alert as he scented the air about them, his ears straining to catch any that sought to intrude. Aware that the shuffling to his left was the Old

119

One approaching, he did not acknowledge her but waited for her to speak.

"Beware. It is too quiet, and there are those who watch and wait."

"Where?" The big wolf growled softly; his gaze searching, trying to penetrate the shadows.

"You can't see it. It just is."

Gabriel snorted impatiently as the Old One threw back her cloak, revealing her staff. The intricate designs cut deep into the wood seemed to glow as they were passed in front of the cool flame.

"Old One, be careful." Jerome leaned forward, his senses tingling as the barest whisper of sound reached him. Chera circled around the fire, her senses alert as Gabriel stiffened, the hair along his back rising.

The Old One stood poised beside the wolf, her black eyes gleaming; one gnarled paw running the length of the staff. She relaxed a bit as the shadows within the cavern lengthened, deepened, and then changed, according to the intensity of the fire which threw welcoming warmth against her robes. Her senses alert for the unseen, she peered into the hidden depths of the flame; one paw grasping the staff to her, as with the other she shielded her wizened face against the brightness of the flame.

§ § § § §

Owen flew low, skimming the treetops, the sound of his passing disguised by the wind as it caressed the leaves of the popular trees softly. As the leaves danced in the moonlight, guarding the passing of the winged watcher, the great owl followed the heavily cloaked figure into the depths of the dark forest; watchful, as the sounds concealed within the darkness enveloped his senses; his night vision coming to the fore as he used the low-seeking wind currents to aid him.

§ § § § §

Seeking the hidden opening, the "*Other*" felt carefully for the lever that would gain him entrance to the passages below. Aware he was being followed by one of the flying forest dwellers, and not wishing a confrontation this night, he slid beneath the rock overhang that afforded a small measure of protection. Amused, he watched as Owen glided soundlessly by his hiding place; then, when the night grew still once again, and only then, did he turn the lever set deep within the stone. High above him, Owen circled helplessly as the grating sound of stone upon stone told him he had lost his quarry.

A-Sharoon stood in the darkness; waiting. She too, had heard the grating sound as the mechanism that controlled the door had slowly opened, then closed to allow someone passage to the secret places below. Whoever it was made no attempt to disguise their footsteps; the sound echoing hollowly through the long corridor as the uninvited visitor approached the main cavern.

A-Sharoon held her staff to her, the incantation already pouring forth from her blood red lips as the visitor moved into the room. Striding purposefully toward her, a hand unerringly covered her mouth, choking off the spoken words. Shaking her head violently from side to side, A-Sharoon tried to twist out of the tight embrace, her fingers raking the length of the strangers face as she lashed out in a futile effort to be released. The deep laughter of her captor echoed hollowly as he laughingly pushed her aside.

"You!" The words were spat out in undisguised rage as she fought to control herself, mentally making a note to severely discipline whoever had allowed such easy passage to an intruder.

"Don't worry; the sleeping spell will wear off, the guards won't remember anything."

Lighting a small torch, A-Sharoon turned on the figure, eyes blazing. "How dare you!" The words were spat with such venom the visitor was momentarily startled.

"I would have thought you would have welcomed assistance." The tall form paused before softly adding, *"Sister."*

§§§§§§

"Why have you come?" A-Sharoon spoke so softly the words were barely audible. The man who called himself brother stood gazing down at her, for as tall as she was, he was taller. He turned aside, his profile was that of a handsome man, but more than that, it was a darkness that was compelling, almost unnaturally so, for as white and cold as A-Sharoon was, he was darkness and comfort and, between the two of them combined, a deadly combination.

"There must be a balance of power, you know that." Tossing his cloak carelessly aside even as he moved swiftly across the room, he leaned down into the darkest corner. Reaching as far back as he could, he found and withdrew a small ornately carved box. A-Sharoon said nothing, but watched thoughtfully as he removed something from inside.

"Lord Nhon searches the forest for you."

A-Sharoon remained silent as she studied him; her gaze intent. A slight rustling sound outside the cavern's entrance barely gave her pause. It was obvious that the potion had worn off. With a wave of her hand, she dismissed the creature that stumbled into the room. Her anger dissipated, now she was merely curious.

"The Living Flame should never have been taken. If it perishes, so then do we. You should never have helped him, A-Sharoon."

"Where is it written that the Flame can die?" A-Sharoon leaned forward, her gaze now inches from her brother's.

"It isn't. It just is."

"And what would you know about it? Where were you these many turnings, brother?" A-Sharoon faced her brother, arms crossed, waiting.

"Where I was matters not. What you have been doing is what matters."

"Well, I am not with him now. You have read the ancient script as well as I. Show me where it is written that the Flame will perish." A-Sharoon arched a midnight brow, her stance defiant.

"Sister, let me share something with you, something that is an unwritten law. It is an ancient knowledge given only to a few." A-Sharoon found herself now inches from her brother's angry glare.

"If, and that's a big If, the Flame's breath is somehow extinguished, not only will the darkness prevail, but time will work backward." A-Sharoon flinched beneath her brother's angry glare. His breath was hot upon her cheek as he hissed, "There will be nothing! Only the earth we now walk upon will be; that and nothing more. A barren piece of molten rock! And yes, the realms within realms will be affected."

"The Flame must be returned."

"Yes, it must. Just as the winged warriors watch, so must we. If the forest dwellers fail in their quest, before the last breath of the Flame flickers out, before the last sigh is heard, this must be used."

A-Sharoon stared at the object her brother held out to her, a forgotten piece of her past. Put aside in her days as a young girl, the darkness now swirled about her as forgotten memories pressed upon her; she shrugged them off. There had been more to think of back then than the contents within the item that was now being held out to her.

"It is time."

A-Sharoon looked at her brother, then at the object that nestled snugly within the palm of his hand. Even in the semidarkened gloom that surrounded them, the tarnished silver glinted with an eerie reflection.

"Remember, you must be discreet, for the power that lies sleeping within this amulet can destroy even the wearer. Use what needs to be used, that, and nothing more. When everything is back where it should be, the amulet must be returned to the stone case where it can rest."

A-Sharoon felt herself trembling as the necklace was dropped into her white hands; remembering surged through her as she slid the heavy chain over her head where it nestled softly around her neck—the feel of the metal a cooling sensation against her skin.

"Where will you be?" Her voice trembled as she clasped her brother's arm.

The man looked down at his sister, his gaze thoughtful; his voice was low, resonating with unleashed power as he replied. "I must return to my realm, and soon." One dark hand reached out to grasp A-Sharoon's shoulder, while the other cupped her face, turning it upward so that she had no choice but to look into his eyes. "You will hear me, but not see me, for that part which is physical must remain in that other place. Dissent is all around me, for even those who are loyal fear the powers of the *Fallen* and I must maintain control. The warriors of the forest guard most of the gates. Their power is great, for they are part of the earth, and the Flame calls them to it, for it suffers greatly."

A-Sharoon drew in her breath sharply, remembering her own encounter with the heart of the Flame; unaware of the strange look her brother gave her, she instinctively clutched the amulet nestled in the hollow of her throat.

"Remember..." The man suddenly dug his fingers into her shoulder, causing her to flinch. "Only a woman can wield the power of the amulet. Never—ever—forget who you are—" The words were grated out from between clenched teeth as his grip tightened.

"Do not use the power unless you must, for it can be used only once before it returns to the one who owns it to rest. Remember, and do not forget!" He released her so suddenly that she nearly fell.

§ § § § §

The figure, wraithlike, moved quickly out of the range of Nickolous's vision. Standing alone in the middle of the circle, the sweet scent of the burned grass still lingering in the air, Nickolous stood, arms crossed, waiting.

"I am not here to hurt you." The words had a hollow ring to them in the stifling stillness.

"Your friends wait in the sacred place; you must return to the Woman of the Flame so she can see you safely back to the others." The disembodied voice was all around him; his gaze swept the hidden places cloaked in shadow.

"Who are you?"

"I and others guard this place and those who sleep in the outer chambers. You sensed my presence; a remarkable thing." The voice was neither feminine nor masculine. Nickolous concentrated on the direction the voice was coming from, trying to find the owner.

"Don't waste your energy." The voice was tinged with laughter as a slight form materialized in the far corner. Nickolous's eyes widened as the lithe form appeared before him. A tiny hand reached out to touch him. It felt like the brush of butterflies against his skin.

"Who are you?"

"Like everything else that exists in between the unknown places, I am." The being answered as it slowly withdrew its hand from Nickolous's arm. The prickling sensation that moved up his arm reminded him of the intricately carved armband that nestled against his arm.

"So, you have the knowing." The voice held approval. "Those dark of heart cannot enter here, for to them I am not what you see." The figure changed as it spoke, becoming wraithlike, then more visible as Nickolous once again centered himself, trying to focus on what he was seeing. Dark skin shimmered with golden flecks as wide eyes set far apart in an elfin face studied him curiously from beneath finely arched brows. Her hair trailed in waves down her back, curling about a tiny waist—it reminded Nickolous of the leaves when they changed from their reds, meshing into browns and gold's. He pulled back, startled at the intensity of her gaze; her emerald eyes reminded him of the forest. He drew in his breath sharply, the need to return to the others nearly overwhelming.

"I must return to the place above."

"Yes, go now. There will be none to hinder you on your return journey." The lithe form leaned forward, her elfin face inches from his, while the scent of cedar wafted around him as he listened to her words. "Remember what you have learned from the place of the dreamers, and take this advice with you on your next journey: Take nothing you see for what it resembles." The lilting voice faded into nothingness. Nickolous looked around him. He was alone.

It was as he reached the top of the stone steps that the realization hit him. The fragrance that had surrounded him since coming to this place, the pixie-like creature with the eyes that reminded him of the forest, her ability to be one thing to one person, and something else to another, the smell of earth and flowers that emanated from her. It reminded him of something beautiful, sad, and ancient. Suddenly feeling overwhelmed, he touched the armband, remembering the sensation that had coursed through him earlier.

"Nickolous, it is time." The flame haired woman stood outside the corridor, waiting.

§ § § § § §

Nickolous stepped out from the circle into the group of waiting companions, the words of soft farewell echoing from the crackling flames that wended their way upward as the woman became transparent within the heart of the burning flames. The companions watched silently as the vision slowly faded into nothingness.

"Here, sit down. There now, here's something hot to drink." Sarah hovered close by, her cure for all ills her herbal tea.

Nickolous drank the contents of the gourd and then held it out for a refill while Jerome waited close by; his warrior's training enabling him to be patient, his knowledge of the old teachings preparing him for what was to come.

"Old One, the Woman of the Flame and the guardian of the warriors cavern, are they the same?" Nickolous had finished his drink but was still huddled by the fire, chilled from the dampness that seeped through the many underground passages.

"Yes and no."

Nickolous turned to look into dark eyes that were fathomless. "Old One, the smell of earth and forest were everywhere. It was not like here."

"What does it tell you? Here?" The Old One asked as she touched Nickolous's chest gently.

"I don't know. It's almost as if there are places that the shadows cannot touch, yet those that protect the sacred places cannot leave, their destiny to remain forever there.

"Yes, there is much truth to what you say," the Old One agreed, one gnarled paw resting softly against the silver armlet. "But remember, for everything there is a time, and for some the turnings are coming to an end. Others, who have the ability to see beyond the gates that keep those confined, can, and must, go forth." The Old One's face was now inches from Nickolous's, her gaze intense as she peered into blue eyes that were fathomless.

"Remember, the beginning was just that. It didn't mean things would not change, that each place of wonderment would not grow, and some of the growing would not be pleasant, but that is the way it is. Things cannot be changed once they have happened, but there are those who are gifted with a knowing that can help." The Old One leaned closer, her voice barely above a whisper.

"All things that are gifted with the breath of life have a destiny, but that does not mean it is always fulfilled. We all have choices to make." She stood up and moved away toward Orith, who was studying them intently.

§ § § § § §

"Jerome, I need to talk to you."

The warrior stood facing the forest, his heavy war club by his side. He had left the cavern's warmth and those inside, giving Nickolous and the Old One their privacy—he had needed to breathe the night air and hear the heartbeat of the forest. A few shrill whistles assured him that his warriors were still in place and all was well. Leaning back against the rocky wall, he had closed his eyes, weary beyond reckoning, his sudden need to absorb the sounds of the forest almost overwhelming.

"Jerome?" Nickolous stood looking up at the big warrior; spoken words were not necessary, as the ability for Nickolous to speak within himself to the warrior became easier with each day that passed. Green eyes the color of the forest leaves gazed down at him as Nickolous returned the gaze knowing that everything he was thinking, everything he was feeling, was being felt by his friend.

"You have seen things that others have only heard about through teachings, or as little ones when they were put to bed for the night." Jerome rubbed his chin thoughtfully as he looked past Nickolous, to the forest's edge. Although he appeared relaxed, he wasn't. The stillness of the night was but a prelude to something darker; he could sense it.

"I know. I know. Because I walk between the two worlds, belonging to neither, yet belonging to both I have the gift of the '*knowing.*' Now, I have to learn to use those gifts," Nickolous replied, his answer surprising Jerome.

"The Ancients—"

"Are what they are." Nickolous closed his eyes as images assailed his memory, the scent of burning grass and sweet earth filling his nostrils as the warrior who had welcomed him within the sacred dreaming circle, once again walked within his memories.

Unable to control them, Nickolous let the images pour forth, knowing that the warrior of the forest was sharing in what he was seeing, an inner part of him realizing that he was seeing things which hadn't been there before. His attention turned inward as the two shared something which neither would ever forget.

Jerome breathed in deeply, his very being vibrating with the realization that everything he had ever been taught—everything he had ever believed—was true.

§ § § § §

The winged watcher remained where he was; concealed, watchful, as Jerome and Nickolous dream walked together, a thing which was only gifted to a few; those who had earned the honor.

The warrior was one of the forest people, old beyond reckoning; ancient in his own right; the ability to see into the darkest heart a gift from the Flame to those who protected the earth.

The boy, a boy no longer, was still growing. His heritage was one of mystery; his mother a daughter of Skye, the ties from the world he had been born in a fleeting memory at best as he found his place among a race of beings struggling for independence.

The winged warrior settled back to wait; he would remain where he was. There would be none to interfere in their journey...

None.

§ § § § §

Lord Nhon waited patiently in the shadows, his dark cloak concealing him from any watchers as he pulled the hood low over a heavy brow so that only his red eyes glinted in the darkness. As the night watcher flew overhead, his wings brushing the tree tops seeking his quarry, Lord Nhon felt the others frustration and smiled beneath his covering as he crouched low to the ground, covering himself completely.

Owen scanned the ground beneath him as he glided above the treetops, his keen sense telling him that his quarry was watching him from below. Frustrated that he could not penetrate the darkened places with his night vision, he veered sharply to the left, his echoing cry a warning to those concealed in the beneath places where the light could not penetrate. Gliding soundlessly, he skirted the small valley, circling around to see if his quarry had moved. Once, landing on a nearby tree that was darkened and dried with age, he thought he saw a shadowy form running, then, it was gone. Breathing in deeply, opening his mind to absorb the night smells and sounds, he waited in the stillness as the moon crept out from the concealing clouds to splay her light softly upon the well worn paths within the forests depths. Great golden eyes widened as the white head swiveled slowly around while wings unfolded, stretched, and then went back into place.

He waited.

Almost directly below him, Lord Nhon covered himself completely beneath the voluminous folds of his heavy robes, for he knew the power of one known as Owen was increasing.

He also knew that he had been foolish to have been caught out by himself; first by one of the forest guardians, and now a night watcher of the forest. Finding what he was looking for in a packet, he placed a small amount of the powdery substance in the palm of his hand. Clutching it tightly to his chest, he uttered a remembering from the before time, then, throwing back the cloak that concealed him, blew the gray powder upward while rising at the same time, his gaze locked on huge golden eyes that glared at him from the top of the gnarled ancient tree.

Owen prepared to lunge, his every instinct telling him that it was now or never, but before he could do anything, the form below him vanished; the fading image of Lord Nhon, smirking as he looked upward at him, then, nothing. Caught off guard, he lunged toward the now empty spot, hoping that the invisibility powder hadn't quite taken affect. Grasping nothing but air, he made a few more futile lunges before giving up, knowing that it would be useless to waste any more time here. Grazing the tops of the trees, he soared away toward the waiting place.

Lord Nhon waited in the stillness, the power of invisibility spell weakening as he fought to maintain control. Below ground, in his cavern, he was in his element, however, here, on the outside, it was a different matter. Finally assured that Owen was no longer a threat, he moved forward into the moonlit night, his thoughts on the task at hand. As he turned toward the darkened places, a shadowy form stepped in front of him, barring his path; the creature bowing low before him as they conferred in the language of the dark ones.

§§§§§

Owen knew that as soon as he left, the way clear, Lord Nhon would retreat back to his lair. The Dark Lord's followers were everywhere; their smell a clinging cloying thing that stuck to one's nostrils, and hard to get rid of. Glancing down, he saw yet another form skulking toward its master's path of return; it glanced up, wary; yellow eyes gleamed with a unnatural light that faded into nothingness as it scurried for cover.

Looking upward into the starry sky, he drew in a deep breath, his thoughts on those who waited back at the sacred place and the sudden prickling sensation that moved up his spine merely another reminder that they were all in danger. Veering sharply to the left, he headed toward the others, the whoosh-whoosh of his wings echoing loudly in the silence of the starlit night.

§ § § § §

Waiting in the darkness, the winged warrior watched as Owen headed back toward the sacred place, then he too lunged skyward, his dark wings all but invisible against the night sky, his form indistinguishable as he veered into the low-lying cloud cover that swept across the horizon.

Aided by the wind, Owen rode the currents as he swiftly closed the distance between himself and the sacred place where the others waited. Now and then, he caught a glimpse of the shadowy being that trailed him but was not concerned. He knew well the purpose of the warrior of Skye and felt safer because of it. Below him, the ruins of one of the ancient places lay, a grim reminder of the battles past. Peering straight ahead, he fixed his gaze upon the distant horizon and those who waited.

§ § § § §

The fire burned, giving little warmth to the two watchers as Nickolous rubbed his arms in an effort to dispel the goose bumps that rose in protest against the chill night air, while his companion grasped his war club tightly as he peered into the darkness—alert for anything untoward this night. Blocking out the chill that bothered Nickolous, grimacing, he rose stiffly; the need to move about almost uncontrollable as, turning, he caught the furtive movement off to the side, then, it was gone.

"Jerome?"

"Yes?"

"There isn't much time, is there." It wasn't a question, but a statement.

"There's enough."

"The others—"

"They must remain here." Jerome turned to face Nickolous, his gaze penetrating. "Gabriel and Chera will guard them. Timothy will make sure the Old One and Orith are kept safe until they are needed. Where we must go, we must journey alone. None will approach without consequences. My warriors will remain, and I seriously misdoubt that the unseen ones of Skye will also guard the passage this night." Jerome lowered his voice so that Nickolous had to lean forward to catch the next words. "There are others who will guard those here. Do not worry." He straightened up, indicating to his companion that he was ready to go.

Sparing a backward glance at the cave that shielded those within it, Nickolous hurried to catch up to Jerome as the night engulfed them gently within its embrace.

§ § § § §

The Old One arose stiffly, one gnarled paw clutching her staff. Timothy, seeing her discomfort, went to her aid immediately, while Sarah stirred sleepily within the robes that had been hastily thrown down as a bed.

Orith watched silently as the Old One stood at the entrance, inhaling deeply of the night air and those that were a part of it.

"They're gone."

Orith nodded as she turned to face him, her dark eyes gleaming as she tightened her grip on her staff, while pulling her cloak tightly about her thin shoulders to ward off the damp chill that pervaded the deepening night. Saying no more, she watched as Orith placed another log on the fire, and then helped her to find a comfortable place among the pile of robes to ease her weary body down. Timothy placed more wood close by so that no one would have to move into the shadows that the fires light could not displace, then he too sat down, his sword resting within easy reach.

Outside the caverns entrance, Chera sat close to Gabriel, her shoulder brushing against his as they gazed up into the starry night. Both knew their purpose and, as much as they would have wished to go with Jerome and Nickolous, they knew they were needed here. When the time was right and everything was in place, they would be ready. The Flame that languished somewhere in the depths below them had reached out from its prison and somehow touched them all. Their thoughts twinning now, the two wolves settled down, alert for any danger, prepared to protect the Old One and the others at all costs.

19

The ancient warrior turned, beckoning as he did so to the two travelers. Nickolous looked up at him and nodded, grateful Jerome was nearby. Drawing in a deeply of the scents surrounding him, he entered the place where the watchers of the eternal waited.

Nickolous stood, awed, at what was before him. Jerome stopped just behind him, automatically reaching for his war club; startled to find it no longer loped about his waist, he looked around, bewildered. Inhaling deeply, he exhaled slowly, his breathing gradually slowing until there was nothing left to distract him, only the scene in front of him.

This wasn't just a dream walk. Once again, two worlds had been bridged. Once again, something more powerful than what Nickolous could comprehend had reached out, pulling him through a veil that went beyond the powers that he had been gifted with. Looking around at the giant ferns and smelling the perfume that wafted through the already sweetly scented air, Nickolous knew he wasn't in the realms of the warriors of Skye, nor was he in the future and certainly not the present. He paused to glance back at Jerome, at the same time realizing where they were...

The before time.

Jerome shared the same thought. The ancient warrior of the forest knelt down, touching the earth reverently; grasping handfuls of rich dark soil, he let them run through his broad hands and trickle to the ground unheeded.

He had dreamed of this place so long—this place of legend and dreams.

They were in a passage, with water trickling from an underground spring, running over the rocks, which were slippery with moss and slime. Nickolous went down, hard, his knee taking the brunt of the blow as he struggled to rise. The warrior didn't even glance back as Jerome bent to help Nickolous up. Limping, trying to conceal the pain, he continued on toward the light at the end of the passage that glowed blue-white.

"Enter." The warrior stood aside so that they could pass.

"Jerome?" Unspoken thoughts spun about them, unheard; but heard. The warrior nodded curtly, beckoning them further into the cavern, and then they were there, with only the rock walls surrounding them, and beyond that—

Both Nickolous and Jerome stood looking upward into an unending vastness of blue sky and distant mountains; their tops rimmed in white mist. To the right of them, water cascaded over rocky cliffs entering a small pool, which nestled at the base of the cliff. The smell of Oleander permeated the cavern, the white flowers hanging in clusters from stems that threatened to break under their heavy burden, while the wild honeysuckle, which clung to the crack's running deep into the rock, added their own beauty. Deep red flowers hung down from slender stems as humming birds flitted in and out. Nickolous stopped next to a fern that was taller than he was, while Jerome breathed deeply of the air, absorbing the scents that stirred memories of ancient times.

"Come. Time grows short." The warrior stood at the edge of the forest; the oak trees within so gnarled and twisted that Nickolous could only gaze upon them in wonder. As Jerome fell into step beside him, the knowledge that this was the place from whence all things had began, humbled him as they stepped carefully onto the path that led into the deepest heart of the ancient place that had been there from the beginning.

§ § § § § §

Orith watched patiently as the Old One stirred the contents from the small leather pouch into the hot water, the steam rising as she pulled the pot off the fire. Sarah, refreshed after her sleep, was there immediately; gently taking it from the Old One, she placed it carefully on the flat part of a rock that had been hewn out for that purpose then stood back so that the Old One could pass.

As the Old One made herself comfortable, Orith remained where he was, silently watching while at the same time caressing his staff. Saying nothing to the others, he touched the wood where the sensation was strongest. The tingling sensation ran through him—a warning that they were being watched; yet at the same time a comfort, because they were prepared and protected. Then he, too, leaned back.

It would be at a terrible cost to whoever or whatever was out there to try and enter this night.

He closed his eyes but did not sleep, his grasp firm upon the staff that hummed gently beneath his touch.

The Old One bent forward, her black eyes gazing into the fire's deepest depths, her mind focusing on what was behind the small flames that licked their way upward toward the small sticks placed crossways against the red-hot embers that glowed beneath. Her attention focused, she withdrew a small amount of powder from the worn leather pouch that hung at her side. Tossing it into the fire, she leaned back, inhaling the pungent odor that wafted upward to curl lazily around the ceiling, then she too closed her eyes. Sleep was an elusive thing, and so, like Orith, she withdrew to that other place that to which only their kind could journey. And like Orith, she also grasped her staff tightly to her, knowing that it would serve her well this night.

§ § § § §

Gabriel raised his head, inhaling deeply of the scents wafting to him on the night's breeze. Instantly he was on his feet, the fur along his back bristling as Chera scented the night wind, the soft growl emanating from deep within not a threatening one; rather a greeting of old friends as the low growl from inside the fringes of the forest begged entrance. The Old One, roused from that place where she had centered herself, opened her eyes briefly before once again closing them; even now she felt the pull of the Flame and knew the wolves would do what was necessary.

"We thought you lost." Chera moved to allow passage to the black wolf who moved slowly into the fires shadowy light. The wolf bowed low before her, and she nudged him gently, urging him to rise, for he was not only the captain of the wolves but a trusted friend. As she drew back, she noted the partially healed wounds that crisscrossed his back, the fur patchy in some places, the scars a permanent reminder of battles past.

"The others? Where are the others?" Gabriel looked past Liege, to the forest beyond, his gaze searching as he waited for an answer.

"Gone. All gone." Liege dropped his head in resignation as the soft sighing of the night wind enveloped them within its embrace; its passage amongst them a telling thing.

§ § § § § §

"The Flame rages against what it cannot escape, my Lord." The shadow creature, a being as old as time itself, faced Lord Nhon across the room, its form as changing as the wisps of smoke curling up from the fire toward the ceiling. There was no heat from the flames, for the cavern was unnaturally cold; the feeling of desolation and foreboding nearly overwhelming as a deep moaning rose up, the echo writhing upward, to trail off against the cold stone that guarded against escape.

Lord Nhon said nothing, his expression guarded as he glanced toward the thick stone wall that separated the two rooms. Muffled sounds, low and keening, sounded from the other side as the walls vibrated with unheard sound. Lord Nhon rubbed his chin thoughtfully, his red eyes glinting in the partial light. He did not care to enter the other room, for the Flame hurt his ears with its incessant moaning, and he had other things to attend to this night. Blocking out the sounds from the other side of the wall, he went about his tasks as the shadow creature watched silently. Once, feeling the presence of the unknown, he rose, his gaze searching the hidden places within the cavern, his senses reeling as he fought the nausea that rose within him. Shaking it off, he shrugged, for he knew his adversary well. He had no doubt that, if he were to venture outside, the winged ones would be waiting.

"Lord Nhon?" Whirling, he caught himself, his expression guarded. It wouldn't do for the creature to see his fear—

After all, he was who he was.

"What is it?" He glared from beneath heavy hooded lids, his red eyes mere slits.

The being before him met his gaze evenly. Searching. He lowered his voice. Even so, in the stillness of the cavern, surrounded as they were by rock that carried ancient remembering, it seemed loud.

Lord Nhon fought the urge to cover his ears, his mind focusing on the ability to shut out all but the immediate purpose before him.

"*Three.*"

"What?" Lord Nhon turned toward the being, his senses tingling.

"*Three.* As long as they are separated, there is no real danger. There must be a joining of power, and for that to happen, they must be together." The being drew closer, and Lord Nhon looked at him as if it were the first time. There was nothing definable about the creature; there wasn't even a face, really, where the eyes should have been, there was only a black roiling that was ever changing in its depth of intensity.

Lord Nhon pulled back as if seeing the creature for the first time; suddenly aware that the being could, if he chose to, look into the depths of his very being. Inwardly he shuddered, even as he closed his mind to the rising emotions welling up inside. When next he faced the creature, there was no indication that there had ever been any indecision on his part. His red eyes narrowed as he asked, "What have you seen?"

"*Nothing. Everything.*"

"You talk in riddles!" Lord Nhon snorted angrily, his temper flaring as he turned away from the creature. He was halfway across the room, yet he still heard the whispered words that were almost lost to the sudden sighing that permeated the cavern. The Flame, the heart of all living things since the beginning of creation, began to scream; the sound nearly unbearable for it, too, had heard the whispered chant of the shadow creature. Lord Nhon pulled his robes tightly about him as he whirled around, an unaccustomed chill creeping up his spine, his mind pushing the fear back as he asked the question; knowing the answer.

"Where is he?"

"*The Warriors. The Ancients. The Seven.*"

Lord Nhon released the glass vial he was holding, the crushed shards biting deeply into the palm of his hand as the remnants fell to the earthen floor at his feet. Wordlessly, he clenched and unclenched his hand, not bothering to stop the red liquid that seeped between his fingers.

§ § § § §

Jerome stayed slightly behind Nickolous, his view so breathtaking that for the moment it seemed that it was just him and the forest that had created him and there was nothing, had never been anything else before…

Not even that which had followed after.

He watched as the path they traveled widened and once, sparing a backward glance the way they had come, and was not surprised to see that the pathway had closed—even a place as ancient as this needed to keep its secrets, he supposed, as he bent slightly to avoid the low-hanging branches of a gigantic willow tree. As the branches touched him, whisper soft and sweetly scented, he stopped, his warrior's intuition telling him that this was where he was to remain.

Nickolous was aware that Jerome had remained behind, but he was not concerned. He too, knew that the rest of this journey was his and his alone to make. When next he looked, the forest was in shadow, so thick was the canopy of intertwining limbs overhead.

"There was a time when all things were like this."

Nickolous turned around as the speaker stepped out of the shadow that concealed him, into the light.

§ § § § §

"Old One, there is the sound of thunder beneath our feet," Sarah said as she crept closer to the fire; its warmth pulling them all toward it as the dampness seeped through the cold gray rock that surrounded them.

"There's nothing to fear," the Old One replied. Adjusting her robes about her; shivering slightly, she moved closer toward the flames that licked upward.

Chera and Gabriel stood at the caverns entrance, while Liege, exhausted, rested nearby. His journey back to them had been fraught with many dangers, and the knowledge that only he had survived would stay with him until the day his own life force was extinguished.

"Hush, child," the Old One said, as she patted Sarah's shoulder gently, trying to calm her as Orith moved toward them, his slow gait a concern to the Old One.

"Come." She motioned to the fragrant boughs of cedar beside her.

As Orith lowered himself carefully down beside her, the tremors beneath them lessoned.

"The Flame calls…"

"And the son of Skye answers; he just doesn't know it yet." Orith finished the sentence, his grip firm on his staff. The tingling sensation did not alarm him; he turned to face the Old One; the elation he felt showed upon his scarred features as he patted her arm gently. Saying nothing more, he leaned back, grateful for the warmth that crept around him. Sighing deeply he nestled into his robes, the crackling of the logs in the fire comforting—but not for long.

§ § § § §

Liege stirred in his sleep, restless and exhausted; the journey that had brought him here had been at a terrible cost; the lives of many lost in the darkened places that harbored deceit and evil. Wherever they had gone, the wolves had seen it—a festering sore that would not heal. There were so many who had followed the shadow creatures.

They were legion.

Liege opened his eyes; then slowly closed them again; his midnight black shoulders shaking as he fought the images racing through his brain. In this semi-state of sleep, it was as if he were back in battle, the howls of rage and pain tearing at him as he watched the others being devoured by the inky blackness that had pervaded the clearing where they had taken a stand.

The swirling darkness had come out of nowhere, a twisting turning writhing mist that held disembodied voices and images of things that darkened and faded as they changed into things even more terrible to behold; they had tried to fight back, striking out at the nothingness that enveloped them. The battle had lasted mere moments and, at the end, only Liege had been able to throw himself out of the shadow's grasp. When everything had stopped spinning, and the world had righted itself, he was alone. Anguished, he had searched for something, anything, that would tell him that there were some who had survived.

It was not to be.

Finally, exhausted, he had tracked the others to this place; however, his rest was anything but peaceful. In his mind he could hear the howls of the others, cut abruptly off as if a door had closed; shutting off their cries and in his heart he grieved.

"Liege."

The call came from a distance and, in his sleep-induced state, Liege had to fight the urge to slip further into oblivion, but the voice was persistent; the speaker familiar. Rising up on stiff legs, he turned to face Chera.

"Liege," she said; her tone soft and low. "We have need of you, can you seek out Owen?"

The big wolf shook his head. He would try.

§ § § § §

"The gate must be closed!" Lord Moshat leaned against the table for support as he looked at the messenger. He drew his thick brows together in a frown, the crinkles in the corners deepening as his eyes narrowed. The messenger stood against the door, his expression unreadable. The shadow being was dangerous, and the Fallen must not be allowed to bring any more through. These creatures belonged in their own worlds; not here with them. The balance must be maintained.

Lord Moshat fell silent after this outburst, for the past hours had seemed endless, the road ahead impassable. He drew in a deep breath and held it, before exhaling slowly, the sound not lost to the messenger, who stood, head bowed, waiting. Finally, Lord Moshat spoke, the words slow and measured, the inner knowledge of the risk he would take a secondary thing. The messenger drew back, masking his shock, but did not argue.

A short time later, under cover of darkness, without even the comfort of the moon's silvery rays to light the way and masked by clouds that to mortal eyes would appear natural, two forms moved stealthily through the night.

§ § § § § §

Lord Nhon shuddered as the long-forgotten emotion washed over him; the shock he felt quickly turning to amazement. His companion looked up, puzzled, as the laughter echoed throughout the cavern.

"So, he would leave the safety of the sacred place to journey below—and for what—a boy who did not know what he possessed and the wood clans who fought a losing battle against what they could not hope to defeat?" He spoke not to his companion, but to the empty air around him.

For untold turnings, he had sought to draw that *one* from his lair, where his warriors could not protect him. Striding alone, into the night, he left the shadow creature to guard the Flame, for he had a score to settle.

A score as old as time itself.

§ § § § § §

Lord Moshat swayed slightly; the journey from the high place to the below had been difficult. The passage of time had brought with it the inability to move as freely as the warrior behind him, who watched, his eyes missing little, even in the darkness.

Chest heaving, Lord Moshat drew in deeply of the night air. Suddenly he stiffened, sensing the presence of an old enemy. With the merest of nods, he released the warrior behind him from his vigil. Absorbing the smells and sounds of the forest; drawing upon the strength of the elemental powers that surrounded him, he stood erect; no longer did age seem to affect him for this night he had been granted the ability to meet his former protégé on equal terms. Not bothering to glance back, he continued on, the sounds closing in behind him as he neared the place he sought.

Owen flew; the wind's current carrying him soundlessly over the rise, for he knew his path lay straight ahead; the sacred place not much further. He was fortunate to be downwind for if he hadn't, the thing skulking on the ground below, in the shadowed places, would have sensed him first. As it was, there was barely enough time to swing out of range of the slashing claws as the creature flung itself upward, talons clawing at empty air.

Owen somersaulted as the creature lunged again, narrowly missing him as he righted himself. Catching his breath the great owl flew straight upward, until the foaming, screaming creature was no more than a small glaring thing, its narrowed heavy lidded yellow eyes mere pinpoints of glowing light in the clearing below.

As Owen began the downward plunge, the creature rose upright; where before there had been front legs of a sort, there were now leathery wings. The whoosh-woosh sounded incredibly loud in the sudden stillness as the creature became airborne.

One of Lord Nhon's elite guard, it had been placed there by the Fallen One himself to guard its masters path; and it had no intentions of letting anyone pass as long as it held life within its being.

Prepared for the worst, hoping for the best, the two combatants struck each other with incredible force, the night pierced by Owens's war cry as he flung the creature away from him, barely having time to recover before he was attacked again. Grappling, the two plunged earthward.

The winged warrior watched as the battle raged.

Owen shook bits of debris off himself as the creature sprang upward, its mouth opening in a scream as it lunged forward; jaws snapping, leathery wings with spiked ends reached out, trying to grasp its prey for the death blow. Its breath was foul, the sounds the open mouth emitted unearthly.

Concentrating on the space beneath the thing's ribcage, Owen let it get dangerously close before striking out, his claws slashing through flesh and bone as the thing pulled back, too late realizing its mistake. Wounded, but not mortally, it scuttled sideways; then, glancing upward, caught sight of the winged warrior behind Owen.

The changeling wavered under their intense gaze as Owen drew in great breaths of fresh air; glad the thing was standing downwind; glad for the respite of battle, however brief. Glancing sideways, he nodded, acknowledging the winged warriors presence, yet puzzled as to why one of the warriors of Skye would reveal themselves so openly.

Before he had a chance to contemplate further, the wind swirled about him, bringing with it the sounds of the night—the howl of the hunter seeking its prey.

§ § § § §

Liege scented the night wind and that which rode upon it, nostrils distended, his head held high; the fur along his spine bristled as a chill ran down his spine; ahead of him the sounds of battle grew louder. Topping the rise, he stood transfixed at the scene before him. Peering through the darkness he made out two struggling forms. Owen! As the two combatants fell apart, he drew in his breath sharply before letting it out in a deafening roar that momentarily diverted the thing's attention. Leaping high, he quickly closed the distance between himself and the creature that turned to meet him; its attention now on this new adversary.

That was all Owen needed.

Too late the creature realized its mistake—too late it turned around to the sound of rushing air as the great Owl took flight, his talons extended.

20

Nickolous studied the figure before him thoughtfully; trying to absorb all that had been said. The warrior turned to face him; his arms crossed over his chest as he looked at him; his eyes reflecting nothing of what Nickolous knew he must feel. The warrior's journeys were timeless, while his, were not yet written.

The words echoed within his mind. He rose from his cramped position as the other clasped his arm in a farewell gesture. The forest around him spun out of focus as he fought to maintain his balance, the words of those others who watched from a distant place ringing in his mind as he fell through the great abyss that reached out to swallow him. Vaguely he wondered where Jerome was, and why the return journey was so hurried, and then for a time there was nothing.

"Nickolous, wake up." Jerome shook him gently, glad that they had both came through the gate in one piece; and as he glanced around at his surroundings, close to the sacred place where the others waited.

Nickolous stirred, his mind groggy as he struggled to sit up, the memories of where he had been and what had been said washing over him in waves as he was helped to his feet.

"You must not speak of the things you have seen. Not yet. Not even to me."

Nickolous stared at the warrior for a moment before nodding. Grasping his war club in one hand, Jerome looked around, cautious, for they were no longer in the sacred place. His senses tingled as he gazed upward at the stars etched against the inky blackness overhead;

feeling the tremors beneath his feet, he knelt down, his eyes closed as he felt the beat of the earth beneath his fingertips, the sensation spreading upward as he absorbed the vibrations.

"The dwellers below? The little ones..." Nickolous voice trailed off into the silence. Watching the forest warrior's expression, he could not feel what the warrior felt; although it was obvious that they were each gifted with certain abilities, and they had shared some experiences as one, this wasn't one of the times it would be so.

Jerome turned to look at Nickolous. He had changed yet again. Whatever had happened back there, where the Old Ones dwelt, had matured him further, and he wished Nickolous did not have to bear such a heavy burden alone.

"The little ones speak of suffering; there is great pain." Jerome paused as he straightened up from his kneeling position. He peered into the darkness as if seeking out a distant sound. "The Flame seeks to be released from its prison, while others weep." He did not look at Nickolous as he said this, but gripped his war club, his fingers spanning the breadth of it as he pushed his rising emotions down.

Nickolous nodded. There was nothing more to say.

§ § § § § §

Owen inclined his head slightly toward Liege.

"Well met; and the others?" He turned away from the still form crumpled at his feet, expecting to see more wolves coming over the rise. When there were none forthcoming, he turned back, his gaze questioning. The question went unasked. He lowered his head for a moment then, looking around, noticed the winged warrior was gone. Certain he had not gone far, he turned his attention back to Liege. The big wolf said nothing, for his eyes said it all.

"How did you know..." Liege growled, the words cut off abruptly as he sensed the approach of something or someone.

Owen blinked, his huge golden eyes reflecting the Moon's pale light. There; he could hear it. Soundlessly he flew upward, scanning the ground below.

"Nickolous. Jerome." He breathed their names thankfully as he glided toward them, leaving Liege to follow; their scent now strong upon the nights wind.

§ § § § § §

Jerome watched the silhouette against the backdrop of the starry night. He knew it was Owen and so was not alarmed. He was more surprised to see the long, loping form that followed. Nickolous, too, was glad to see the captain of the guard. The memories of that night in the clearing when Liege had risked his life for him came flooding back with a bitter sweetness as he greeted the big black wolf.

Liege was amazed at the change in Nickolous. Gone was the young boy. As he allowed a hand to caress him in greeting, calm overtook his senses, and for a moment he leaned against him for support, the need to let his guard down for one moment of peace nearly overwhelming. Then, remembering where he was, just as quickly pulled back, once more on guard, alert for anything untoward.

"Don't worry." Nickolous looked down at the wolf, studying him intently. *"The darkness cannot hold them in forever."* The words drifted upon the night wind for him alone to hear

Liege drew in his breath, letting it out slowly, hardly daring to hope that what he was hearing meant his haunting dreams were correct.

"Nickolous speaks the truth," Jerome said as he drew close, for the warrior had just now realized what the little ones, the earth dwellers, had been trying to tell him—

Somewhere below them, deep within the earth, there was a fierce battle for freedom being waged. Jerome felt powerless to help and wondered how so few could defeat so many alone. He turned away, trying to draw strength from the knowledge of where he had been; cautiously guarding his thoughts.

Liege nodded in understanding. Had he not been so blinded with emotion, he would have seen what Jerome and Nickolous already knew.

"Come." He turned aside, tilting his head to one side, listening intently.

"Chera calls."

The far-off cry carried on the night wind to the rest of them as Nickolous stepped forward to follow Liege.

"Wait!"

Jerome yanked Nickolous backward forcefully as he swung his war club in a wide arc. Whatever it was that the club connected with—it went flying unceremoniously through air to land somewhere beyond their sight. Jerome grunted in disgust as he wiped his war club against the long, damp grass. Nickolous didn't ask what it was, for in the split second before the club had made contact, he had glimpsed the narrowed yellow eyes glaring downward. Devoid of any humanity, they were empty of all save the madness that drove them forward to obey their master.

"Are there any more? Were we overheard?" Owen peered into the darkness, silently berating himself for not having been more vigilant. Liege nudged him gently; the big wolf suddenly impatient now, for there was an overwhelming restlessness growing within him. As Owen took flight, the others followed closely behind, Nickolous being placed in the center, flanked on either side by Jerome and Liege.

§ § § § §

Lord Moshat stayed at the edge of the shadows, the air around him was thick, almost suffocating—somewhere behind him, someone followed. He smiled in the semidarkness that cloaked him, for the moon hung full and round in the sky, its pale light casting shadows where the trees bent gently in the night breeze. It had been turnings beyond remembering since he had been here; he had almost forgotten. He turned left toward a grove of trees. He was there. The gate stood open, invisible to most, but not to him. Gripping his staff firmly, Lord Moshat turned to meet his enemy.

Lord Nhon threw off his heavy cloak as he flung himself through the air to intercept his enemy—too long had he waited for this moment—too long had the hatred festered and grown within. He had become weary over the turnings; the longing for revenge a terrible thing that had burned within him until he had lost all ability to reason when it came to his former mentor.

Lord Moshat knew this, had been prepared for it; for he had known, had felt the hatred that burned within his former protégés breast these many turnings. He stood in the gateway's center, the incantation already cast as the dark form hurtled toward him. Lord Nhon spun around at the last moment; his arms raised high, the staff he held sparking blue-white as it collided with that of Lord Moshat's.

§ § § § §

"Wait!" Jerome hissed as the night was filled with unearthly shrieks. Pivoting around he gazed upward into the eastern sky—the shadows dancing against the velvet blackness of the night warning him.

Nickolous shifted uncomfortably; beneath his jacket the silver armband burned hot against his skin as he peered into the shadows and pulled back; startled. For a split second, the winged warriors gaze burned into his, then the night was filled with the sound of rushing wind and the wailing of something unclean as it passed overhead.

"Hurry; to the cavern!" Jerome shouted as he jerked Nickolous forward, half dragging, half carrying him in his panic.

Liege followed swiftly, for as much as the big wolf would have liked to turn and face whoever, or whatever, was behind him, he knew their safety lay ahead; in the sacred place where the others waited.

"No." One word. Nickolous pulled out of Jerome's grasp, startling the big warrior. Jerome looked down at him in shock.

"No." This time the words were breathed out softly as Nickolous reached out to touch the warrior of the forest gently, his gaze seeking understanding. "I cannot go back yet. Tonight is only the beginning of what is to come—I will not run away." He turned to face Liege as Owen hovered overhead. Jerome gazed upward at Owen, his eyes begging for help.

Owen said nothing, for he had a feeling that things were about to take an unwanted turn. Sighing deeply, he glided toward them, momentarily unmindful of the prying eyes that watched.

§ § § § §

Lord Moshat leapt clear, narrowly avoiding the piercing light that flamed from Lord Nhon's staff—a staff that he himself had given him. Inwardly, he drew upon the knowledge that although his former student knew much, he did not know all. The thought lent him little comfort as he parried the next thrust that was aimed with deadly accuracy.

§ § § § §

Instinct drew Nickolous forward, his unwilling companions following behind. Guided by something he did not quite understand, he plunged forward into the forest, unmindful of the branches that tore at his clothing and scratched his face. He was near; he could sense it. Feeling the silver burning against his skin, he rolled up his sleeve, for once unmindful of who, or what, might see.

Light, brilliant white and scorching hot, shot upward, nearly blinding those behind him as a wailing rose overhead, causing Jerome to shudder. Not knowing what they faced, he hurried to catch up while Owen glided soundlessly on the wind currents, his eyes peering deep into the darkness for something they could not find; ever mindful that, somewhere behind them, a winged warrior watched. He suddenly found himself being flung backward as the wind became a screaming thing. Not seen—but heard. And as they were soon to find out, a force to be reckoned with.

§§§§§

Lord Nhon somersaulted backward as the staff flew from his grasp, while Lord Moshat stood firm within the center of the gate, his stance defiant, both hands grasping the staff in front of him as he used it as a barrier between the two of them.

Landing on his feet, Lord Nhon twisted around with incredible agility. Bending down, he retrieved his staff then, turning, faced Lord Moshat. Words, muttered behind clenched lips, tumbled out as Lord Moshat stood, unwavering against the anger. Closing his eyes, he inhaled then exhaled as he turned the staff slowly around, twirling it around and around as Lord Nhon took one step, then another toward him, his breath foul from the darkness that festered within.

"So, you would think to interfere with that which is not your concern!" Lord Nhon spat the words out as he struck out at the staff that Lord Moshat now used between them as a shield.

"You have betrayed all that you were, and for what?" Lord Moshat thrust the other's staff aside. Ignoring the smell, he drew close to Lord Nhon so that they were mere inches from one another. Guarding himself against what he might see within the darkened shell of what was once a being of light, he gazed deep within—and pulled back reeling.

Lord Nhon struck the staff aside, at the same time grasping Lord Moshat by the throat. Flinging him aside, he drew the two staffs toward each other; nearly touching, the two glowed with an unnatural light. As Lord Moshat struggled to his feet, Lord Nhon turned to face him, his face a twisted mask of incomprehensible evil.

"I have betrayed nothing." Lord Nhon's eyes shone red in the pale gloom that surrounded him. "Look at you. You have grown old and weak over the turnings, while I have remained the same."

"No; you have not remained the same. The strength you possess is one of despair and longing for that which you will never find!" Lord Moshat struck at the two staffs as he spoke, breaking their connection. The staffs, freed from each other's embrace, spewed light skyward, entwining, the colors merging into a brilliance that was a combination of hot and cold.

Memories of the before time poured forth into the sudden silence that was nearly overwhelming; and then the noise was nearly more than they could bear as the voices screamed within their minds…

Around them. Over them. All the entities of untold turnings. The Ancients. The Lost Ones.

Even in the abyss of dark despair into which they had been thrown, the battle still raged as untold voices screamed—seeking the way to freedom while the others, the Ancients, fought to hold them back.

Each staff possessed its own power, its owner putting much of himself into its center. Those powers now released pulled at each other, each one trying to envelope the other.

One to put back. The other, to possess.

"No!" Lord Nhon leaned forward to grab the staff, but it was too late.

The gate had begun to close in upon itself, while the air above him shrieked with sounds that threatened to drive him mad. Turning, he drew his cloak about him, the incantation already cast; when next Lord Moshat looked, he stood alone while the two staffs smoldered at his feet; their power broken.

The voices dimmed into nothingness as he knelt down and sifted through the blackened remnants of what had been.

§ § § § § §

"Nickolous!" Jerome swept the air in a wide arc, his club thudding against something he could not see. The wind shrieked around him as something passed overhead brushing against him, the sensation nearly causing him to lose his balance. He swung wildly, hitting nothing as huge droplets of sweat beaded on his forehead, then dried as the wind assailed him.

"Run—"

"No, wait." Nickolous bent low as the air above them carried the haunting cries of unseen things into the quickening silence. "It's over." He turned toward Liege; the big wolf stood by his side, his expression guarded. Owen flew low, alert for anything that might be near, the feeling of unease causing him to shiver.

"There, beyond those trees." Liege nodded toward the darkened forest, but Nickolous stepped forward, intending to go around him. The big wolf nudged him gently. "Patience," Liege cautioned. "There may be others who tread places we are not prepared for."

Nickolous stopped where he was, his expression questioning. Jerome nodded to Owen, for with his immense height he could see what the others could not. Light, blue-white, emanated from within the confines of the forest. Owen, too, was alerted to the nuance that had not been there before, for he knew this part of the forest well. Tilting slightly to one side he glided low over the treetops, keeping to the shadows.

"Someone comes," Nickolous whispered as Liege crouched beside him, the fur along his back bristling as the scent of unknown things assailed him while Jerome stood in front of them, his war club held loosely at his side, nevertheless, prepared for whatever was approaching.

"*Nickolous.*" The words wrapped around him, carried upon the warm wind. The urgency was unmistakable as, unbidden, he moved forward toward whatever beckoned.

"No." Liege edged ahead of the big warrior. Placing himself between Nickolous and Jerome, he motioned them back as he approached the forest's edge, the warm air that blew over him and around him sending shivers through him as he crouched low to the ground, waiting. He peered into the moonlit night as the sounds of someone slowly approaching carried to him upon the night breeze.

§ § § § §

Lord Moshat moved cautiously toward the outer edge of the forest. The staffs were destroyed and he grieved for their loss, but the gate to the world below had been closed and that was all that mattered. Lord Nhon, for all his power, would not be able to open it again. The thought gave him little comfort as he threaded his way carefully along the winding path that led away from the gateway; away from the memories.

§ § § § §

"No. I must go in there." Nickolous tried to go around Jerome but the forest warrior blocked his path.

"You cannot." The big warrior looked down at his young charge; into blue eyes that held the knowing of the ages deep within their depths. Nickolous reached out to touch him gently.

"*They call,*" he whispered softly, moving around the warrior as the way was barred once more.

Jerome studied him intently from beneath heavy brows, a small part of him acknowledging it was useless to argue in the face of such power. Gazing upward into the night, he inhaled, drawing in deeply of the fresh air, his keen hearing picking up the nuances that drifted upon the nights wind; releasing his breath in resignation he moved aside. Grasping his war club firmly, he followed silently behind his young charge; nodding to Liege as he passed by, the understanding unspoken that the big wolf would stay behind to guard for their return.

The pathway was littered with fallen debris. Broken limbs, big and small, lay scattered about the forest floor. Jerome gazed at the mess thoughtfully. Whatever had torn through this place had left in its wake total devastation and, as Nickolous followed the warriors gaze, it was obvious that they would have to choose their way carefully. Beneath his feet, the earth dwellers beat out a steady rhythm against the earth. The vibrations reaching upward until the sound resounded like a heartbeat, rushing over him, around him, through him; Jerome shook his head, drawing in a deep breath as he fought the sensation that washed over him. Something dark had passed this way, and it didn't take much to guess whom.

"The small ones seek to speak their thoughts."

Jerome looked at Nickolous in surprise.

"They seek to be heard—to be remembered." Nickolous tilted his head to one side; drawing the emotions seeping upward from the earth to him. When he spoke again, it wasn't to Jerome; but to himself. "The ancient places have been breached while the darkness treads within sight of the light. The earth weeps this night." Nickolous turned away, the helpless feeling climbing upward, threatening to suffocate him.

"We are not defeated yet."

Startled, Jerome reached for his war club, only to watch in amazement as it flew from his grasp to land a short distance away; as he bent to retrieve it, a shadowy form slowly detached itself from the shadows.

"Lord Moshat." Nickolous inclined his head slightly, surprised that the elder would have left the safety of Skye.

Lord Moshat strode quickly toward them as Jerome studied him from beneath half-closed eyelids. There was something familiar about this elder—a memory tugged at him from his youth; then broke free as he drew on those memories—

A terrified youngster had wandered away from his clan and couldn't find his way back while the day had vanished; in its place, the darkness had come, bringing with it the sounds of the night wending their way around him—over him—through him. He had closed his eyes, trying to shut out the fear that had threatened to overtake him; the need to flee overpowering his emotions, when strong arms had grasped him and lifted him up—he had not opened his eyes until his feet had once again touched solid ground.

"It is good to see you after so many countless turnings." The oldest of the elders of Skye stood before him, and even in the shadows of the darkness he knew that Lord Moshat was looking up at him; gauging him to see if he was worthy. He bent down slightly to catch the next words, spoken so softly that only he heard them.

"It is good to see the stripling has grown to honor the forest and protect those who dwell beneath. It is good to know the gifts given were honored." Lord Moshat pulled away, but not before Jerome caught the whispered; "To grow within is to grow without. The circle grows smaller, yet the light in the center survives."

Jerome nodded mutely. The big warrior was at a loss for words. After he had been returned to the forest as a youngling, he had many dreams and had seen many visions. The need to seek out those who could teach and explain had nearly consumed him, so great had the need become to be aware of the unseen ones that dwelt among them.

As he stood before Lord Moshat, he was glad that he had sought out the things that had brought him here, to this place.

"Nickolous; we must see him safely to the others. If Lord Nhon knew he was here…"

Jerome nodded mutely. The knowledge of the truth the elder spoke, combined with the knowledge of the danger they were in lay heavy within his being. He hadn't approved of coming this way from the beginning, but his warrior's heart had trusted Nickolous's judgment.

"We must go. Now." Jerome strode quickly ahead, not bothering to look back; knowing the elder walked with the boy, he trusted that Liege sensed their coming. Above him, the air stirred with the beating of wings as Owen soared above him; his eyes the mirror that reflected the night and those who threaded their way within it.

§ § § § §

"Chera, come inside."

"Where are they?" Chera turned her gaze toward her mate. "They should have been back long ago."

"Do not worry. Jerome will protect him and Liege won't fail us. Come." Gabriel nudged her gently. He didn't want the Old One to worry. Both Orith and the Old One seemed a little frailer with each passing day.

"Chera." Gabriel stood at the entranceway, his tone firm. It was time to gather everyone together for the days dawning was but a few hours away.

"The night deepens into a blackness that smothers." Chera stood poised beside him, her stance reminding him of the Chera of old. He nodded assent; the urge to hunt now a growing hunger, he scented the air, seeking.

"They come." Chera looked at him, her expression guarded. "They are not alone. Tell the Old One and Orith to prepare."

§ § § § §

The fire burned high, the heat comforting after the dampness of the night. Sarah had already prepared the tea, which was accepted gratefully, the need for spoken words not necessary as the hollowed-out gourds were quickly emptied then refilled.

Nickolous leaned against the wall, exhausted from his journey; for now, he was content to draw in the welcome warmth from the fire. He watched as Sarah bustled about, making sure no one lacked food or a warm drink while Timothy stood close by, his dark eyes missing little as the silence that surrounded them deepened.

Lord Moshat hadn't been to this place since the time of the Ancient Ones; but the power remained. He turned his head, listening, glad that he had stopped here for a little while before returning to Skye. The earth beneath him beat out a steady rhythm that he had almost forgotten, and for a moment he contemplated defying the unwritten laws and staying...for these few stood against many.

He sighed deeply, closing his eyes for a moment.

"Lord Moshat. My Lord?" He opened his eyes. Luminous dark eyes peered up as Sarah knelt before him, her curiosity getting the better of her, for she dared what the others would not.

"Was it you then, I mean, back at the cavern?" Remembering the unexpected visitor, and the crystalline tears that had fallen in such sorrow, she waited breathlessly, sure of the answer.

Lord Moshat leaned forward, studying Sarah intently, her childlike innocence was intriguing.

"Sarah!" Timothy was shocked at his sister's behavior. Lord Moshat was, after all, an honored guest. The rest of the companions looked on, amused.

"Hold." Lord Moshat motioned Timothy back.

"It's all right, little one," he said as he drew her close. Sensing her awe of him and her blind trust that he could help was nearly too much. He patted her arm gently.

"Small one, there are many who hold the knowledge within—the decision to share a careful one. Each guardian holds a part of the knowledge within themselves—but not all. It wasn't I you saw but one who holds the knowing of the before time and foresees the possible ending because the middle is not yet written."

Sarah looked at him, her expression confused. Lord Moshat stood, and when he spoke, it was to them all.

"There is no riddle, for the words I speak are true. The end is not yet written, for the middle is not yet set. Lord Nhon should not be here, but then again, neither should I."

He smiled in the half light.

"I decided to even things out a bit. The gate I closed will prevent any more dark shadows from coming through. They don't belong here. They belong to their own realm; their own time. Even the Daughter of the Night flees this festering sore. Even she has seen the darkness that shrouds the land as an unwelcome thing that threatens her existence."

"A-Sharoon brought this evil to us, and now she hides from what she has done." Chera paced the length of the cavern, her frustration evident.

"The evil was already here, Daughter of the Forest." Lord Moshat spoke gently as he stirred the coals at the outer edge of the fire. "It would have only been a matter of time before '*That One*' made himself known, for the darkness is an insidious thing that gathers power as it goes." He lowered his head and closed his eyes against the sudden sensation that pervaded his senses.

"It's forbidden that one such as you help those of the forest clans."

Lord Moshat kept his eyes closed, knowing that only he was hearing the words. He clenched his fists, wondering how Lord Nhon could peer through the living rock as his thoughts turned outward, seeking the speaker. There was nothing; and so he turned aside, his features concealed by the shadows; his decision made. The Fallen's powers were even greater than he had realized.

"I must leave, for the time grows short and my own warriors grow impatient." He drew the heavy woolen cloak about his shoulders, wanting to leave as quickly as possible, before something happened—on the off chance that Lord Nhon could channel his power through him to harm even one of these was unthinkable.

"Wait." Nickolous placed a hand on his arm. "Are they safe? Are they together?" Blue eyes met blue.

"Yes to the first. No to the second." Lord Moshat placed a hand on Nickolous's shoulder, the warmth was penetrating and comforting at the same time.

"Your Mother waits beyond the misty places, her power to protect those within the necessity that holds her there. Your sister is safe elsewhere; her destiny a different path that calls her. She answers that call with a fierceness that will serve her well in the future—whatever that future may be." He lowered his head as he drew the hood forward to conceal his features, then, nodding to the others, went into the night; the wolves following at a distance until, turning, he waved them back.

Chera stayed awhile longer, even after Gabriel and Liege had went back to the others, her silvery-gray eyes searching the shadows for danger; then, satisfied that the elder was safely away, she turned and in a few minutes was back at the cavern's entrance.

§ § § § §

Lord Nhon threw his tattered robe to the floor, grinding it into the cold earth as he hurled oaths at the empty air around him. The shadow being wasn't there; which was a good thing, given the mood of the host. Anything that could be thrown was, and the broken shards were left for an underling to clean up.

As the fire flickered, then caught, the flame burned low, the ice-cold chill pervading the cavernous room as Lord Nhon bent to his task. It was much later that, rising, he stretched wearily, the task done.

"Where have you been?"

The shadow creature was suddenly there, watching him almost warily, his attention on what lay in front of the ice-blue flames.

"That meddling fool closed the gate." Lord Nhon snarled. As he turned to face the being he hissed. "But then you would already know that, wouldn't you?"

"And what would I do to stop such a being? You who studied under him for so long know him better than I. Remember; I am here only to assist you. There are other gates. We will find them."

"We don't have time!" Lord Nhon glared from beneath his hood, his eyes mere slits that glowed red in the dim light.

"You fear what they can do." The voice was tinged with surprise.

"Only a fool would not fear such powers as they have. Together, combined, they will be formidable," Lord Nhon retorted, as he picked up what he had been working on.

"Ahhh, a new staff, and need I ask what happened to the other one?"

"No. You need not!" Lord Nhon snarled as he turned away, one arm sweeping upward as he held the staff above his head. Twirling it round and round, faster and faster, until the high-pitched shrieking was nearly unbearable.

"Enough." Wheeling about, the being shot a nearly translucent web that struck the staff, knocking it out of Lord Nhon's hands. Reaching out, the Fallen caught it in midair as the creature drew back, wary, watching, ready to lash out if need be.

"Relax. The power of the staff is guided from within my own being. It is not as powerful as the one I lost, but who knows?" Lord Nhon shrugged his shoulders and then turned away, leaving the other to his own thoughts.

§ § § § § §

"Lord Moshat is safely away." Jerome bent low to enter, the small space not to his liking but the need for companionship greater. Besides, he needed to speak of things best not overheard beyond these walls. Feeling more at ease, but not entirely, he crouched beside the fire, motioning Nickolous close.

Not much had been said during Lord Moshat's visit, for Orith and the Old One had no need to ask questions; for what the Old Ones had taught had come to pass. True, they had no way of knowing everything, but that, too, would come in time.

Nickolous grasped the armband, carefully sliding it off his arm. Turning to Jerome, his voice low, he whispered, "Watch." Then, turning back to the fire, he turned the bracelet slowly over and over, the metal seeming nearly transparent against the flames that reflected back.

Jerome drew closer; his attention caught by a reflection within the silver grooves that had been etched at the beginning of the turnings, made by hands that had known what was written of that time that was now coming to pass.

"The Flame shows the way," Nickolous whispered breathlessly as he moved closer to the fire.

"There. See that?"

Jerome bent nearer to see the reflection that danced against the light; hardly believing what his eyes saw. He had been so blind! The answer had been in front of them all the time.

"The bracelet is a beacon that guides the way. It will guide us to the three sleeping forest warriors and to the way in."

The Old One and Orith nodded knowingly. The path was set; the way in clear. The bracelet was more than an ornament—

It was a guide.

The Old One closed her eyes, for she had to rest. Only part of their journey was complete, and the night was melting away into the pre-dawn of the morning. She yawned, settling against the backrest that Sarah had so carefully made for her, and dozed off.

Orith made to rise, then, thinking better of it, settled back. Let those younger prepare for the dawning's light, he thought to himself as a gnarled paw patted him gently. Looking over at the Old One, he nodded, and then he too settled down for a sleep that was devoid of images to startle him into wakefulness.

"Guard the bracelet well. No one else must know you have it. *No one.*" Jerome leaned closer, his gaze searching; trying to impart the need to not speak aloud of things that might be overheard.

"*It's too late for that.*" The voice whispered.

Both Nickolous and Jerome looked at one another.

Then at the others.

The Old One and Orith were sleeping; as were Timothy and Sarah, while the wolves were outside; their preference to be in the night air, for the cavern had grown too warm for them.

"Who are you?" Nickolous asked; his head bowed as he concentrated, trying to locate the source.

"*I am who I am.*"

"Are you a friend?"

"*For now—yes.*"

Jerome concentrated; he could feel the unseen presence. It was close by…

The warrior drew in a deep breath before exhaling slowly. A shiver ran through him as the realization of whom the voice belonged to hit him. Then the voice was blocked out as Nickolous spoke; his words breaking through the concentration.

"Jerome; we need to listen."

"What…" Jerome looked at Nickolous with incredulity; forgetting his desire to not speak aloud. Quickly recovering from the shock of what he had just heard, he turned a startled gaze on his companion.

"What are you thinking?"

Nickolous placed a finger to his lips, as Chera peered in; her gaze questioning. Nickolous smiled at her and, seeing the reassuring look on his face, she withdrew her head, and it was just the two of them again.

"I'll ask it one more time. What are you thinking? Nickolous, are you mad?" The warrior's voice was low, measured, as he stared at his companion, hardly daring to think that he had heard him correctly.

"No, I'm not. Lord Nhon is not only a danger to the woodland clans, but he is also a danger to A-Sharoon and anyone else who walks the land. We must trust no one—but use what we have to our advantage."

"There can be no alliance with something so dark and evil, Nickolous," Jerome replied; the warrior shivered, despite the warmth cast by the fires flame in the center of the cavern.

Nickolous, not sure of how long they could block out the "*Other's*" thoughts, or, for that matter, if they had; chose his words carefully. "Our world shrinks as we talk, and a new day dawns; with it the unknown of ages past. What we saw and learned serves no purpose if we don't see what is in front of us, Jerome." Nickolous's voice was anguished as he lowered his head. When he looked up, Jerome saw the answer, there, in the fathomless depths of eyes that had saw so little—yet so much.

The big warrior nodded. Wisdom wasn't something that always came with age; and innocence wasn't something that you could dismiss when it was combined with the latter. He sighed...

So be it.

Nickolous turned his thoughts outward to the faceless voice draped somewhere within the shadowed places, so that they might hear its words.

"*I will not interfere with anything you chose to do; neither will A-Sharoon. You need not fear our either of us in what is to follow; beyond that, when everything is done, I will make no promises—in everything, there must be a balance.*" The voice faded away into the silence.

Nickolous let his breath out slowly; unaware that he had been holding it.

"Well, at least we know wherein our danger lies," Jerome muttered as he moved a rock absently out of his way with his foot. Sweat beaded his brow as he wiped at it; mindless of the fact that it only beaded up again. "We must prepare. Trust no one, and use our instincts."

He rose to go, and he was partway out of the cavern's entrance when he turned; the far-off trilling carrying faintly through rock and earth. "My warriors call; I must go. I will leave Chera and Gabriel to guard the entrance. Nickolous?" Jerome's voice softened as he looked at his young companion.

"Yes?"

"Try and get some rest." The warrior smiled; despite the worry, he knew things would turn out the way they should.

Nickolous leaned against the wall; the coolness that seeped out a temporary relief from the heat from the fire. Crossing his arms over his chest, he closed his eyes, wondering what the days new dawning would bring; then, like the others in the cavern, he drifted, his slumber broken by dreams of mystical places; outside, the soft trilling of the forest creatures had began.

On a grassy knoll a short distance away, Jerome and the others watched in silence as the eastern sky began to lighten; the warrior posting his warriors in strategic places where they could remain unseen.

§ § § § §

A-Sharoon waited in the darkness, her senses alert for anything untoward; a sense of foreboding lay heavy within her. *Where was he?* She paced impatiently back and forth, the waiting nearly unendurable. How she wished that she had never involved Lord Nhon in any of this. She sighed. It was too late now. She threw up her arms in resignation knowing that when her brother chose to communicate, he would; beyond that, there was little more that she could do. Clutching the amulet tightly, she closed her eyes, reciting the words deep within so she would not forget. Feeling the power surge through her, she smiled in the half light, the shadows cast by the cold flames set within the circle strangely comforting.

"Have a care, sister. Even you are unschooled in the power of that which you hold within your hands."

A-Sharoon whirled around, her eyes glittering. "Where have you been?"

"I have been doing what is necessary." The disembodied voice was all around her as she turned about, dark eyes searching for what was not there; her voice, when she spoke, dripped of sarcasm, the words bitter against her tongue.

"And did you accomplish anything?"

"Have a care, sister." The voice held an underlying menace to it. A-Sharoon started to say something then thought better of it, her concern now for herself.

"And?" The question was directed at the empty air that whirled around her, seeping through the fissures within the rock. She waited in the stifling silence for an answer.

"Enter into this only if you must sister, for it would be unseemly for those born to the darkness to battle another like yet unlike themselves. Let the one who walks between worlds do what he must; there will be other opportunities. If you must use the amulet, direct its powers to Lord Nhon." The voice lowered, and A-Sharoon stiffened as her brother used a tone she had not heard since she was a young child.

"Remember this: the one born of light who turned to the darkened places is no kin to you or me—let things go back as they were—" The words of farewell faded as A-Sharoon crossed the length of the cavern in long strides that carried her outside the caverns entrance, to gaze upward at the night sky.

The moon hung round and silvery white just behind the treetops that stood close together; entwined tightly against each other, their heavy limbs cast shadows against the rocks as the wind pressed against her. Looking to the east, the slight lightening of the sky promised morning wasn't far off. A-Sharoon moved back; pushed by the force of the wind she stood just within the cavern's entrance; her face deathly white; her long, slender fingers stroking the amulet clutched tightly to her breast. Only when the moon had crept further down, hidden from view by the great trees that guarded the entrance to the valley, and the rosy hues that signaled the days new dawning began to streak the eastern sky, did she retreat back to the confines of her dark cavern, her expression thoughtful.

It was there, in the darkest corner, an incantation was cast, and the grinding of stone upon stone reverberated in the hidden places below; the rumbling reaching upward into the open spaces where the clans of the forest—the four-legged and winged—walked.

§ § § § § §

Stretching upward, the little ground dweller scented the air, his long whiskers flicking back and forth as he turned slowly around. Dark eyes, wide with disbelief, scanned the valley below, seeking the source of the disturbance that had stirred him from sleep and sent him from his den; eyes that could peer into the darkest corners sought out the hidden places, and stopped where the entrance to A-Sharoon's cavern had been. A few more small rocks tumbled down, then silence. The entrance was completely hidden from prying eyes, the occupant within safe from any enemy who might seek to enter from above.

A few moments later, small feet beat out a rhythmic tattoo against the earth in the tunnel below until the sound was picked up, and passed on until it became the heartbeat that joined the below places to the above.

§ § § § § §

"What is it? What do you hear?" Gabriel, alerted by the low rumbling, had sought out Jerome. The big warrior knelt down; placing a hand upon the dry earth, he let the sensation pulse through him as he listened.

"A-Sharoon takes refuge within the living rock. There will be no interference from her. It is as we were told." Jerome rose slowly and turned to face the silver wolf, his voice resonating throughout the little clearing as he spoke. "The Daughter has no stomach for this fight. Although we must still be on our guard, our worries have just lessened a bit. The little ones will watch her. Their eyes and ears miss little."

"The dawn comes, little comfort to those who hide within their forest homes, thinking an army goes out this day," Gabriel mused thoughtfully as he looked to the eastern sky. The rosy hues were creeping upward; dawn mere moments away.

"To the sacred place, my friend." Jerome loomed above the silver wolf; his need to say more suddenly failed him as he looked into the blue eyes that, like his own, had seen so much in the turnings that had brought them here; to this place. He sighed deeply.

Gabriel nudged his stalwart friend gently. He and he alone knew of the secret things that burned within the forest warrior's breast; although they were not born of the same family, they were brothers nonetheless. It mattered not what was on the outside, for inside they were the same.

§ § § § § §

Nickolous stood just inside the entrance of the cavern; watching the sunrise; his emotions within as changing as the hues that surrounded the sun as it climbed higher, while the moon, paling, receded into the azure background.

"You're wondering if you'll see another dawning such as this…"

Nickolous looked down at the small form of the Old One. Reaching out he drew her to him; her presence had a calming effect that he welcomed, for their journey together had been fraught with danger and learning. He closed his eyes against the emotions that welled up within him. Knowing that he had to rely on his own abilities, what he had seen, what he had been taught, all would come to nothing if he did not focus.

"Jerome comes while the others prepare; as must we." Orith stood beside them, his staff held out in front of him.

The Old One nodded; her own staff now in full view as Nickolous acknowledged the pulsing of the silver armband. Although it remained covered, he had no doubt of its power.

"We are ready, then?" Jerome asked; pleased to see everyone prepared for the journey. His own duties called to him as he turned to one of his warriors, his head bent slightly as he spoke; the words inaudible to those watching. Nodding, the warrior called to the others as, one by one, they parted, each heading toward a predetermined destination.

Nickolous watched them go, his mind on his own duties, then he too turned aside to busy himself with what was necessary.

§ § § § §

"Why? Why do I have to stay behind?" Sarah stood facing Gabriel, her stance defiant.

"Little One, you will be safe here. We have much to do and others to watch over," Gabriel replied, his tone soothing as Sarah stood her ground while the others looked on, amused.

"Oh? And I suppose I can't do anything to help?" Sarah retorted, her voice betraying her anger as she looked at her brother for support. Timothy remained where he was, saying nothing; knowing it would be useless to argue with either Sarah or Gabriel.

The big wolf shook his head from side to side exasperated with the little female standing before him. "Sarah," he said, nudging her gently. She didn't budge, but remained where she was, glaring at him. "Orith and the Old One are in great danger, and Nickolous even more so. Your heart has great courage, and you have borne great responsibility, but you must understand—you cannot go—"

Sarah stared into Gabriel's eyes, her emotions evident to all who watched.

Nickolous encircled her shoulders and drew her close, for he had a great fondness for her. His own heart aching at the sight of the tears pooling within the liquid depths of her eyes, he turned her toward him and cupped her face gently as he whispered something in her ear that only she could hear.

Sarah tilted her head to one side, her expression thoughtful; then, sparing a glance at Gabriel, she nodded. "Very well, I won't argue anymore; I'll stay here and wait for your return."

"I'll remain also." As much as it pained him, Timothy felt obligated to stay in case Sarah needed him.

"No; you most certainly will not!"

Timothy drew back in surprise at Sarah's outburst, shocked that she would refuse his protection.

"It's all right, Timothy," she said as she hugged him to her fiercely; releasing him, she stood back. "You must go. They," she motioned to the others, "will need you."

"Sarah…" Timothy looked down at his sister, not knowing what to say. Deep down, he knew that she was right. He also knew that she would be safe, here, within the living rock that surrounded her. Once he and the rest of the companions were gone, there would be no need for any others to gain entrance; for it was, after all, a sacred place. He hugged her tightly—letting his breath out slowly, he turned, and without a backward glance, followed the others into the mornings light.

21

"Is all in readiness?" The form bent low over the strewn pieces of parchment that were spread haphazardly across the table. The candle with its spilled wax flickered erratically, yet this did not seem to bother the reader as he poured over the ancient incantations; his eyes seeing everything, yet his mind focusing on what needed to be done.

"Yes, my Lord." The creature bowed low before its master.

"Where are they?" The question, not unexpected, still caused the messenger to stiffen in anticipation of its Lord's displeasure, should the answer given not suit.

"They have left the sacred place, their footsteps covered by the warriors of the forest; their passage guarded from above by the winged one called Owen. The wolves go in front cutting a deadly path for those who seek to impede their journey to the place of the 'Three.'"

The silence grew as Lord Nhon studied the parchment laid out in front of him. The news the messenger brought was not unexpected. He rose slowly to his feet, aware the messenger watched him warily.

"Go. Wait outside with the others. We will attempt to intercept them at the place of the joining." Lord Nhon dismissed the messenger with a curt nod before returning to the table.

As the footsteps receded down the long passageway, he found the document he sought, and with a long drawn out sigh rolled it up; tying it with a piece of leather. Concealing it beneath his robe, he rose, his attention now riveted to the sealed passageway before him and what lay beyond it.

§ § § § § §

It was a hard thing to do, this thing of not moving—not thinking lest the thoughts be heard. To those who watched, there was nothing to indicate that the prisoner was poised to strike at its tormentors, the need for freedom nearly unbearable, the pain of confinement excruciating. Where once the fire flared there was nothing save the tiniest glow.

It was this sight that greeted Lord Nhon as he moved soundlessly into the room; his eyes narrowed into near nothingness as he gazed at the center of the room where the prisoner was.

"*No.*" Moving quickly to the inner door, Lord Nhon placed his hands against the transparent wall that guarded the prisoner—the heart within the Flame flickered slightly.

Waiting—

§ § § § § §

The little earth dweller moved swiftly; silently; pressing himself against crevice and jagged edge as he moved around the waiting sentinels that guarded the doorways from above to the places below. The need almost overwhelming as he, and those who followed, answered the Flame's call.

§ § § § § §

Lord Nhon listened to the drumming that told him the Flame continued its life cycle. Not daring to release the last barrier to get closer, he stood, watching; his concentration on listening. Frustrated that he could detect nothing, he backed slowly out, his eyes watchful as he picked up the fallen parchment; his gaze darting around the room, seeking out the hidden places. He felt them—the little ones. Yet he could not see them. The sudden howling startled him; its closeness alerting him to danger as he wheeled about, his hand pressing against a hidden lever as he hurried to intercept whatever it was that tore at his being. It was not a physical presence that reached out to touch him in the hidden places... No; this was an intrusion of something that he could not see and could not battle alone.

§ § § § § §

The little ground dweller let out a long sigh, unaware that it had been holding its breath. Long moments after Lord Nhon had left, it waited—waited in the silence that crept around it—waited as the shadows about it dispersed. Finally, timidly, it crept out; away from the walls dampness; away from the musty smell that spoke of untold turnings of darkness. It turned to look behind it at the others. They were there—hundreds of them. In the semidarkness they poured forth, their soft breathing filling the room with warmth as they gathered about the barrier.

All had answered the call of the Flame. All had risked much to be here. After a time, the first of them, the one who had been the first to heed the voice that flamed within the deepest heart, inched slowly forward until the first threshold had been passed to the inner circle.

A soft, high chattering filled the room. The Flame flickered and then sparked to life as the room brightened.

§ § § § §

"We cannot fight what we cannot see, my Lord." The sentinel stood, breathless, his sides heaving, before his master. Lord Nhon flung his cloak over one shoulder so that his staff was exposed. The wood shimmered with an unnatural sheen beneath his gnarled hands as he caressed its length; the wood smoothing beneath his touch as the tingling sensation traveled up the length of his arm.

"Come." He pulled the cloak about him, drawing the hood forward so that his entire face was covered. As he stepped outside into the early morning mist, he looked up at the brilliant hues that streaked across the horizon and bowed his head; while those closest to him heard an uttered oath that promised this would be the sun's last rising.

Keeping to the hidden places, they moved forward; careful not to stray too far into the morning's light, for they were lovers of the deep-est darkness, and they chaffed beneath the warmth of the rising sun. The stench of unwashed bodies permeated the air, leaving behind the scent of death in its wake. The howling that had drawn Lord Nhon forth from the cavern's depths receded into the distance. Its soulless echo imbedded itself into the essence of those living creatures that pursued it.

§ § § § §

"Chera; behind you!" Gabriel's shouted warning was appreciated, but not needed as Chera wove in and out of the dense foliage. Those few who hid themselves within the forest's emerald walls could not evade the wolves' sense of knowing for long.

Cutting off the creature's snarled hiss of rage, Chera tossed it aside; her senses already telling her where the next intruder hid. Gabriel cut a wide swath of destruction as he swept to the sides of the tree-rimmed path, Liege following in his wake as the three of them took a heavy toll on Lord Nhon's scouts. Behind them, the others followed.

The Old One, Orith, and Nickolous were so cocooned within the circle that wound its way to the sacred place that they walked unafraid; trusting in the warrior's ability to keep them safe.

Jerome walked ahead, his warriors bringing up the rear—so many, yet so few—the big warrior smiled to himself. Their numbers might be small in comparison to the dark race that dwelled below, but there was no lack of courage amongst them. He swung his club; the whistling sound carrying through the air to warn others following; those ones who remained unseen, sheltered by the hidden places, that warriors of heart walked the path to their destiny.

"Jerome." Nickolous whispered into the stillness.

The warrior was there in an instant, bending down to gaze at the changing hues within the carved metal.

"It shows the way to The Three. There; past the stand of oak trees, there is a valley we must cross where nothing grows and none of the clans dare enter. It is a place of nothingness. Not even my people go there." Jerome frowned as he spoke. "It has always been barren for as long as I have had a remembering and those I have known that have passed before me. Our abilities to sense those who walk the '*beneath*' are as nothing in this place of deadness we go to!"

"Still, we will go." Nickolous looked straight ahead, appearing more confident than he felt. Somehow, they would pass safely through this place of bleakness. Of one thing he was certain: there would be watchers guarding the passageway through to the other side.

§ § § § §

"They come, my Lord, and there are others; dark ones from the lower realms; their stench of evil precedes them."

The form remained slouched, the hood placed so far forward that the face was invisible. They were in the clearing. The Old One, ancient beyond remembering, and the other, young, untried.

One was the student, the other the teacher.

"None has dared to cross the valley since the beginning of the time of remembering." The voice was neither young nor old. The speaker could have been male or female. The head stayed bowed as slender hands dug deeply into the earth.

"What say the others, those of the earth; the little ones; and the warriors, the winged ones, who wait in the high places?"

The young one, thoughtful, paused for a few moments, thinking, choosing the words carefully so that nothing would be lost in the words about to be spoken.

"All say to allow them entrance..." He paused for a moment; letting the silence settle between them. Leaning forward, he stretched out a thin hand to touch the master then, straightening up, he looked around, taking in the view that others saw with their mortal eyes; their mortal hearts.

"What else do they say?" The master turned ageless eyes upward to the red-tailed hawk that watched them from its perch atop the ancient oak tree.

"Well?"

He waited while the hawk bobbed up and down upon the branch, the high-pitched *screeee-screee* echoing over the green valley; for that is what it was, an ancient place of wonder to those, who, like the master and the student, could see. To others, who the seasons aged and time withered beyond recognition, there was only the tinder-dry brown earth. Nothing moved; nothing grew; and to their eye, it was a vast expanse of death and mystery and so they had kept away these many turnings—

Until now.

The student followed his gaze; his appreciation of what they were seeing no less so than the teacher who had taught him so much. For a time he had left—the master—to walk upon the vast expanse of earth where the clans of the two legged lived; to seek out the one who walked between worlds; the one who one day would take the master's place. He closed his eyes against the vision of there ever being another other than the one before him. Then, remembering himself, he answered:

"They say that there shall be one amongst those who come who will see what others do not. And if he is the first and passes the test, then he, and those with him, shall go in safety."

"And those who follow?"

"Will find no welcome."

"So be it. Let us prepare. For a time, the ancient laws will be forgotten." Bowing his head, the elder began to speak in the language of the sky people as the hawk listened, its eyes bright and alert with understanding. Then, opening its wings, it took flight; its own cry echoing, mingling with the cries of countless others of its kind.

"We are close." Jerome stood next to Gabriel; the two looking down upon the distant valley. To their eye, it was a vast expanse of brown grass and boggy places—that and nothing more. Timothy stood behind them, his sword grasped tightly to his side as he looked upon what lie below them; he too, saw what the others saw and wondered how they could cross such an open space where they could be seen; yet at the same time be unprotected. For even with the forest warriors to shield them, they would still be vulnerable without the forest to further cloak their presence.

"Things are not always what they seem." The Old One stood close to Nickolous, looking up at him; her eyes bright with understanding. They had paused for a moment while Jerome was talking to Gabriel. Orith had taken the opportunity to rest a little apart from the others; while Chera lingered close by, alert for anything untoward that might threaten.

Nickolous knelt before the Old One, his gaze resting on hers. "Old One," he spoke the words softly, his arm going about her to offer support as she leaned against him; one paw clutching her staff, the other patting Nickolous gently as he looked at her, his blue eyes questioning.

"Remember, things are as we perceive them, each thing being different to the one who observes from a different place." She placed his hand to her heart; her eyes speaking for her as she tried to convey something to him without words.

Nickolous patted her gently, his touch letting her know he understood what she was trying to tell him. Then, turning, he left to walk ahead to the rolling rise where Jerome and Gabriel stood, waiting.

Jerome turned at the soft sound of approaching footsteps; even though he knew it was Nickolous, he stood, watching, wondering within himself at the change in him. Gone was the boy; before them stood a man. Untried, true, but a young man, soon to be a warrior, the likes of which had not been seen since the warriors of Skye had departed to their high places, the guardians of those who dwelt in the lower places. Exchanging glances with Gabriel, he moved to let him stand between them.

"There, beyond the barren plain, the three sleeping warriors that guard the gate wait." The big warrior pointed to a distant rise.

Nickolous shielded his eyes against the suns glare as he peered down the deep incline that led into the valley. "We will have safe passage through the valley to the other side. The forest walls are deep and thick, they will hide us from the prying eyes of those who follow."

Jerome turned; startled at the words. Casting a glance toward the big wolf that stood on the other side of Nickolous, he looked once again across the desolate plain, searching for what Nickolous saw.

Finally, seeing nothing but a barren place of deadness, he turned back toward the Old One, his gaze questioning. Black eyes peered up at him with a knowing in their depths that startled him.

Turning back to Nickolous, he couldn't help the feeling that fluttered deep within his chest. A distant remembering, long forgotten, struggled to rise—to surface within reach of his ability to know—

"Jerome, use your warrior's heart to see!" Nickolous reached out to grasp his friend's arm, his touch burning as Jerome pulled back, startled at the sensations that coursed through him. Beside them, Gabriel growled, the sound low and rumbling deep within his chest as he sensed what the warrior felt, his own primordial instincts coming to the fore as he glimpsed a vision draped within the misty places where it had all began; then, just as quickly vanished. He shook his head.

"I do not know what it is you see, but I will trust your judgment," Jerome said, not quite believing the words were coming from his mouth, yet nonetheless finding himself following Nickolous.

"What is it that he sees?" Orith asked as he fell into step beside the Old One, his gaze questioning as he stepped carefully over fallen limbs that blocked their path.

"It is a knowing from the Old Ones. Discernment that few have, yet even fewer know how to use. He has it. He knows how to use it. We, on the other hand, can only glimpse a little, yet he sees the whole." The Old One wheezed heavily from the exertion as she accepted Orith's help to climb over the debris. Saying no more, they walked quietly side by side, for the way before them was clear.

Orith nodded—as many turnings as he had, and still he must learn!"

§ § § § §

"Well? What do you see?" Jerome looked down at Nickolous from his great height; his brows furrowed together, waiting.

"I see a forest full of life. I see a place that has been here since the beginning," Nickolous replied, his tone succinct.

They were standing in front of a wide expanse of dry grass and boggy places, and as hard as Jerome looked, that's all he could see.

§ § § § §

Nickolous stood just within the forest's edge; his breath catching within his throat as he looked around him. Beckoning the others to follow, he didn't bother to look back, the need to go into this haunting place of beauty something that drove him forward, unafraid, knowing that there was nothing here to harm him or the others.

§§§§§§

"He sees with eyes of knowing."

"They shall pass through protected; let none molest. Close the gates behind them. Any who follow will be stopped."

"But my Lord—"

The robed figure glanced up, his eyes fathomless. "Through countless turnings we have not interfered; we have obeyed the ancient laws set out from the beginning. Even now as we speak, a terrible darkness threatens the clans of the forest, while the Daughter to the Night covers herself within the earth, away from what she has unknowingly unleashed." The elder's voice shook slightly as he continued, his voice betraying the emotions that coursed through him.

"Our own warriors wait in the hidden places; the ability to walk upon the land a forgotten thing, while behind our doors we keep time as it once was; before the greed and deceit that plagues those who have the knowledge to grow festered like an uncontrollable sore. Now, it is time we help those who see these things for what they are; who want to change their destiny." The elder rose from his kneeling position; looking down at the other, he spoke more softly, the tone in his voice broking no argument.

"They shall pass in safety." The elder turned aside; his voice rising to a high-pitched cry that was immediately answered.

The great golden Eagle, talons extended, landed gently upon the outstretched arm. Bobbing its head, it looked into its holder's eyes, a feeling, a thought, passing between the two as the forest itself listened, the slight trembling of the Eagle's body the only indication that the message had been heard.

The Eagle turned its head slightly, his gaze focusing on the eastern ridge that jutted straight upward past their valley; a place where none had entered without impunity…

Until now.

"That's it, old friend. *Go.* Tell the guardians of Skye that those who come are to be protected; also, tell those who dwell within the earth that those who follow will not pass through. Nor will they return the way they came."

The Eagle bounced slightly on the outstretched arm. His gaze questioning; the need to be sure of the elder's commands beyond all certainty, something that had to be confirmed.

Dark eyes that had seen the world from its beginning bored into the other's; the color of spun gold. Then, the Eagle soared high, his high keening cry echoing, reverberating throughout the unseen forest that had from the beginning remained silent, invisible to the prying eyes of other realms until now.

§ § § § §

"Nickolous. Wait."

Gabriel pulled ahead of the others, his concern for his young charge evident while Orith and the Old One followed behind flanked on either side by Chera and Liege. Strangely enough, the wolves, although uneasy, felt no sense of danger when normally they would have. Jerome walked behind them; his warriors to the back of him, wary and alert, his war club thronged loosely at his side within easy reach as Owen soared above them, gliding sideways, the winds current warm and soothing to his senses. The warrior closed his eyes against the sensation of warmth and when he opened them, he was in the middle of an emerald green forest.

Orith blinked, his eyes adjusting to the sudden shade, his body to the coolness that surrounded them. To their left a stream ran, trickling over rocks and fallen logs; the moss growing beneath the surface a rich, dark green, the pungent smell of flowers was everywhere.

The Old One inhaled deeply; remembering. Not since her youth had she seen such a forest! Looking about, she absorbed the scents and sounds, not bothering to wonder how all this came to suddenly be—just accepting that it was.

Nickolous was slightly ahead of the others, his long strides taking him quickly and deeply into the center of the forest; even so, when the figure stepped out of the forests shadow, he was not surprised. He stood, waiting for the others; he could hear their footsteps, quickening their pace, as they hurried to catch up.

"Welcome."

Jerome and the others paused; the figure that approached was familiar and, as he slowly drew his hood back, was recognized. Timothy wished that Sarah were here; she had often wondered who the visitor to the cavern had been.

Owen landed soundlessly; folding his wings tightly to his side; acknowledging the robed figure, he bowed his head slightly. He knew who stood before him; but was amazed that this place was home to such a being. He turned to gaze at Orith and the Old One.

Truly, things were not as they seemed.

§ § § § § §

"I can offer safe passage through the valley but not beyond." The elder, hands locked behind his back, walked beside Jerome, the two of them following Nickolous while the others followed behind; the Old One and Orith accepting this as just one more thing that was to be. Timothy, more cautious, stayed farther back, not quite ready to trust completely, his sword gripped tightly beneath his cloak.

"—and for that we shall be grateful," Jerome replied as he glanced toward Nickolous, ever watchful. His companion, noting this, nodded.

"Do not worry for your young friend; he is safe here, guarded by those watchers whom even your eyes cannot see." The elder paused before continuing, his voice lowered so that only the warrior of the forest could hear the words which were spoken. "Be at ease; there will be none to follow through this valley. None." He turned toward Jerome, his gaze searching...

Jerome nodded. He understood.

§ § § § § §

Standing upright, the creature stood; nostrils flared, scenting the wind. Seeking out the hidden smells; listening intently for even the slightest of sounds that would betray its intended prey.

There were none.

Cautiously the sentry stepped forward onto the barren plain, the hair along the nape of its neck rising with each step it took; the impending sense of doom growing; yet, driven by the need to obey its master, it motioned the others, those hidden within the long grasses, onward.

The Eagle glided silently upon the wind's currents, his amber eyes narrowing as he watched the intruders pass into the heart of a place they could not see—into the circle of waiting warriors. Then, as the sounds of battle erupted, he veered eastward, toward the gate and those who guarded its secrets.

§ § § § § §

"Hold! Your weapon is powerless, as are you!"

Jerome stared down at nerveless fingers. His club lay on the grass where it had fallen. The high keening cries had trailed off to a soft sighing, then, nothing.

"*There will be none to follow...*" The words were carried upon the wind that blew around them, falling off into the silence as the companions remained where they were, temporarily frozen in place.

Jerome bent to pick up the war club, but the tingling sensation remained, slowly lessening as moments passed. Trusting his instincts, he looped the war club at his side and walked with the elder as Nickolous paused at the top of a grassy knoll, his attention on the great Eagle who sat perched above him, its snow-white head turning from side to side as if studying him.

"See? He has the memories of the Old Ones. Buried deep within him they may be; but they are there. Waiting." The elder from the hidden place turned to Jerome. "He has to but draw them from within himself..."

"A terrible burden for one so young," Jerome sighed as he turned away from the sight of the great bird with its head bowed, communicating with Nickolous in the manner of the Ancients. His heart welled with pride at Nickolous's willingness to listen; to learn; there was no question in his mind as to who was the true warrior of heart.

"Do you see beyond our journey, Elder?" Jerome asked as he turned his attention back to the path in front of him.

"My friend, there is no answer for that; for the balance of all things lies not with one being. There is always a combination of events that lead up to the final result."

Jerome shook his head, acknowledging what he already knew. There was no way to know how this day would end or what tomorrow would bring. He sighed wearily.

"This is where the path ends; it is not safe for me to travel beyond the boundary now, for it is being watched too closely."

Jerome blinked in the bright light. They were standing at the edge of a heavily overgrown path, littered with debris from countless turnings of the seasons.

"There, beyond this grove, lies the path to the *Three*. Watch carefully the way the light falls in this place, for it will show the way." The elder saluted the forest warrior, then, turning, approached Nickolous.

Head bowed, Nickolous listened to the words being spoken, and when the white staff was thrust toward him, took it, ignoring the tingling as bracelet and staff recognized their own.

"The Staff! Do you see what the elder has gifted him with?" Orith was incredulous as he helped the Old One to step over the fallen log; covered in moss, it was half rotted. Grabbing Orith, she leaned against him for support; breathless, she could only nod; even she had not expected such generosity. She turned, her dark eyes moist with emotion, and gently patted her companions shoulder.

"The sacred staff is powerful, but he has to listen—to learn—to hear it when it speaks. Let us hope that when the time comes, he will know what is necessary." She bowed her head, hoping. That was all she could do.

Jerome stood looking down at the debris strewn along the path. It was obvious it had not been used for many turnings; either that, or those who had walked in this place had chosen their footsteps carefully, lest the dark ones follow.

Turning around to bid a final farewell to the elder from the hidden place, Jerome was not surprised to see that the valley had returned to its former state, and where the elder had stood, there was nothing but a large gray rock beneath a shrub tree that was curled and twisted with age. The Eagle perched on the top branch looking down at the little group, turning its head from side to side, listening, the only sound the soft sighing of the wind as it blew gently through the trees.

Nickolous turned; the staff held before him. Raising his hand in a partial salute, he watched as the great bird took flight, before moving to where Jerome waited.

"Guard the staff as you would your life, my young friend." Jerome lifted a low-hanging branch out of his way, careful not to break it. He wanted nothing to mark their passage to the sacred place. Nickolous nodded as he tucked the staff inside his coat, partially concealing it as he walked beside Jerome, unafraid; while Owen soared high above them, his eyes searching.

§ § § § §

A-Sharoon waited in the stillness as the water pooled about her feet. The amulet was clutched tightly in one hand as the other hand held her woolen cloak to her. It was cold here—even for her. She squinted in the half light, her eyes adjusting to the gloom that swirled about her. Wishing she knew more about what was going on outside her self-made prison, she bowed her head and focusing deep within herself, found that secret place where the knowing was. She drew in a deep ragged breath as she felt the Flame's presence, pushing upon her senses. It called out. She sighed, wishing; then just as quickly pushed it back, her senses overwhelming her as the heart of the Flame called out once more.

No—she would not—could not—she turned in the darkness, stumbling against the jagged rocks; trying to shut out the remembering as she fell; the smell of earth and mold clogged her nostrils as she struggled to rise. Muttering beneath her breath, she lit a candle, the flame flickering as it struggled to burn; the cavern so tightly sealed that there was barely enough air to keep it from dying. Summoning her strength, she pushed against the lever imbedded into the slime-covered rock; cursing her brother for abandoning her to this terrible solitude, with not even her followers to keep her company.

Angrily, A-Sharoon pushed the lever up and out while uttering the incantation that only those closest to the earth heard. The earth trembled as the rocks around her cried out their protest while the earth heaved beneath her feet.

Rising, blinded by the sunlight that streamed through splayed fingers pressed against her face, A-Sharoon swayed then, catching herself, swung around. Ever mindful of the fact that Lord Nhon was still searching for her, she sought refuge in the darkened places, deep within the forest, hardly daring to pause even as she drew in deeply of the fresh air—a welcoming change from the foulness she had breathed in the closed chambers that now lay in ruins below her.

She had made her decision.

The amulet. It had been passed down through the darkness of eternal memory to those who guarded its secrets. A woman's weapon, its use was forbidden by all others except a Daughter of the Night.

A-Sharoon was next in line.

§ § § § §

The little earth dweller moved slowly, careful to avoid anything that would alert the woman to its proximity; its duty—to watch and see if the earth kept its secrets. Not knowing why the Daughter would have emerged from her hidden lair after so short a stay it drew further back, into the dense foliage and when A-Sharoon had disappeared into the dense underbrush, it knew she was returning to her lair.

§ § § § §

"Wait." Jerome stood still—listening. Tilting his head to one side, he centered himself; the soft, almost inaudible sounds were coming from beneath his feet.

"She returns."

"We need not fear her in this battle."

"The Other?"

"The *Other* spoke the truth. The Flame calls to her in its distress. She will not see it extinguished. I think," Nickolous said, turning to face Jerome, "that even she, with her dark heart, sees the truth in the

Flame's freedom, for with its freedom she gains her own." He stayed where he was, looking up at Jerome, a peculiar look on his face.

"*She regrets!*"

"What?" Jerome snorted, the sound loud in the silence, hardly believing his ears. "She is of the darkness. Born to it. How can she regret?"

"You cannot have the light without the dark. Even you and I have a dark side. We all do. The difference is that we control it. For some reason, I think that even she realizes what she has unleashed and wishes to have things back as they were. Perhaps the Flame has touched a part of her that is unknown to our way of understanding."

"Whatever happens, there will be no truce between us. When this is over—if we still stand—we will still be enemies."

"So, we exchange the greater for the lesser." Coughing into a ragged piece of leather, the Old One stood there, looking at them both. "Now," she commented dryly, "is not the time to stand there wondering at A-Sharoon's motives. Whatever help we have, take it with the knowledge that all things return to their proper place. Lord Nhon was unforeseen. He could destroy time as we know it. A-Sharoon now realizes this. The Flame always knew this. Now, are we going to finish our journey or not?" She sighed wearily. Muttering beneath her breath, the Old One turned from them and returned to where Orith waited.

Nickolous watched her go, his expression one of amusement. "Well, on that note, we had better continue on."

§ § § § §

Gabriel leapt ahead of Chera; veering sharply to the left, he plunged into the dense underbrush. A strangled cry was heard, then silence. Behind him, he knew the others followed. Jerome's warriors were spread out, creating an outer circle to protect those on the inside, while his duty was to find the stragglers that evaded their grasp. Hearing a noise he looked up, Liege stood there, his breathing ragged. The big wolf had been sent ahead to scout. Gabriel growled, the sound low; inquiring.

"The warriors are there. Just as the legend foretells; they sleep."

Gabriel let his breath out slowly. They were so close... He turned his head as a new sound assailed him and then relaxed as Owen flew low, his wings brushing against the treetops, while above him, Gabriel focused on something unexpected but welcomed. The great Eagle soared high above them on the warm air currents, expending little energy as it saw what they could not with its keen eyesight. The wolves relaxed, knowing for whom the great bird watched.

"It would seem that we pick up reinforcements as we go," Liege commented as he fell into step beside Gabriel.

"Perhaps," Gabriel replied thoughtfully as Chera caught up to them. She, too, had seen the great bird of prey and was visibly relieved at its presence but, like her mate, was wary.

"See. There. The great bird watches." The Old One stepped carefully around a fallen limb, at the same time absorbing the power that the forest offered. Drawing in deeply of the scents that assailed her, she turned dark eyes on the two who walked ahead.

"While we may gather others about us, do not be deceived, old friend, as to their intent."

"Yes, yes, I know," Orith replied, his tone thoughtful as he reached out to push a low hanging branch out of the way.

"The Three Fallen Ones, were they once like you?" Nickolous asked, his fingers stroking the length of the white staff idly, wondering at the way his fingers fit into the grooves as if it had been made for him. Jerome, noting this, didn't answer right away. Instead, he continued on, his concentration on the path before him. It was some moments before he spoke, and when he did, his words were measured, the tone low, words spoken from a memory of a childhood telling.

"It is said that *The Three* were ancient warriors sent by the watchers of Skye—like us in form, but there the resemblance ended. Powerful shamans, mystic warriors, their knowledge combined out of a thousand beginnings and endings. They guarded the entrance to the eastern gate so that none could enter or leave. No one knows what happened, for it has been lost to mortal memory, but they finished their time here, and the forest clans buried them facing the entrance. Since that time, I and others of my kind have tried to live by the ancient code as we believe The Three would have it."

"If they guard the gate, then how are we to get in?" Nickolous asked, and then regretted the asking as the familiar tingling began. Even as Jerome answered, he knew the truth—what he held in his hand, and wore on his arm was part of the answer; part of the key that would get them in.

He bowed his head, wondering how he was going to do this, and hoping he would not have to do it alone. Inwardly he drew on the vision granted to him by the *Seven* when he had entered the dreaming circle.

§ § § § § §

The mist had came; rising, swirling about them as they had picked their way carefully through the forest; the trail had tapered off and the going was much more difficult as Chera and Gabriel, joined by Liege, scented the air warily. The fog had come out of nowhere, and there was the feel of the unknown hanging heavy in the dampened air. Without a sound, they began the short journey back to meet the others.

Jerome shouldn't have been surprised, but he was. Too surprised for words; he looked from Orith, to the Old One, then back again. Behind them, his warriors waited, just out of view while before him, Nickolous stood, amazed at what he had done. He had only thought about it, and it was there. Yet it was more than a thought. It was a need to protect those he held close to him, for he sensed an ill wind rising, and it was close.

Jerome saw what Nickolous saw, and then it was a blur of translucent form and a smothering darkness that was impossible to fight physically, for it had no tangible form at which to strike out.

"Where did that come from?" Nickolous asked as he ducked low, the tendrils trailing behind the creature nearly touching him.

"Lord Nhon, no doubt," Jerome muttered as the wolves rushed in; Gabriel standing shoulder to shoulder with Chera as Liege pushed to the rear. The blanket of fog grew thicker; wrapping itself about them; unearthly shrieks filling the air as something unseen passed overhead, its frustration evident. The shrill *screeee-screeee* of the Eagle blending with the war cry that was Owens's was still ringing in the companions' ears, even as the fog tightened its grasp about them.

The Old One nudged Orith. "The staff of Knowing; it breathes with its holder."

Orith looked up, as did all who were gathered about. The staff had taken on the same translucency as the bracelet; the air charged with energy as Nickolous held the staff aloft, the white mist swirling about it—or from it—no one was quite sure.

"Hurry. The shadow being cannot be held off for long." Nickolous turned to Gabriel. "How far to The Three?"

"Not far, and we are under the forest's cover most of the way." The big wolf tilted his head to one side, listening to the fury that raged above them. He wasn't sure, but he thought that there was something else—something other than the faceless being drawing near. He growled, the sound low and menacing.

"What is it, Gabriel, what's out there?" Chera nudged him gently.

Gabriel drew in deep breaths of air even as the tendrils of white mist began their slow downward descent to curl about him. The scent was hauntingly familiar; still, he turned to Chera, his look questioning. Silently she turned, disappearing into the mist, which by now was so thick the companions could easily lose sight of one another.

"Hurry!" Nickolous's voice rose above the rest. The urgency unmistakable now, Jerome whistled, the pitch so high it was barely audible to all but those with the keenest hearing. He turned toward Nickolous.

"Where? Which way?"

Nickolous paused; concentrating. The staff was pulling him, tugging at him from somewhere deep within.

"Follow." The words were whispered; barely heard, but the meaning clear as he strode swiftly away, into the deepest depths of the ancient forest. Without question, the others followed.

Only Gabriel held back; the need to protect a strong instinct which tore at him as he watched the others disappear beneath the protective canopy of trees. Above him, the beast raged as tendrils reached out, searching, grasping nothing but empty air. He ducked low as the creature searched about, once coming so close that he could have touched him. Gabriel shrunk back from the intrusion, instinctively knowing that to suffer this creature's touch would be disastrous.

The shrieking had faded, yet the mist remained. Gabriel crouched low, waiting. Someone was out there, waiting; watching. The fur prickled along his spine, washing over him in waves as the feeling grew. Somewhere ahead of him there was a soft shuffling as something inched slowly toward him. Peering through the whiteness that now reached the ground, he saw Chera creeping toward him, her silvery-gray eyes speaking for her. Waiting 'til they were nearly touching, Gabriel remained silent.

"There. Something walks in the light which once was confined to the darkened places," Chera whispered, nudging him.

Gabriel looked at her, puzzled, then as realization dawned, shook his head in disbelief.

"Come." He turned to her, the urge to catch up to Nickolous and the others now overwhelming.

§ § § § §

Black eyes followed them as they disappeared into the dense underbrush. Then, stepping out, the figure peered upward, concentrating.

The shadow creature swung around. Something was calling to him, something dangerous. Whirling about, it began a slow spiraling downward descent.

Looking up, A-Sharoon watched calmly as the tendrils reached out for her and embraced her. Even as she welcomed the embrace, words spilled forth from bloodless lips, and the air was filled with unspeakable things.

§ § § § § §

Nickolous kept moving, driven onward by something he could not control. When at last they stopped, they found themselves at the edge of the forest. Blinking in the bright light, Nickolous saw that the staff was no longer translucent; the mist no longer swirling about them. Concerned for the others, he turned; relieved that the Old One and Orith seemed to be all right, albeit exhausted from their hurried journey.

"There." He pointed to a sheltered place ahead of them. Wordlessly, the others followed his pointing finger.

The Old One squinted, her gaze focused. She knew without being told where they were. Ahead of her were the remnants of the three ancient warriors of a race lost to remembering. Long ago turned to stone, resting where they had fallen, their tomb the ground upon which they lay. Filled with unexpected emotion, she brushed at the wetness that rested upon her face as Orith hugged her reassuringly.

"Well, old friend, we have come full circle. Of all our paths we could have chosen, this one is the one that will see us to our destiny." The Old One remained silent, taking in the spectacular scene before them.

Orith nodded; too lost for words; too awed by the legend that had become reality. He looked around him.

At the others.

At the resting warriors.

He turned, his gaze locked on that of Nickolous, who had removed the book he had gifted him with from its tattered covering. He watched as the pages, once undecipherable, appeared to be covered in words of understanding. He moved closer as Nickolous sat down, the staff that had once belonged to one of the Ancient ones now his. Wordlessly, he turned the book toward Orith, the passage clearly written.

One by one the others came to gaze upon the pages filled with words that were suddenly understood; while above them, the great

Eagle soared, its keen eyesight missing little. Turning its golden head from side to side, it gave one last cry, the keening sound carrying to those below it. Nickolous turned his head to look up as the bird swept sideways, drifting on the warm air currents that carried it back toward the hidden valley.

"He leaves to go back to his valley." Jerome shielded his eyes against the bright light. Chera and Gabriel stood beside him, watching as the Eagle fell out of sight, below the treetops. Gabriel shook himself. The Eagle had called to him. Spoken to him. Chera nudged him, her body language telling him he wasn't alone.

The wind blew soft and warm against their faces, while the pages seemed to turn of their own accord. Nickolous put out a hand to still their movement, his eyes widening at the place where they had stopped. Bending his head, he studied the words beneath the pictures.

At the Old One's gentle touch, he looked up; her black eyes shone with affection as she patted him gently; her thoughts reaching him in the ancient way of the elders. "We have come full circle, you and I. Soon, it will be time for the fledgling to fly."

"Old One, I am not ready."

"Orith and I will guide you in, but the rest of the journey is for those who are warriors of heart."

"And I am?" Nickolous looked at the Old One beseechingly, feeling as though he were sinking into an abyss of dark despair.

"Look inside, to that place where we all go." The voice was soothing, and Nickolous relaxed for a moment, his thoughts turning inward, taking him to the place of the warriors—the dreaming place. His eyes widened in surprise at what he saw.

The Old One smiled.

Wisdom had many faces.

Nickolous let his breath out slowly, relieved. He understood now. Everything revolved in a circle, ever changing; the evolution of things yet to be still evolving even as he thought about it. He smiled at the Old One as she struggled to rise. Then the others, Jerome, Chera, and Gabriel, crowded around them, their concern evident for the Old One who rose stiffly, refusing any help as she straightened her aching body, her staff aiding her.

Orith stood a little apart, waiting patiently. Soon they would face someone worse than the Daughter of the Dark Lord. Soon their numbers would dwindle, for they could not expect to come through this unscathed. He drew himself up, the motion painful as he straightened his aching body. The breeze that blew around him carried the scent of something putrid upon its back. Jerome saw him coming and moved aside so that he could draw closer to the Old One.

"Well?" The forest warrior looked down at Orith questioningly. Orith merely nodded his head, an affirmation that didn't need to be spoken of aloud.

"The dark one races to his destruction..."

Nickolous stood holding the book aloft; its pages turning, flipping against the breeze that enveloped it, while he changed before them. His knowledge and understanding of the things he had seen, the remembering of the before times that abide within all living things reaching out, and up, to seek a new remembering.

Everyone stared in awe and admiration as the wind changed direction; coming out of the east, swirling about them to encase them within its safe embrace. Meanwhile the Ancient Ones, those who had gone before them, watched from their sacred place; as Nickolous, born of two worlds, one of man, the other, the whisperings of legends and dreams; the place where the imaginings of their minds kept them sane or not; accepted himself for who he was.

Taking his place among the watchers, one day to join them in their high place.

But not today.

Nickolous lowered the book. Slowly, carefully, he turned around, the staff held tightly within his grasp. Now his own, made for him at the beginning; it had waited for him; kept carefully by those who had seen. Who had known this day would come.

Nodding to Jerome, Nickolous waited while the big warrior called everyone to him. When all the warriors were in place, creating a semicircle so that the three were within that circle, they closed ranks.

Nickolous looked about him—at the solid mass of warriors— seemingly now ancient oak trees that surrounded him. Knowing that Lord Nhon would soon be upon them, he turned to the others. Bending down, he grasped the Old One in a tight embrace, then, nodding to Jerome, watched as the warrior effortlessly pushed aside some boulders, revealing a hidden place big enough that whatever was placed there would be safe. Intent now, he gently picked the Old One up, placing her inside the hidden place. He waited while Orith followed. Although Orith was not feeling the passage of time like his companion that went before him, the scarring to his body had taken its toll. Looking up, he nodded as Owen swept down, the rush of his wings whispering as they folded inward against his body.

"Keep safe, my brother." Orith looked away, so filled with emotion that he could say nothing more.

Owen could only nod as the boulders were placed back upon themselves, carefully, so that the Old One and Orith would be safe.

"*We will be back...*" The words were whispered against the cold, gray stones.

22

"The power of the three must be combined!" Lord Moshat paced back and forth; agitated, he whirled around, grabbing his cloak.

"My Lord. You cannot mean to go back. Things must unfold in the way they were meant to. We have already broken our own laws repeatedly to help those of the forest clans. The boy must find the way."

"Do not quote what is written within the ancient runes to me!" Lord Moshat turned angrily toward the speaker. "It was I who wrote them; I and the others who have gone before me."

The messenger looked down at the floor, ashamed he had been disrespectful to the elder. When next he looked up, he was alone.

§ § § § §

Clouds frosted at the outer edges with silver skirted overhead as the Eagle balanced itself on the dry limb of the dead tree. Turning its head from side to side, it watched the figure below as it moved stealthily along the hidden path, stopping every so often to listen. Launching itself into the air, the Eagle soared high, disappearing into the canopy of clouds that hid it from view.

Lord Nhon looked up as the Eagle soared out of sight. Shrugging his shoulders, he continued on, his confidence growing. He had not wanted to intercept them in the cavern, for there was ancient magic there. There was bound to be an awakening if the peace within the earth was disturbed. No, it was better this way, and if the *shadow being* had done his job...

Lord Nhon stopped as the distant cry, familiar and tugging, reached him. Beneath his hood, red eyes flashed, and as the cries died, choked off and stifled, a hand raised, clenched, as words known only to a few spewed forth from lips taut with rage.

§ § § § § §

Hurrying, A-Sharoon slipped into the shadowed corridor that ran the length of the canyon. She could feel Lord Nhon's presence and knew that, if he could, he would reach out to try to destroy her where she stood. She drew in deeply of the damp air as she slid the lever that pushed the heavy rock back into place. There were many such places as these.

She smiled to herself in the half light.

Search as he might, the Fallen One would be hard pressed to find them all.

§ § § § § §

Nickolous knew that Orith and the Old One would be safe, but still he hesitated. Jerome, seeing the flicker of indecision upon his face, spoke his thoughts aloud.

"They are as safe in there as anywhere. When the time comes, things will unfold as they must."

Nickolous stared straight ahead, his thoughts on what the warrior was saying. It was hard to leave them here, unprotected; while they waited for a battle that could sway either way.

"The Ancient's protect their own. Nickolous, you know that." Jerome knelt down while, around him, the warriors of the forest tightened the circle.

Nickolous looked up at Jerome, at the wolves, then past them to where the warriors were. He saw beyond them, into the wooded places. He saw A-Sharoon, shadowed within her place of concealment, saw Lord Nhon, the Fallen One. He *saw*. Back to the beginning; before greed had darkened the Fallen One's heart and poisoned his soul. He saw the Flame in its place of concealment.

He saw what the Eagle saw, he knew where the Fallen was, and he knew that he would be prepared for him.

"We must get inside; Lord Nhon comes."

"But how…" Gabriel stood looking perplexed, for before them stretched a solid wall of rock, certainly nothing to indicate an opening.

"The entrance lies not within your sight, but beneath."

Jerome drew his eyebrows together in a frown. "But The Three—"

"Point the way." Nickolous finished; turning, he removed the bracelet to gaze intently within its depths. Within the intricate carvings, there was a map. He turned to the others.

"See." He pointed upward, shading his eyes against the sun's glare.

Following his pointing finger, Jerome saw it first. As the sun had risen with the days new dawning, the warriors' shadows had crept slowly toward one another; now they were almost touching, and in a few more moments...

Jerome drew in his breath sharply. The others saw it, too. In the same instant. In the same heartbeat.

Gabriel and Chera growled softly, their keen hearing picking up the sound of something approaching. A little beyond them the warriors of the forest tightened their circle, the movement so subtle it was noticed only by a few. Jerome exhaled slowly. Lord Nhon would have to get through his warriors first, and that would give them enough time to gain entrance to the caverns that lay below their feet. His senses told him that Lord Nhon had little desire to fight them in the sacred cavern.

Nickolous looked up, then down. The shadows, carried by the morning's sun, were merging; meeting in the place where the entrance lay buried.

"How do we gain entrance?" Jerome knelt down, running a gnarled hand over the earth. At first he could feel nothing except the dirt, then, digging a little deeper, he felt the stone resonating beneath his touch. He looked at Nickolous questioningly.

Saying nothing, Nickolous placed his hands upon the place where the entrance was; listening. Feeling the vibrations that rose up to meet his touch, he concentrated, while beside him the staff began to change, turning nearly translucent as he reached out to grasp it. Holding the staff, he gently touched the earth with it; beginning at the eastern point, then south, then west and, last, north. Standing back, he waited as the wind blew warm upon his face and the earth before him gave way to reveal steps leading downward.

Without a backward glance, he disappeared into the dark, foreboding depths. A few moments later, the others followed while, from their hidden place, Orith and the Old One waited.

§ § § § §

Lord Nhon paused at the edge of the clearing, knowing that he was too late. Unbelieving, he stared at the solid wall of forest warriors before him then, turning, he signaled something as yet unseen to him. The air about the waiting warriors changed, bringing with it a putrid smell; a clinging, cloying thing that heralded the arrival of something dark and dangerous.

The warriors tightened their circle, waiting.

§ § § § § §

The cavern was dark, the steps slippery. Cautiously picking his way along, Nickolous held the staff before him, trusting his instinct. Jerome, bent nearly double in some places, wished to be at the end of this journey, while the wolves and Timothy followed closely behind. There was no danger here; just dampness and the unknown...

"Wait." Nickolous was standing upright in a large cavern; the staff had begun to glow, but strangely it remained cool to the touch, even as it turned white, illuminating the companions as well as the room in which they now stood.

"What is this place?" Nickolous held the staff high so that there were no shadows to conceal things unwanted.

"It was—is—a place of all knowing; a place of renewal." Jerome turned to look around him.

Once there had been warriors here. Once Lord Nhon had access through the chambers that led to the outside; Jerome knew now why the Fallen had tried to stop them from entering here. Once they gained entrance, he could not bar the way through the underground passages—once the fallen guardian had walked these passageways, studying the writings upon the wall; a telling of ages past—once—but no more.

The walls were lined with ancient weapons. He slid his fingers along the edge of an ornately carved sword, the edge still razor sharp after countless turnings beyond remembering.

"What happened to them?" It was Chera who spoke, her voice breaking the silence; her thoughts mirroring that of her companions.

"Who knows?" Jerome rubbed the accumulated dirt off his fingers, his gaze thoughtful. "These warriors walked in this place long before our time began. The weapons here were left for those who came after. The ones who protected the circle made sure there would be a legacy to follow."

"Except something happened, and they had to leave; everything was left exactly as it was. There has been no one in here since that day. The entrance was sealed, and the warriors that fell outside became the guardians of the cavern's entrance." Chera finished thoughtfully as a remembering of the ancient times, dormant, sprang forth—memories of those who had been here before—guardians—protectors. It was they who had watched over those of the forest clans while the four-legged and winged clans grew into what they were now.

Nickolous tensed as the staff in his hand flared with a white-blue light, temporarily blinding him, the intricately carved silver bracelet burning into his skin with an intense knowing.

"There." He pointed to a pictograph etched into the rock. The others stared at the ancient painting, their expressions questioning.

Nickolous turned to Jerome, his need to confirm with his eyes what his heart knew—knowing that what was on the wall was a map, drawn out for him and those who followed the path to their destiny.

"What do you see?"

Jerome peered closely at what was depicted upon the walls. It was a journey of a race of beings that had been here before he was even born—his first breath drawn. It was a telling of a people who had to leave but had left in their wake a confirmation, a legacy, of who they were and what was to come.

Jerome pointed at the drawings. "I see the telling of an ancient race, I see what you see; each place where life is had a beginning." His eyes widened as he traced the drawing with a finger. He turned wide green eyes on Nickolous.

"We are all the same, just different," he whispered into the dampness as the others crowded close to see what was written upon the walls.

"So, this is why the *Fallen* does not want to fight us here. Better for him to intercept us then have us pass through the passageways where the Ancient ones watched and left a record for those who came after." Timothy murmured softly, his mind trying to absorb what his eyes were seeing.

"Look. Here and here." He pointed to the etchings that were cut deeply into the rock. "The journey of the forest dwellers and how we came to be."

"They still watch." Nickolous turned to face them. The staff in his hand was emitting a sound unlike any he had ever heard. So, too, was the armband. He instinctively raised his hand to cover it as his whole body became attuned to the vibrations.

"We must go. Move nothing. Everything must be left as it was."

"But the weapons, to leave them here..." Timothy's voice trailed off as Nickolous spoke softly, his voice carrying to the others by an unseen breeze. "This is not the time to wield the weapons of light." Nickolous leaned closer to Timothy, the rest of his answer whispered as the staff glowed brighter.

"There will be others."

Carefully and in silence, the companions moved along the corridors, the dampness chilling them as each step took them further into the earth. Finally, reaching a place where the cavern branched off in three separate directions, they paused, unsure of which way to go. It was Chera who felt the first breeze as it rippled through the darkness, finding them.

"We must go that way," she said, her face turned upward, inhaling the warmth it brought with it.

§ § § § § §

Breathing deeply, the little earth dweller moved forward, its companions following as they moved as one, pushing against the barrier that kept the Flame imprisoned. Inside, the Flame flickered, then grew, the brightness nearly too much for them to bear as they pushed against its prison.

The barrier held.

Finally, the first of them, the one who had led them here, stopped, his senses alerting him to a far-off sound. Someone was coming. Scattering, they hid in the small places where they could not be seen, preparing for what was to come.

§ § § § § §

Lord Nhon strode angrily through the dense forest, knowing that he had failed in his quest. His hands clenched and unclenched as he fought down the rage that threatened to choke him. Knowing that he must regain control, he breathed deeply, composing himself. More than a quarter of his army had already been decimated, while A-Sharoon had destroyed one of his shadow beings.

He had underestimated her power.

He had underestimated her.

Throwing a backward glance over his shoulder, he moved swiftly to push the heavy, stone door aside; inwardly cursing himself for not having had the foresight to see this coming.

"You cannot stop the prophecy or alter the course of its destiny." Lord Nhon whirled around, his staff raised, its ebony darkness starkly visible even in the subdued light.

"You!" He hissed through clenched teeth. "What are you doing? Why are you out here?" He glared at the shadow being.

"Why would I wait for my own destruction?" The creature turned to face Lord Nhon. "The earth echoes with the footsteps of the Old Ones. They have risen from their sleep and come to aid the Flame."

"Bah! That's impossible!" Lord Nhon snorted in disbelief. He flung his cape aside as the rush of warm air hit him.

"Already the boy turned man calls the Ancients to him. Even he, with his innocence and youth, does not know yet the power he holds within himself!" The shadow being moved slowly upward as it spoke, putting more distance between itself and Lord Nhon—away from the cavern and what lie deep within its depths.

"Where are you going?" Lord Nhon shouted as the creature began to dissipate in front of him.

"The earth moves beneath your feet. Can you not feel it, Lord Nhon?" the being asked as it rose higher. There was nearly nothing left, it was now so transparent. A leaf swirled slowly down to rest at Lord Nhon's feet as the whispered words echoed within his mind:

The army rises. The Ancients awake. By your own hand, you have unleashed an awakening that could change the course of things as we have known them since our awareness of the beginning. You should have known better. In all things there must be a balance. Draw your dark ones to you... those that are left.

The words died away as the sudden stillness alerted Lord Nhon to his own danger. Pulling the lever that released the rocks to fall against the opening, he strode angrily away.

§ § § § §

Lord Moshat moved cautiously, concealment being necessary even as he hurried toward the sacred place. As he approached his destination, he called to the watchers—the others.

The time of the awakening was upon them.

It was time to put away the old laws. It was time to face one another so that each race could draw strength from the other. He sighed. It was the sigh of one who has seen too much and grows weary. Ahead of him was the grove where he knew the others, like and unlike himself, waited. As he passed beneath the emerald-green canopy, he heard the whispers following him and knew he would not return this way.

§ § § § § §

The little earth dweller drew in his breath, waiting. The sound of stone grinding on stone reached him as the sounds echoed around him and the others. As the footsteps, soft and nearly inaudible, drew closer, he shrank even further into the crevice, hoping that they would remain undetected. The footsteps paused and then faded into the silence. The little watcher let his breath out slowly, relieved.

The wind, unseen, touched the case that held the Flame within its prison. Splaying itself across the barrier it searched for a weakness within the shield, anywhere where it might enter.

The Flame flickered higher as the second of the elemental powers sought entrance.

§ § § § § §

"I tell you we can no longer observe in silence what could be our own destruction!" Lord Moshat paced angrily. The watchers, gathered from the four corners, listened in silence. To break their own laws was unthinkable.

What does it concern us, this matter of the forest clans and the one who walks between?" One of the watchers asked, his face concealed within the voluminous folds of his hooded cloak.

"Do you not think we have our own realms to see to? Of what concern is it to us what transpires in the realms that are held in the 'Between?'"

There were murmurings of assent as the others nodded their agreement. Lord Moshat shook his head, incredulous at the attitude being displayed. They had not always been watchers. Long before that, in the beginning, they had been like those of the forest clans. Growing in knowledge, reaching out to grasp the truth, eager to learn; to achieve the knowing that one day would earn them the right to be a watcher. Now here they were, dismissing the danger that lay at their own doorsteps, waiting to spill inside.

Lord Moshat grew angry. Throwing his cloak over his shoulder, he brought the staff up over his head, then down upon a large piece of smoky quartz that lay at his feet. The vibration, as it struck, echoed within the fragile layers so that it split into pieces. Leaning down, he prized a piece of it up. Holding it high, he turned it, first this way, then that way, so that the sun's rays caught, then held, within the prism it created.

The watchers fell silent as the shafts of light spun against each other, creating a vortex of colors that intertwined, then separated, only to meet again in a never-ending dance.

Lord Moshat's voice rang out in the clear air as he addressed the ones he had summoned from the high places.

"*Watch!*" He turned the crystal slowly so that the colors slowed, were distinct. He moved the crystal a little faster. The colors rolled toward one another, melding slightly at the edges.

"Do you forget? Have you all grown so complacent that you forgot the struggle that brought you to your place of watching? Have the turnings taught you nothing. Well?" He placed the stone carefully upon the ground, at the same time his gaze raking the circle of watchers. One by one, the bowed heads raised as each watcher placed his staff before him. When all the staffs were placed in front of their owners, they formed a circle, and Lord Moshat nodded. They had all voted as one, without any dissent. The elder let out his breath, relieved.

From the four corners to the center, they would lend their strength and their wisdom to help the companions.

Knowing that there was one more thing to be done, Lord Moshat took his leave.

There must be *Three.* Always. There must be *Three.*

23

Orith shifted so that the Old One could lean on him more comfortably. The shadows outside were lengthening, the shafts of light moving slowly across the rocks that concealed them.

"Shhhh." Orith leaned forward to peer out, the shrill whistling of the forest warriors a telling thing. Danger approached. Feeling helpless, he leaned back as the sounds of battle reached him. Knowing that Nickolous was safe within the caverns deep below offered little comfort as he held the Old One to him. Too late, they realized the foolishness of staying behind, for if they were discovered...

§ § § § § §

Lithe and deadly, the feral creatures attacked in packs, worrying their quarry with darting attacks, moving swiftly in, then out, as Jerome's warriors struck out blindly, their deadly blows missing their mark with irritating frequency. As one was struck down another took its place to weary the warriors so that an opening might be found.

However, the warriors of the forest stood their ground, neither defeating nor winning, the barrier holding, keeping the passageway to the three fallen warriors impenetrable. Finally, a trilling cry was heard, and the invaders turned back, their master calling them. The warriors watched as the last of them slunk into the forest, leaving their wounded to find their way or not, as best they could.

§ § § § § §

Orith leaned back, relieved as the shadows passed over their hidden place, the silence welcoming as he let his breath out slowly, then easing himself forward, listened. Someone approached; the soft tread of their footsteps heard even though they stepped carefully over the dry twigs and leaves while the Old One clutched him; her sharp nails digging painfully into his side as she pulled herself forward, just as the footsteps stopped and someone softly called their names.

§ § § § § §

"The sentries return, my Lord."

"Prepare them. We must intercept them in the cavern, before they reach the chamber."

"Yes, my Lord."

Even as he spoke, Lord Nhon moved toward the darkened passageway. Knowing that the others would soon follow, he went to prepare himself. He knew that it would take the companions awhile to find their way to the center where the Flame was imprisoned. He also knew he had to stop them before they entered the cavern, for even without the other two, the Old One and Orith, he could not risk that they might get past him. As he began the long descent into the depths that held his prisoner, he extracted a large silver medallion from his robe. It had been a gift, given to him many turnings ago. Within its center, a blood-red stone lay nestled.

Chanting an ancient incantation given him from those who dwelt below in the shadow worlds, he caressed the stone, peering into its depths. The light from the torches positioned on the walls behind him glinted against the stones surface, reaching the heart that was deep within.

Lord Nhon threw back his head, laughing.

The stone wept.

§ § § § §

Nickolous felt the pull of the stone even as the Fallen awakened it from its eternal sleep. He leaned against the damp wall for support, his head spinning as he fought the images racing through his mind.

"Nickolous?"

"Something calls to me. Something ancient."

"What is it, what do you see?" Gabriel leaned close, the feeling of danger prickling along his spine. Chera and Liege, sensing this, positioned themselves beside Nickolous while Jerome felt the hair on the back of his neck rising as the first cold draft of air hit him.

"Listen." The big warrior leaned forward as the smell of something putrid reached them, the cold draft causing Nickolous to shiver as he held the staff in front of him. It glowed softly in the semidarkness and then flared brilliant white as the first form leapt toward them, only to fall, lifeless, to the earthen floor. Then the others came and the air was filled with shrieking forms as the companions defended themselves. Jerome pushed one away only to fend off another as Nickolous held the staff out in front of him, unsure of how to awaken its powers.

He need not have worried. Even as he drew it back toward him, the words came unbidden. As he swung it in an arc, the blue-white particles that drifted out from it landed carelessly here and there, where they glowed like tiny coals set free from a burning log that has rolled from its place within the circle of the fire.

The screaming died away in a soft sigh, so quickly was the creature consumed, leaving only a tiny pile of ash in its wake. No one noticed the first, or the second, or even the third as it perished alongside its fellows, so hard was the battle being fought, the battle cries ringing throughout the cavern carried deep into the depths where few—two-legged, or four-, had ever trod.

"Chera, to your left!" The words were shouted as Gabriel flung off another creature.

Nickolous swung the staff around as the sparks hit their mark, and still they came. Even with the aid of the staff, they were on the verge of being overwhelmed.

Leaning down, Nickolous drew the staff in a circle, his thoughts reaching Jerome, the big warrior fighting to reach his side. Calling the wolves and Timothy to him, they turned back to back to meet the enemy, only to see them disperse as suddenly as they had appeared, the distant call of their master fading into the sudden silence, the only sound now that of their own ragged breathing.

§ § § § §

Orith shoved the Old One back, his body covering hers protectively as the stones guarding their hidden place were removed. As the last one was rolled away, he shielded his eyes against the bright light that streamed in through the opening.

"Lord Moshat!" Orith pulled himself up as the elder knelt down to help the Old One.

"The others? The council?" Orith asked; too surprised to say anything more, for he knew the Ancient laws well.

"There comes a time when there can be no differences between us, for it is one of our own who brings this danger to the forest clans. This is an ancient evil; awakened by one who risks all for the power he hopes to gain through the suffering of others. There had to be an awakening within the circle. This is it. Come." The elder stood at the opening of the cavern, where the others had entered, it seemed, but a few moments past.

§ § § § § §

"They come, my Lord." The creature bowed low before its master. Lord Nhon nodded. He was not surprised at their failure to stop the companions from entering the sacred place; yet, he had hoped. He shrugged; it did not matter. There was still the stone to call upon. It could not refuse him, for it was bound by the ancient calling of the before time to obey him.

"Tell the sentinels that guard the lower levels to be alert. Has there been any sign of the woman?" Lord Nhon asked as he fastened the heavy woolen cloak about his shoulders, placing the hood over his head so that his features were hidden from prying eyes.

"None, my Lord," the creature replied.

"Be watchful, and remain guarded at all times. Now go." Lord Nhon dismissed the guard with a curt nod and returned to his work. There were certain places he was forbidden to go, and the knowing was festering within him. He drew himself up, his eyes glinting as he went to the opening and peered into the bright light. Somewhere beneath him, he knew the companions moved toward the Flame, while A-Sharoon waited above. He could feel her presence. Knew she was close. Angry, he turned aside. He would seek her out later. Right now, he had to deal with the others, and if that meant destroying another entranceway to the *"Beneath,"* then so be it. Calling the others to him, he disappeared into the darkened depths that beckoned.

A-Sharoon watched Lord Nhon go. He sensed her, she could feel it, but she knew he would not find her. As much as she loathed the forest dwellers, she loathed him more. As the last of the feral beings followed him back into the cavern, she stepped out into the open and, guarding herself against the bright light, followed.

§ § § § § §

Nickolous let his breath out slowly, relieved that they were gone.

"There will be more where they came from," Jerome said as he turned one of the creature's over, checking for signs of life. There were none. Straightening up, he fastened the club to his side, looping a long, thin strap about his wrist so that he could swing up and out more easily should the need arise. Nodding, Nickolous drew the staff to him, partially concealing it beneath his cloak, then, motioning the others to follow; he started down the winding corridor.

"Well, which way do we go from here?" They were standing at a place where the cavern branched off into a maze of connecting tunnels. Each one they peered down seemed darker than the rest, with no indication of it ever ending. Nickolous looked at the bracelet; it was glowing an iridescent hue that was comforting. "We go that way," he said, pointing down a long length of corridor that seeped wetness from a hundred places.

The smell was nearly overwhelming as they made their way slowly along; the way before them slippery with things that had been there since the before time. Moving carefully, they began the slow descent into the deepest part of the cavern, Chera and Gabriel flanking Nickolous while Liege and Timothy stayed a little behind, their ears straining for anything untoward. Jerome moved ahead of them, the luminescent light from the staff shadowing everything in front of him so that his senses were heightened as he concentrated on even the most innocent of sounds that wafted toward them.

The farther they went, the colder it became; the chill creeping upward until even Jerome felt it. The big warrior stopped suddenly, tilting his head to one side, listening. The far-off sound of rocks tumbling down upon one another, echoing through the partial darkness, reached him as he turned in the direction from which they had came. He turned to face the others. Motioning to the wolves and Timothy, he moved quietly into battle position as the sounds grew louder. Whoever, whatever, it was, was not bothering to cover its approach.

"Hold!" The voice pierced the darkness as Jerome hefted his war club effortlessly, readying himself.

"Lord Moshat?" The big warrior slowly lowered his weapon, shocked into speechlessness as Lord Moshat, followed by Orith and the Old One, came into view, obviously weary from their hurried journey.

Nickolous moved ahead of the others, relieved that they were all together again, for deep within, he knew that they should never have separated. He had sensed almost as soon as they had left them in their hiding place, protected by the living rock, that their power was in being united.

He hugged the Old One to him.

"We don't have much time." Lord Moshat grasped Nickolous's arm in greeting, his grasp firm. Nodding to the others, he turned his attention now on those crowded about him, his gaze missing nothing as he noted how weary they all looked and how hard this journey must be.

"For now, the old laws will be put aside. The dark ones begin to gather from the nether realms to assist Lord Nhon in his evil." Lord Moshat brushed the dampness from his brow; the hurried journey from Skye to where he was now had made him realize that he, too, was growing tired. He turned to Jerome.

"Use the old ways of speaking to one another from this point on." Lord Moshat turned to face the rest of the companions; his blue eyes piercing, his brow furrowed as he listened, even as he spoke, for anything, anyone, that might be close by. He drew his staff to him, drawing comfort from its presence, the power that emanated silently from it flowing through him, renewing him.

"Chera, Gabriel, you must draw from the memories given you by your ancestors. What was gifted to the elders, to the warriors of the forest, and to the watchers beneath as their birthright, is also yours by remembrance." He drew the staff in front of them, the pale blue light washing over them, bathing them with its soft light.

Timothy shook his head as the color washed over him, the words coming to his mind unbidden, unspoken. He looked at the others in disbelief. He was sharing his thoughts in the ancient way, a way that had been lost to his kind for untold turnings. He drew himself up proudly, his weapon clutched tightly to him. Like the others, he stood, ready for whatever was to come.

The elder was speaking again, the words in the ancient language of the Old Ones.

Nickolous nodded, understanding. What was once forgotten had been reborn. He looked at the Old One and Orith. He understood this much at least; within all breathing things, there was a memory of the beginning, which most had forgotten, their memories buried deep within to resurface as dreams and visions except to a few.

He turned his gaze on the elder; old beyond reckoning by human standards; older even then Jerome's race of beings. He touched the staff to his forehead, momentarily lost in his own thoughts. Drawing in a deep breath, he went inside himself, something he had never done at will before, and he saw where the Flame was hidden; felt its anguish, heard the soft sighing of the wind, knew the little earth dwellers waited with stalwart heart for help to come. Looking up he saw the others, watching, waiting for him.

Lord Moshat said nothing; there was no need for words. The Ancients had seen...had known. The weariness swept from him as he stood gazing at those gathered about him—knowing that the turnings he had lived were nothing more than a preparation as he centered himself, preparing himself for the battle to come. He looked at Nickolous—at the others—

§ § § § §

Lord Nhon moved silently from corridor to corridor, his gaze searching as, ahead of him, things scurried from crevice to crevice, seeking out the hidden and destroying them. Lord Nhon waited impatiently for them to finish. As each corridor was swept clean, something darker was left behind to guard against intrusion. Lord Nhon leaned against a moss-encrusted wall, unmindful of the foul odors emanating from it—unmindful of the fact that behind the wall stood another; hidden from prying eyes, white hands clenched tightly around a silver pendent that in turn held its own secrets within...

"Lord Nhon?"

"What is it, what have you found?" He turned toward the speaker.

"The elder, he is with them."

Lord Nhon drew in his breath sharply. He had not expected this. Interference in the lower realms was expressly forbidden. He let his breath out slowly. There was no sense in worrying about it now, for there was much to do. If his former mentor had called the others to him, they still would not interfere directly, and he had grown powerful enough that he personally need not worry. He looked around him, his gaze sweeping the cavernous room—at the dark feral things that milled about him, unmindful, unless given a purpose. Drawing his cloak tightly about him, he went forward.

No, he thought to himself as he turned down the next long corridor—he need not worry.

As for the rest? Let them look to themselves.

§ § § § §

Black eyes glittering darkly, A-Sharoon waited in the darkness, her nails digging painfully into the palms of her hands as she restrained herself. Now was the not the time to reveal herself or her intentions. She would wait; would see what the forest dwellers did. As much as she despised the one who now walked away, she would not jeopardize herself. As she stepped out into the opened corridor, yellowed fangs snapped at her, catching her cloak in powerful jaws, then relaxed as words, whispered low and soft, soothed it. Panting, it lay down, its narrowed eyes following her as she moved out of sight.

§ § § § § §

"Careful, the way from here grows dangerous," Jerome cautioned as he placed a hand on Nickolous's shoulder. They were standing on a narrow ledge looking down. Holding his staff out in front of him, Nickolous watched as it glowed blue-white; its light dispersing the shadows that danced in front of it. He drew in his breath sharply. It was a long way to the bottom.

Easing himself backward, he leaned against the jagged rock that protruded outward from the wall, exhaling slowly. Then, taking a deep breath, he leaned forward again. Never one for heights, he pushed back the fear that gnawed at him and, holding the staff in front of him, leaned over the edge once more, his eyes seeking a way down.

Lord Moshat watched as Nickolous fought down his fear, doing what needed to be done. He himself could have easily found the narrow set of stairs that would take them down, and he would, should Nickolous fail. He drew in his breath and held it as he watched him fight his fear to help the rest of them.

Good. The pupil was learning without realizing he was being taught.

"There. You can hardly see them, but they're there."

Jerome peered over the ledge as the others crowded close, their gaze following the light as it reflected back. Stairs, hewn by a knowing hand, followed the natural slope of the rock in a downward spiral. Nickolous looked at the others; fighting down his unease, he started forward, slowly, carefully easing himself over the ledge. The others didn't hesitate as they followed.

§ § § § § §

"What is this place?"

The companions were standing at the bottom of a deep ravine while water swirled about their ankles. The Old One shrugged. At least it was warm. She turned at the touch of something being placed around her shoulders and looked up into Lord Moshat's eyes. The elder smiled at her as she nodded her thanks for the gift; the feathered cloak was warm, and she had felt chilled. Squinting into the gloom, she made out the shapes of the others as they pressed close together. She drew in deeply of the air as it blew through the darkness, swirling around them and over them...

"I think, Nickolous said, "that we are at the bottom of the chamber. Lord Nhon's army will be looking for us up there, along the precipice." He pointed up, back the way they had come; the staff lighting the way.

"We had better use it to our advantage, then. At some point, those tracking us will realize what we have done and come after us," Jerome urged, anxious to be on his way. His senses were tingling as he tried to peer through the darkness.

The others agreed. In silence now, and as quickly as possible, they made their way along the bottom, careful to avoid making any unnecessary noise. Once, pausing for a rest, they heard the far off tinkling sounds of small rocks as they tumbled down the steep sides of the ravine, as the searchers scuttled back and forth, probing.

§ § § § §

"They can't have disappeared."

"My Lord, we have searched everywhere."

Lord Nhon whirled on the creature, his face mere inches from its. "I would suggest, then, that you search again." The words were ground out through clenched teeth as the cowering creature, terrified of retribution, nodded mutely.

"Fools! Idiots!" Lord Nhon raged as he paced back and forth. Where could they be? The caverns ran deep, true, but there were only so many hidden places. He paused, his gaze resting on the rock floor he stood upon.

Far below the Fallen One, the companions moved silently, the need for spoken words unnecessary as they hurried toward their destination.

§ § § § §

Out of sight, hidden behind a wall of ancient stone, A-Sharoon traced the outline of the amulet with a slender finger as she waited. Sensing that the Fallen was close, she had veiled herself so that she would remain unseen; the need to be near the Flame something she could not explain, even to herself. As the searchers moved around her, they gave no indication they saw her. She ignored the dampness, drawing from it as she waited in the shadows for the Fallen to make the next move that would determine the course of action she would take.

Lord Nhon swung around, his gaze penetrating the hidden places for whatever had caused the unease that rose within him, the feeling increasing as he reached out, touching the walls in front of him. Listening to the pulsing of the earth around him, he pulled back.

"I know you are near." The words were low, measured, as Lord Nhon placed his own amulet against the living rock. Seeking what could not be seen.

So, she thought to play a game of cat and mouse, did she? His eyes narrowed thoughtfully as he moved away. He didn't have time for games right now. He would deal with the mistress of darkness later.

This time, as the footsteps receded down the darkened corridor, A-Sharoon did not follow.

She had nearly been discovered this time. She clenched and unclenched her hands in the darkness, angry at herself for having been so careless, yet at the same time wondering how Lord Nhon had came to possess something as powerful as what she held tightly clenched in her hand. Hers was older, but not by much. Made by different hands, the purpose remained the same—to protect the wearer. A-Sharoon frowned, wondering.

The amulet she wore was hers from the beginning. A birthright. What she had sensed from Lord Nhon's amulet as it had slid silently over the stones, seeking, was different. Her eyes widened in the darkness.

The red stone that nestled within the silver bed that held it prisoner was of Skye. It was not the Fallen's by birthright, but by deception! Closing her eyes, she drew in deeply of the air that suddenly swirled around her as the amulet warmed her with its strength, recognizing its own.

§ § § § § §

Liege followed slightly behind the others, his senses attuned to the nuances that rose and fell around him. The air was still down here; in this place of running water and moss covered rocks. More than once, he had nearly lost his footing as he had felt his way carefully along the slime-covered rocks as the others had moved ahead. More than once, he had paused to listen, his keen hearing picking up a far off distant sound that was hauntingly familiar.

"Your brothers call to you."

The voice, unexpected, startled him as he shuddered at the memories of that day. A battle, fiercely fought, the casualties so terribly high. The far-off sighing drew closer, carried by something unseen, and in that moment the big wolf recognized it for what it was.

"You must go to them. Free them. There will be none to bar your way. None..." The words fell off into the stillness as Nickolous reached out to touch him, the light caress something that he allowed from the young warrior—for warrior he was. Warmth coursed through him as Nickolous turned away, the faint glow from his staff lighting the way; back to the others.

Liege blinked in the half light cast by the staffs light reflecting off the walls on either side; unsure that Nickolous had even been there, he caught the whispered: "*Go.*" Moving quickly now, he went back the way he had came, stopping now and then to listen, his keen senses directing him to where he must go; the high keening, although still distant, was reaching a fevered pitch. Liege didn't pause in the direction he chose as he hurried along the narrow corridor, trusting in Nickolous's instincts.

§ § § § § §

"We must hurry. Lord Nhon will soon realize which way we have taken..."

"...And by that time we will have reached our destination," Lord Moshat finished, looking upward as he measured Jerome's immense height against his own, his thoughts on what a formidable warrior he was. Sparing a quick backward glance, he noted that Nickolous had dropped back to walk with the Old One.

Lord Moshat bowed his head, deep in thought, while Jerome tried to measure his stride so that the others could keep up. Still, he worried about the two old ones. They grew weary; this he knew without being told.

"Don't worry. All will be as it should be. The Old One and Orith can do it." Lord Moshat looked up at Jerome with his startling blue eyes. Sensing the unasked question that the warrior wanted to ask, he nodded his head, giving permission.

Jerome weighed his thoughts carefully, choosing his words with care. Once the great bird of prey had aided them to protect her own, would she aid them again? What relationship to the warriors of Skye did Nickolous really have? He turned his gaze from the elder's, clearing his throat as he debated the asking of things that maybe should remain unknown.

Lord Moshat smiled in the half light. So many unasked questions these forest folk had, and there had been none to answer them—

Until now.

"Ask."

One word. Jerome drew in his breath sharply. It was enough.

"He is of Skye." It wasn't a question. The warrior was seeking confirmation of what he already knew. The elder nodded, waiting, for he knew there was more.

"How?" Jerome let his breath out slowly as he turned to face the elder.

Lord Moshat studied the staff in front of him, wondering how much he should reveal. For turnings beyond count, the origins of his race had been kept secret, but that was before. His brows furrowed together thoughtfully as memories coursed through him. Ahhh, he straightened up.

The Old Ones had known. They whispered the answers even now. He held the staff tighter, the words forming in his mind even as he uttered them out loud.

"Nickolous's mother was born to a dying race once of Skye; which was why her form was not quite the same as ours." The elder flicked a midnight wing so the tip was revealed to the warriors gaze. Jerome nodded; understanding as Lord Moshat continued.

"Like you, we too, waited for things foretold to come to pass. Unlike you, we watched through the veil that separates, unable to interfere with what was occurring in the mortal world where those of the two-legged clans dwelled. We watched as the girl-child grew, her abilities all but absent in a foreign land, her memories of who she had been becoming nothing but a vague remembering."

"Could you not draw her back?"

"It was against our teachings. To have done so would have caused a further rift between our time and hers as she knew it. Things, once written, cannot be undone except by those who can affect the outcome by free choice." Lord Moshat fell silent for a moment, his thoughts traveling back over the turnings.

Jerome waited patiently as the elder reflected on the events that had brought them here. When Lord Moshat once again began to speak, the forest warrior was amazed at the emotion he sensed emanating from the elder of Skye.

"The child that had vanished returned to us a woman, more powerful then we had ever supposed she would be…"

"And her son?"

"Nickolous is pure Skye. He merely needs to throw off the mantle of the human race that girds him to that other place."

"Easier said than done; what happens if he doesn't?"

"Then, my friend, there is no hope that the circle elders prophecy will be fulfilled. Nickolous must come to terms with who he is on his own, then, and only then, can he truly learn." Jerome looked at the elder, his expression questioning.

"And the battle to come?"

The elder drew his brows together in a frown; exhaling slowly, the answer barely audible.

"'Tis merely the awakening..."

Jerome brushed at something that fluttered against him in the darkness; the brush of velvety wings against his cheek diverting his attention temporarily from what the elder was saying. The words seemed whispered as the air about them was suddenly filled with hundreds of small, flying creatures.

"*Bats!* Follow the little winged ones, for they lead the way to the Flame." The Old One, aided by Orith, had moved with surprising agility to stand beside Jerome. Her staff was glowing—a blue luminescent glow that lit the way of the holder.

"Hurry! Do as she says." The elder motioned the rest ahead and was not surprised when Nickolous took the lead.

Far above them, atop the precipice that overlooked the chasm, the watcher, cloaked deep within the darkened shadows, followed their progress, his midnight wings drawn tightly against him. Tensing, he remained where he was as the sound of running feet reached his ears; the dark ones all but invisible as they sought out their prey.

§ § § § §

A-Sharoon waited in the darkness, her breathing steady; her hands still clutching the amulet. Lord Nhon had vanished into the labyrinth long moments before, the others following him into the distant places; as the silence grew around her, she wondered at the wisdom of being here. The amulet burned in her palm as she clutched it tightly to her, for it gave her a small measure of comfort, the knowing that if she chose to, she could destroy the dark one here and now.

"Have a care, sister." The words seemed to echo hollowly off the walls.

Blood-red nails dug into white hands as A-Sharoon fought the urge to throw the amulet, and the memories that it evoked, from her.

24

Liege picked his way carefully, the big wolf wary as he edged through the musty corridors and shadowed places that concealed those who watched from their hidden places. Yet, there were none to bar his way, and it was only after he caught sight of a small, brown form as it moved swiftly back into shadow that he realized why.

The watchers. The little ones. The eyes and ears of the earth. Liege let his breath out slowly, relieved.

§ § § § §

Lord Nhon paced back and forth angrily as he waited for the sentry to return with news. Once he was certain his quarry was beneath him, he had sent the best of his assassins to intercept them, hoping that it would end there—but knowing it wouldn't, because nothing could be that easy.

He had once been one of them—a watcher of Skye—a guardian—
He knew what he faced.

"My Lord?"

The Fallen turned; startled, so lost was he within his own thoughts.

"Yes, what is it?" Pushing back the hood that concealed his face, he studied the creature before him, his red eyes with their black pupils glowing even in the half light.

"The Caverns below, we searched, there are many…" The creature's voice trailed off as Lord Nhon darted forward. He was furious, his rage uncontrollable as he struck out blindly, the need to punish overwhelming.

The shrieks of terror rent the air, echoing off the stone walls before fading into the dank dampness of the cavern.

Flinging the limp form from him, Lord Nhon drew in deeply of the air around him. Fools! He was surrounded by fools! The wind whirled about him unnaturally as he clutched his cape to him, his red eyes searching for the source of the sound reverberating throughout the cavern.

The winged ones—those who flew in the darkness, their incredible senses guiding them as they listened to the sounds that reverberated through the shadows carried by the night.

Lord Nhon drew in deeply of the air around him, scenting it deep, listening for more; his own keen senses now picking up other sounds as he hurried down a long, winding corridor, his staff glowing to light his way.

A-Sharoon watched as the Lord of Darkness moved swiftly away, toward the secret place that held the Flame. Black eyes glittered in a face unnaturally white as red droplets of liquid seeped between her fingers as she opened her palm, slowly, to gaze upon the amulet nestled within.

Silently, without hesitation, she followed. Ahead of her, Lord Nhon paused briefly, his nostrils distended like a feral beast as he smiled in the half light. So then, he would fell them all in the same place. It mattered not to him.

Darkness or light, it was all the same to him.

There could only be one master to rule the night.

A-Sharoon knew he felt her presence but was not afraid, for she, who had been born to the darkness, feared little. She also knew Lord Nhon had no knowledge of what she concealed within her palm, so it mattered not. Her choice had been made.

The Flame called to her, and from the depths of the darkness that reigned within her and before her, something had awakened. Not sure of what it was, she hurried forward, this new feeling that struggled forth not entirely unpleasant.

§ § § § §

"Wait." Jerome pulled Nickolous back. There was something ahead of them and, even though the little watchers—the winged ones—flew above them guiding the way, his warrior's training cautioned him as the prickling sensation rolled up his spine. Lord Moshat swung his staff upward, commanding the darkness to dissipate that they might see what lay in the darkness beyond them. Behind him, the Old One paused, her own staff clutched tightly within her grasp.

The wind shrieked about the companions as they gazed down into the chasms that lay below them.

"There must be another way." Nickolous blinked against the sudden light as the others crowded around, disbelief upon their faces. Lord Moshat had stepped back and now stood a little apart from them, his keen eyesight scanning the area about them as Nickolous turned about, his gaze searching. His penetrating blue eyes met those of the elders.

"Listen." Jerome motioned the others to be silent. The distant sound of water rippling over moss sodden rocks sounded faintly in the distance. Gabriel inhaled deeply, his keen sense of smell seeking the direction they must go. Chera nudged him gently even as she leaned over to gauge the depth of the chasm that was seemingly endless.

"There." Chera leaned over even further as Nickolous knelt down beside her. The Old One and Orith moved back to give them more room. Small rocks tumbled down the sides as Nickolous held the staff over the ledge, while behind him Lord Moshat drew himself up to his full height as he listened. The high-pitched keening in the distance was growing louder.

Everything is not as it seems. The words echoed in Nickolous's mind as he drew on the thoughts the Ancients had shared with him, and from deep within himself, words, not his, poured forth as the Seven, from within their sacred place, gave aid.

The air was suddenly filled with chanting that came from a hundred places as an untold number of voices sounded; reminding the companions of who their ancestors had been; the sudden light blinding, forcing the companions to close their eyes against the images that assailed their senses as words, whispered, became images, and the images, memories.

"Jerome." Nickolous motioned the big warrior closer as he leaned over the edge. Lord Moshat stood behind the Old One and Orith, his staff poised above their heads, the light blue-white and comforting. Timothy, aware of the protection the elder offered moved closer, his senses warning him to be cautious, yet he was curious nonetheless.

Orith nudged the Old One gently. Like the elder of Skye, they had no need to see with their eyes what their hearts already knew. Each gazed at the other in understanding as the light from Nickolous's staff flamed white. The sudden flame arched upward, to spiral downward into the depths below.

Nickolous drew in his breath sharply, then, without hesitating, disappeared over the edge into the darkness below.

"The warrior has awakened. The boy is no more." Lord Moshat exhaled slowly, his grip on Timothy tightening as the little warrior tried to fling himself over the edge after his young charge.

"Easy, my young friend." The warrior of Skye lifted Timothy to one side as he flung his cloak off, revealing himself fully to the gaze of the others. Knowing that the Old One and Orith would fulfill their destiny, he nodded at the forest warrior, his gaze momentarily locking with that of Gabriel and Chera before he, too, disappeared over the edge; the wolves following without hesitation in his wake.

"To the gateway. Hurry." The words echoed faintly against the rocks before dissipating into silence as the Old One leaned over the edge, her gaze sweeping the darkness below.

Jerome longed to follow Nickolous but knew he had to see the Old One and Orith safely below. The sudden beating of wings startled him as Owen landed beside them, his golden gaze locking with that of the warriors.

"Go." He motioned beyond the precipice.

"Go." The words were softly spoken, brooking no argument. Jerome nodded as he plunged into the darkness, disappearing instantly.

The Old One let out her breath slowly as Orith guided her into a sitting position, his concern evident as he knelt down beside her.

"Are you all right?" Green eyes peered into black as he waited for her to speak.

"I'm fine; just tired." Old eyes looked through him as he drew back, surprised at the strength that he saw there.

"Old One?" Owen peered into old-young eyes as realization dawned.

"Things are not always what they seem." The Old One nodded as she withdrew the staff. Nodding to Orith, she smiled as he drew forth his staff. Both were glowing softly in the semidarkness.

"We will follow, but slowly."

Owen nodded, understanding the other's purpose—Nickolous needed time to reach the Flame. Glancing at his brother, he couldn't help but admire the courage he saw there, for despite all the pain he had endured, his heart remained true.

"Timothy, we need you here with us. There must be a diversion."

Timothy nodded, understanding. The Old One and Orith alone were strong, their powers ancient, but they were two. With Owen and himself to give aid, there was strength with arms. The four combined would be formidable indeed.

"Well, then, how long do we have?" Timothy looked up at Owen as he unsheathed his sword.

"There's no telling," Owen replied, his gaze scanning the darkness for things foul and evil. The air around them had changed; the atmosphere stifling as the stench of things unseen and dark swirled about them.

"They've found the way down," the Old One spoke softly, as she calmly placed her staff beside that of Orith's. Taking the two staffs, Orith raised them high above his head, his thoughts going to the sacred place of remembering. Bowing his scarred head, he searched for the words that needed to be spoken, for they were not his—

But the remembering of a race long gone.

"Hurry, my friend, for our destiny approaches more swiftly then we are perhaps prepared for." Owen moved to stand in front of the Old One, his body shielding hers from the sight of the first of the creatures that scurried toward them, its eyes a phosphorous yellow. Its mouth working silently as it stared at them, blinking stupidly as the light flared from the staff toward it, enveloping it within its fiery embrace.

"Hold fast. There's more," Owen yelled as he took flight, his talons cutting a deadly swath as he bore down on the shadowy forms that skittered toward his companions. The light arching over and around him as he dispatched as many as he could while the Old One and Orith stood as one; their staffs now joined. Knowing what was coming, Owen flew low, his talons reaching out to grasp Timothy in a gentle embrace as he flew over the two elders.

§ § § § §

"There will be more of them," Orith spoke softly but still his voice echoed in the vast cavern.

"Those were only the scouts." Owen exhaled slowly as he turned to face the others. "That was nothing compared to what's coming." The sound of small rocks tumbling from their unseen places caused them all to reach for their weapons.

Timothy looked around, his sword withdrawn, prepared for battle. They were still at the edge of the precipice, and he was still recovering from his unexpected flight. The power of the staffs combined was an incredible force indeed, but he knew better then to feel secure, for if they were attacked by a hoard of those dark things, even the staffs would not hold them all safe. There would be casualties.

The Old One drew her staff away from that of Orith's, the wood no longer glowing, its surface now as dark as ebony. She drew in a deep breath. Turning at the light touch on her shoulder, she gazed up at Orith. His scarred face reflected only a little of the pain she knew coursed through him.

"Soon, my old friend. Soon." She drew back so that she could look up at him then patted him gently as she turned away, her eyes dark and luminous, her thoughts now her own. The earth turned beneath them, yet they did not feel it, for it was a silent thing. As each day dawned and each day set, they watched it; not appreciating its beauty enough.

The Old One sighed heavily, turning inward with her thoughts. The knowing that was gifted to her race was coming to the fore as she drew in her breath, letting it out slowly, watching, as it was caught and held by the cooler air. Now vaporous, it hung seemingly suspended in midair.

She heard Timothy's shouted warning and turned, moving swiftly even as the others started forward to her aid. Fingers reached out like tendrils to grasp her but missed as she turned her body around, the words rising from within her as she struck out, her staff connecting with the unseen. Whatever it was, it crumpled into nothingness as the air was pierced by its dying shriek.

Timothy blinked against the flash of light, his senses tingling. He leaned forward. Concentrating. There, in the shadowed corner, just beyond his vision, something moved. Something that did not wish to be seen—

Orith.

Timothy had not spoken the words aloud, merely thought them, but Orith had heard and had moved with surprising agility to his side.

Orith peered into the darkness, his night vision heightened by their danger. The form moved farther out from its place of concealment but remained in shadow. Orith focused, his green eyes boring into the darkness, ripping away the cloak that held the intruder in its safe embrace, while the Old One held her staff in front of her; its white light arcing upward to reach out with long tendrils to caress the intruder.

Timothy blinked against the sudden light, as did the rest of the companions.

"*You.*" The Old One let her breath out slowly, her staff tingling in her grasp as it recognized one of its own.

"Old One. Orith." The figure moved easily toward them, his tall form identifying him as he threw back his hood. Owen breathed in deeply of the scents surrounding them as the Master from the hidden forest joined them. Amazed that another of the Ancient Ones had left his haven to risk himself, the companions could only stare; the words they were going to say falling off into the sudden silence.

"There is no difference between us, my friends. The circle elders bowed to the wisdom of the elder of Skye; for now, we all traverse the path that leads to the Flame." The elder from the hidden place held out his hand for the Old One to take, and she did so gratefully. The distant sound of rocks cascading down the steep rock walls caused them to hurry in the direction the others had taken.

§ § § § §

Liege stood, silent and still, waiting. He was close; he could sense it. The fur raised in a ruff along his back as he scented the air. Nothing. Undeterred, he moved quickly to stand in front of what appeared to be a solid wall of rock. Behind him, the little ones, the earth dwellers—the smallest of the earthen clans—waited. Not knowing what to do, in desperation, Liege flung himself against the barrier, which held fast. He knew they were there—knew they were alive and waiting. Frustrated, he sat back, wishing Nickolous were here.

"Wait." The words carried through thoughts to the wolf as the earth dwellers moved forward. It was they who had waited guarding the entrance. Waited for Liege to come and free those imprisoned behind the cold grey rock.

The largest of them, an elder, bent and withered by many turnings, touched the wolf gently. Looking down, Liege watched as a multitude of the little ones gathered at one spot and began digging away at the base of the rock wall.

Surprised at how easily the rock disintegrated beneath their small claws, he looked closer and, as the little ones moved away, began digging until he hit something hard and sharp; his claws catching on the jagged edge of rock that peeled off in small shards, causing tiny cuts which stung; he pulled back, shaking his forepaw in disgust.

The eldest of the earth dwellers moved forward. Placing himself in front of Liege, he bent his head, concentrating. Liege pulled back, surprised, as thoughts formed within his mind. There was a weakness here, at the base of the rock, but more help was needed. He nudged the little earth dweller gently. Leaning against the cold, grey rock, he pressed the side of his face against its moldy dampness, listening; from the other side came the reply to the unasked thought.

§ § § § §

"*No!*" Lord Nhon leaned against the table, scattering the parchment as it tipped precariously to one side. Crumpling a piece of yellowed paper, he flung it into the corner, then turning, righted the table and its contents. He had returned to the cavern frustrated that he could not find a mere *halfling* and now this—

"Are you sure?" His gaze fixed on the messenger who at this moment was wondering at the wisdom of being there. There was an underlying scent of danger lingering in the dankness that permeated the stale air and something more.

Death.

The creature peered into the gloom and saw.

"Remove it." Lord Nhon caught the barest flicker of anger in the creature's stare. It would not do for these creatures to start thinking for themselves! Dismissing the thing with a wave of his hand, he turned away, his keen hearing telling him that the thing obeyed his command; removing its dead comrade.

So, they were still in the lower caverns, were they? Red eyes glittered in a gaunt face dangerously as Lord Nhon picked up the crystal flask. Turning it from side to side, he stared at it thoughtfully, his mind undecided. Some things should not be rushed; the timing critical to their success; or failure. He held the flask up to his face as the contents encased within the crystal rolled together, blending, before settling back.

No...

He turned away from the cavern's entrance. He still had allies to call upon. He paused briefly as a thought, fleeting, crossed his mind then just as quickly dissipated. Shrugging off the feeling, he hurried to the center of the cavern where the fire had died down to glowing embers. Stirring the center of the fire, he knelt down, blowing softly until the flames stirred, awakening.

§ § § § §

"Hold." A-Sharoon let her breath out slowly as the creature, pressed closely to her side, waited for a command. From their place of concealment they could see Liege and the earth dwellers as they leaned against the cold grey rock that would not give. Exhausted, tired, they waited for their strength to return to themselves so the tedious task could begin again.

A-Sharoon knew what lay behind the walls, imprisoned by the Lord of Darkness and by she, herself. The distant sounds that carried through the silence stirred her with a feeling she hadn't felt before. Moving out of the shadows, she pushed the wolf aside, the earth dwellers needing no such urging as they parted to clear the way.

Moving swiftly to the wall, A-Sharoon felt along its center 'til she found what she sought. Then, running her hands across the breadth and depth of it, she stood back, her arms spread wide, her lips forming words that the eldest of the earth dwellers had never thought to hear again.

Knowing instinctively what to do, and unafraid of this woman for the first time in their long remembering, the little ones joined their thoughts and minds to that of A-Sharoon, while Liege stood, transfixed by the seeming apparition before him.

§ § § § §

Nickolous stepped over the debris strewn about the caverns floor, carefully, so as not to disturb anything as the companions moved silently behind him.

The little flyers were gone.

Nickolous listened to the heartbeat within himself as the bracelet turned luminescent against his arm; the staff answering with its own warmth as the light dispersed the dark shadows that threatened to follow in their wake. They were close. He could feel it…The Flame called with a silent fierceness that drew him unerringly onward; toward it and whatever fate awaited them.

"Lord Moshat?" The elder had moved forward, and Nickolous looked at him questioningly.

"The caverns run deep into the lower depths, and the unknown is unspeakable for those lacking the knowledge to understand."

Nickolous held the others gaze with his own; his understanding of himself an awareness that no longer frightened him. Acknowledging the elder's concern for not only himself but the other companions as well, he was surprised nonetheless when the other reached out and clasped his shoulder in a firm grip.

"There." The elder gazed past him, seeing what the others could not.

"*Old One.*" Nickolous let his breath out slowly, relieved to see the Old One and Orith safe and seemingly well.

"See; the worlds within worlds began to unite." Lord Moshat nodded at the travelers.

"It's the elder from the hidden forest." Gabriel nudged his mate in wonder as the last of the companions came into view.

Orith pulled the Old One to him while Gabriel and Chera stopped their journeying to stay at a distance; while the elder of Skye and the guardian from that hidden place silently greeted one another. Neither one was surprised that their paths had crossed once again.

Nickolous turned and faced them; his thoughts bridging and filling a void that had remained veiled to most since the beginning of remembering; the veil falling from him as he remembered who and what he was—the darkness no longer holding him captive as he struggled to understand what lay beneath the shadows of his forgotten memories.

As the elder's hand slid from his shoulder, he looked into the others eyes and saw himself, mirrored deep within the depths of another being. Letting out his breath slowly, he turned away.

He understood now. Turning, he faced the companions, his stance telling them he had changed yet again. Gone was the child. Gone was the boy; before them stood the man. Changed, yet unchanged; his very presence speaking thoughts beyond words as he held the staff aloft.

The Old One nodded to Orith as they brought forth their own staffs. Wordlessly they held them out toward the one staff that glowed with a translucency that was nearly invisible to mortal eyes.

"The power of *The Three* lies not within our tired bodies but within the staffs themselves," The Old One whispered as the wind found them; swirling about them in a cold fury even as the light temporarily blinded them.

Nickolous reached out to retrieve the staff as it flew from his grasp, unerringly toward the other two, then he, too, bowed to the fury that engulfed them.

§ § § § §

Lord Nhon watched in silence as the flames swept upward, arching against the ceiling; returning to their center, the low hissing emanating from deep within. The shadow being had been powerful, but in the end unreliable. He turned toward the form that grew within the depths of the ice cold flame and, as the two separated, watched as the flame withered into blackened coals. His concentration now on the being before him, the low hissing, at first nearly inaudible, steadied

itself as it sought to center itself in its new surroundings. Sensing
Lord Nhon, it turned to face its new master, even as it changed yet
again. Wraithlike, without features of any kind, primordial beyond
remembering—thoughts passed like quicksilver between the two as
the creature rose higher, the high keening nerve shattering as it hovered near the ceiling, scenting its prey.

"*Go*. Do not let them enter the chamber that contains the Flame."
Lord Nhon rose to his full height, trying to read the others thoughts as
the creature stilled its movements as if weighing the command it had
been given. Beneath his hood, Lord Nhon's eyes glowed with an
unnatural light as he drew deep within himself; seeking the power
which would bind the being to him without thought to question his
command.

"My Lord?"

"What do you want?" The words were hissed as Lord Nhon turned
to the wolf-like creature that had entered the chambers unheard. For a
moment more, the other-world entity hovered above them before disappearing into the darkness that surrounded them.

"Well, what is it. Have you found them?" The Fallen moved
toward the feral creature as he spoke, his intent clear as to his intentions if the interruption had been unwarranted.

The beast moved back, wary. "They come, through the passages of
the Old Ones." The thing hesitated, then: "They do not travel
alone..."

Lord Nhon made a strangled sound as he choked back his rage.
Fighting for control of his emotions, he inhaled slowly; centering his
thoughts. So, they had traversed the hidden places and were being
aided by the warriors of Skye, were they? Well, it made no difference,
for the die was cast, and the Flame would survive—or not. He
shrugged; the first tremor struck him at the same time that the wind
rushed through the connecting tunnels; carrying with it the whispering of things long forgot. As Lord Nhon fled down the chamber that
led to the Flame, the sounds of battle followed him, spiraling down
into the empty darkened places.

§ § § § §

A-Sharoon stood, her back pressed against the cold rock, her hands
clenched tightly as she drew the forbidden power to her. From their
hidden places, they came to heed the call of an ancient spell cast from
before the beginning. Hesitant at first, groggy from their awakening
after endless turnings, they came. Countless of them; waiting to do as

they were bidden. Unsure, like children taking their first steps into the unknown, they shrank back into the darkness only to be urged forth. Their combined strength was needed for the task ahead.

Liege watched as the Daughter of Darkness worked her ancient spells. Confusion had quickly given way to understanding as to what needed to be done. The stone could not be moved by the earth dwellers and him alone. The big wolf moved in the half darkness to stand beside the woman who had been his enemy from the beginning, his understanding growing as he sensed something different about her. Green eyes looked into black as the woman met his gaze, and for a moment their minds met in understanding.

Liege bent his head slightly as he acknowledged their temporary truce. Turning his attention to the wall and those behind it, he lent his strength to the others, ignoring the bits of debris that rained down as the hidden door slowly, reluctantly, gave way.

§ § § § § §

"The balance is tested yet again." The Old One shuffled forward to stand beside Nickolous as the wind rushed about them; not touching them—for it was an ancient thing; bidden to protect those who held the staffs and the bearer of the bracelet.

"It would seem that we have allies in the unseen places," Lord Moshat commented as he retrieved the staff, for that's what it now was. Gone were The Three. In their stead a solid staff entwined, the memories of countless turnings combined into one. The power contained within incomprehensible.

"Here." He held the staff out to Nickolous who took it without hesitation, his grasp firm as he nodded to the elder. A silent affirmation that he understood...

Lord Moshat stood; waiting, as the man—for man he now was—held the staff high above his head; the blue-white light that emanated from it surrounding them all. Pulsing gently it enveloped them within its protective embrace; returning to the staff, it surged upward, then back to the wood that was living. The power shared. The three complete

The Old One sighed softly as she leaned against Orith for support. Jerome stood back with Owen; the great snowy white Owl's golden eyes blinked and closed as the memories assailed him. His thoughts reaching out to the others so that he was not alone as the wind swirled around them—through them—seeking as it passed over them; the thin wailing as it pressed against the crevices made them shiver in the dampness.

"She searches the farthest reaches," Jerome spoke; his voice rising, carrying as the wind rose, shrieking above his head.

"Something approaches." Chera, fur bristling, stood with her mate, her senses alerting her to an unseen terror. Gabriel nosed her gently, his own senses reeling. It was everywhere as they stood powerless beneath its wrath.

The unknown—but not—for it was they who were the ones untaught. It had always been there—from the dawning—back to the beginning—dormant, 'til now—one more remembering to be learned.

And it was to this end that the staff would serve its purpose, for the power contained within its living wood had been there from the beginning—waiting to be called and to call—

The companions suddenly found themselves lifted with the wind; the blue-white light surrounding them, soothing them. Jerome shuddered as even he, weightless against the strength of it, rose, and as if from a great distance saw and the seeing strengthened him and he was not afraid; for his kind had long been guardians of the secret places.

The light struck the companions, flowing through them as a river flows along the river bed—smoothing the rocks beneath its flow so that eventually they are worn smooth; the learning complete.

"The Flame," the Old One whispered as she felt the ebb and flow of the power coursing through her.

Orith nodded as he grasped her to him tightly, for as sure as he was to what was happening to them, there was still the knowledge that there was much to be understood with the learning. He raised his head, the cowl falling back, heat coursing through him, into the Old One, and back again so that they shared the learning.

25

Lord Nhon stood just inside the mouth of the cavern; the rage building within him as he surveyed the carnage. His dark army had been well met; their adversary stronger. Emotions, long buried, rose to the surface as the Fallen stepped into the light; his gaze sweeping the clearing for the one he knew who watched. The silent challenge thrown out—to be grasped—to be met—

The forest warrior—he who was once the guardian of the sacred flame—watched as Lord Nhon raged. His own ability to become one with the surrounding forest an advantage that did little to comfort him as he fought the urge to reveal himself. Long and long had he waited to draw the Fallen One out—out of the shadows, into the light where there was equality for both combatants.

Lord Nhon stepped back; further into the shadows as if reading the others thoughts.

Feeling helpless as the cavern protected the one who had once been a warrior of Skye; the warrior shrugged indifferently, for he knew what they had to do. Already the earth dwellers, the little ones, beat out a steady tattoo from deep within the earth; their message reaching up and out through ancient layers of soil and rock to reverberate through to those above who understood the ancient code. The warrior smiled as the others, like him, drew close together; their thoughts combining to communicate with those below.

"The wolves have been freed to seek their enemy." The warrior straightened to his full height; his attention drawn inexplicably back to the cavern where Lord Nhon had been. There was nothing there that he could see and yet—he withdrew from the others as he went to his warriors' place of knowing. It was there. Concealed within the darkened places; the slight roiling of the shadows near the ceiling...

His senses reeling, he threw himself toward the vaporous creature that came hurtling toward them. With the element of surprise now gone, the creature that had been so recently called to do the dark one's bidding threw himself into the waiting warriors midst.

§ § § § § §

Lord Moshat walked beside the watcher, their thoughts joining as the sounds of battle reached them. It was Lord Moshat who spoke first, his thoughts going up and out to the forest warriors. He sensed their thoughts, saw what they saw, and knew the enemy they battled was formidable.

"The Fallen seeks to have those occupied who could defeat him."

The watcher from the hidden place acknowledged the other's words; the knowledge of what the warriors faced a concern. The power the creature possessed was formidable and old; a creature drawn through time from the imaginings of the darkness that sheltered the unknown, now brought into the realm of light. The watcher shrugged, his thoughts centered on the one who walked ahead of him. The three staffs combined, their powers melded into unimaginable strength, grasped tightly to him like a shield.

"The creature will be well met by the forest warriors while the one who bears the staff will awaken the Ancients."

Lord Moshat glanced at Nickolous, who now walked ahead of them, flanked on either side by the two wolves—companions from the beginning—Guardians to the hopes and dreams of those long passed into the memory; those who carried the knowledge of their forbears within themselves.

"The battle will be fierce."

"But well met."

"Not all of us will survive."

Lord Moshat turned a narrowed gaze on the elder. The warriors of Skye, and those that were like, yet unlike them, lived turnings beyond those of the forest clans and others.

"And Nickolous?"

"His mother's blood runs through him. Her legacy to her son is a powerful one." The elder's gaze rested upon the bearer of the staff. Yes, he decided to himself; the women of Skye; the one called Aleta, would be proud of the young warrior who strode fearlessly toward his destiny.

Liege paused at the top of the precipice, the white ethereal mist swirling about him as he nosed his way carefully to the edge. The others had passed this way but a short time ago; their scent still heavy against the dampness that clung, unmoving, in the air above him. He lifted his head as the sounds of falling rock reached him; they were being followed—Nickolous, and the others. Liege turned to the white wolf that stood behind him, the words whispered as he told him what to do. The second in command nodded curtly before leaving with half of the wolves, the other half to continue on with Liege. They would go around, through the caverns and meet again. By doing this, they would hopefully eliminate those who waited in shadow. Liege turned as another scent came to him. Sickly sweet, cloying, it clung to his senses, nearly suffocating him with its intensity, while the unbidden rose within him. There was fear here, buried deep within the living rock that surrounded them. Terror had walked these caverns long ago; leaving its imprint for those who would follow the same path; a warning to tread carefully. Out of the corner of his eye, Liege caught a shadowy form, tall and lithe, moving to the left of him.

A-Sharoon stood at the edge of the precipice; watching; her dark ones beside her. She had her army; her power was now restored. Liege acknowledged her presence, his own army behind him, waiting to go forward; fear not an option now, they would do what was necessary.

"Hurry, the caverns narrow into nothing that way." A-Sharoon pointed to the right. Her pale skin a contrast to the darkness they were surrounded with. She held up her hand in a gesture of peace.

"Go now, for you need not fear me or mine while we are here; our battle is now the same. In the hidden place the Flame waits. Go." She let her hand fall as she pulled her cape about her, using the hooded robe to conceal her features—the dark cloak rendering her invisible so that she now seemed to be a disembodied voice.

"*Until we meet again.*" The farewell echoed hollowly in the poignant silence as Liege shifted uneasily; his every instinct warning against complacency. A-Sharoon could not be trusted. True, she had helped him free his warriors; had even spoken the ancient dialect known only to a few and had worked beside the earth dwellers. The little ones, those who were the heart beat of the earth.

Liege threw off the instinct to send some of his warriors to follow. There was no time, and as much as he hated to admit it, the Daughter to the Night seemed somehow changed.

Deep down, the big wolf had his own unvoiced thoughts as to how the sacred Flame affected those who touched and were touched by its spirit.

"Go." Liege dismissed half of the wolves to do his bidding, then, turning began following another path to seek his own journey.

A-Sharoon watched the wolves go; her thoughts centered. From this point on, she should no longer interfere in the battle between the Fallen and those of the forest clans, for she could not risk the loss of self. From the beginning of remembering, she had been the darkness that warred with the light. It was as she turned away, her intention to once more go to earth, that she heard it. The *Flame;* its soft sighing within her—whispers that none could hear but her. She stood still, silencing those who walked behind her. Her thoughts, her memories—she silenced them all.

There could be no imagining what would be if she did not put things back the way they once were and again become who she was.

§§§§§§

Nickolous felt the power of the staff as it coursed through him; sparing a glance for Chera and Gabriel, he wondered if they too felt what he felt. The staff hummed slightly, the vibration sending shivers through his body as the armband responded to its kin.

Memories.

Nickolous shook his head to clear it; the whispers of the seven from the sacred place calming him. He inhaled deeply, his senses heightened, his hearing more acute as he turned his head, listening; behind him, Lord Moshat and the guardian from the hidden place also paused; their senses attuned to that of the bearer of the staff.

"We're being watched." Gabriel moved closer, the fur along his back rising.

"Smell that?" Chera asked, her breathing shallow as the air around them suddenly became thick with the unmistakable odor of a change-ling.

"There's more than one." Jerome was suddenly beside them, his war club in his hand, his mind peering into the darkness; locating the hidden enemy.

"You must continue on. Don't stop." The Old One was looking up at the Jerome, her black eyes crinkling at the edges as she too scented the stale air. "They must not know we sense them. We have to prepare ourselves."

"There is another passage ahead. There." Nickolous peered ahead into the darkness that fringed the outer edges of the caverns walls. His grip on the staff tightening as the warmth spread up his arm, into his neck.

The guardian of the hidden forest touched his shoulder. Words—unspoken—heard.

Nickolous nodded, his awareness heightened; the staff flared blue-white as the shrieks ebbed into nothingness.

"Hurry!" The shouted words were nearly drowned out by more shrieks as the changelings, partially concealed within the shadows rushed out. Some were still turning, growing into forms that would have terrified most, but not the bearer of the staff.

Eyes half closed against the light that was nearly blinding, Nicko-lous pointed the staff at the cold grey rocks in front of them. Beside him, the Old One, her paws clasped in front of her, uttered words unheard beneath her breath while Orith, his hooded robe thrown back over his shoulder, joined her. His scarred features softened by the glow of the light from the staff as it flamed upward and out toward the wall; the shattering sound muffled by the howls of the changelings as they sought their prey.

Gabriel threw off the creature and met the next one head on as Chera, fangs barred, leapt to intercept the midnight form that had lain in wait amongst the ledges overhead; while Jerome protected Nicko-lous's passage through the narrow opening in the cavern's wall. Quickly, the others slipped through; their thoughts not on what were behind them—but ahead.

Pushing the Old One and Orith through the opening, Jerome turned to face another changeling; his war club finding its mark with deadly accuracy. Caught midair, the creature somersaulted backward, the need to protect itself, to change, to grow stronger, to defeat. There wasn't enough time, however, for suddenly Owen was there ahead of Jerome, his sharp talons grasping, tightening, until the creature fell limp and was dropped to the ground.

The forest warrior breathed in deeply; the air around him suddenly charged with a heavy musky smell. Knowing they had to hurry now and seal the opening behind them, he called the elder and the protec-tor of the hidden place to him as Nickolous held the staff high, the soft blue-white light emanating toward the scarred opening. Creeping upward, its soft tendrils of mist touching the newly opened places, the fissure slowly closed, much to the dismay of the shadowy beings on the other side. Their howls of protest reverberated through the heavy air, for there were places that even they, with their powers, could not traverse once the way was closed against them.

"We must be close; else the Fallen One would not be calling the forbidden ones to him," the elder spoke softly; his words for the warrior of the forest.

Jerome mopped his brow, the sweat beading up as fast as he wiped it away. Darkness, unseen, moved over him, threatening to suffocate his senses. He turned at the elder's touch. Slowly his senses calmed. He bent down, his craggy face inches from the others, his mind reaching out to touch; to see what the elder had seen.

Startled, he pulled back—the vision of the Flame struggling against an unseen barrier—the little ones, the earth diggers, futilely pressing against an invisible prison, waiting for those stronger than they to intercede.

"Liege waits on the other side with half of Gabriel's warriors while the rest approach from the lower caverns." The elder closed his eyes, concentrating, seeking out the oldest of the earth dwellers. It was some moments before he found him, the ability to communicate with the eldest of the protectors of the earthen realms a gift to be used for the good of them all.

"They wait for us." The elder lowered his head as if listening to whispered words. He looked up, startled, his gaze locking with that of Jerome's.

"The Flame—the heartbeat that is of all living things begins to weaken." The elder turned to the protector of the hidden forest, his hand reaching out to grasp the others arm.

"We must hurry." The sudden urgency in his voice startled the others as his grip tightened. "The elder of the earth dwellers; those of the clans beneath, speaks of the Elemental powers striking the prison. The wall weakens, but more is needed, and quickly."

The air about them resounded with sound as Liege, with half of Gabriel's best, struggled through a narrow opening in the wall. Looking tattered and worn, Liege acknowledged Gabriel, his head high as he stood proudly before his leader.

"Well done, my friend." Nickolous touched Liege gently and the weariness washed out of him. The big wolf was grateful for the strength that had been lent.

Nickolous leaned down until he was level with Liege, his gaze meeting that of the black wolf.

"It was your strength and yours alone." The words were whispered. Liege bowed his head, for he felt the power emanating from the speaker as well as the staff.

"Nickolous, the cavern opens the way to the Flame. We must hurry." There was an underlying urgency in the elder's tone as he moved forward. Nodding, Nickolous rose and followed; leaving Liege to follow.

"Quickly now, we don't have much time." Jerome waited until the others were through. Then, swinging his club in an arc, he struck the wall, causing it to crumble, covering the opening in debris. He stood back. Still...

Moments later, two silver wolves took up their places on opposite sides of the shattered doorway.

There would be none to follow.

"There, the path narrows, and beyond that is the doorway to the Flame." Nickolous held the staff high, its light reflecting off the walls down the long darkened corridor. Gabriel stood beside him; his senses tingling; Chera, flanking Nickolous on the other side, felt the subtle changes around them as the unseen ones watched from their hidden places.

"*Go.*" The words were whispered.

Silently the journey was begun, the blue-white light from the staff reaching out, grasping and melting the shadows that danced in front of them.

"*Lord Nhon,*" the Old One muttered beneath her breath as she labored to keep up. Behind her, Orith followed, his focus on the others ahead of them; the need to reach their destination overpowering the fear that he kept pushing down. He was getting old, he thought. Too old. Wearily he pushed his hood forward, concealing his features as he kept ahead of Jerome, the forest warrior's own silhouette masked by the shadows wavering light.

"We're at the end of the corridor." Lord Moshat stood beside Nickolous as the watcher from the hidden place flanked him on the other side.

"Everything is not as it seems." The Old One pushed forward, her brows furrowing as she pressed herself against the wall in front of them. The sensation coursing through her was one of darkness. It was a trap. Before the companions had a chance to react the wall simply disappeared, and they were surrounded by darkness so complete that the light from the staff was smothered.

26

As the darkness pressed down, Nickolous struggled to bring his arm up, while around him swirled the unimaginable. Inwardly he shuddered at the brush of wings against his cheek, the knowledge of what was behind the feather soft touch spurring him on. The ability to draw on the strength the Ancients lent coursing through him as words, remembered, poured forth.

"Orith. Old One. Where are you?" Owen called into the darkness, his ability to see hampered by the unnatural blackness that pressed against him making it nearly impossible to discern friend from foe. Disoriented, he struck out blindly, his senses guiding him as he struck something.

"Owen!" The Old One rasped beside him as she grasped him, pulling him off balance.

"*Down.*" The words were hissed as she pulled him to her.

As he fell something brushed past him, soft tentacles caressing the side of his body. Almost immediately, he felt the pain as the acrid smell of burning skin assailed his senses. The Old One, recognizing the odor and what had caused it, wrapped her body about that of Owen, at the same time drawing the ancient words forth from that hidden place of her kind.

Almost immediately, Owen felt the power flowing through his body as the burning sensation ceased. Recovering quickly, he pulled away from the Old One, his concentration now on the assailants above him. From beside him, the Old One poured all of her remaining strength into focusing on what she must do.

As the Old One battled alongside Orith, Owen flew high, out of reach of the fanged ones that sought to pull him toward them. Power flowed through him and over him as something unidentified coursed through the caverns with a sudden rush of sound; unheard by the dark hoard that poured forth from the hidden places, their intent to destroy the companions before they reached the Flame.

"To me!" Nickolous held the staff above his head as streams of white-blue light shot out from its tip, dancing along the jagged rocks above them, the shrieks of agony echoing in their wake—seeking out the darkened places where the unseen ones had hidden, waiting.

Orith, struggling against something he could not see, broke free of the unseen thing that gripped him; hurtling forward to be grasped by the Old One, her gaze fierce as she focused on what was taking form in front of them.

"There." Nickolous steadied the staff as it writhed with a life of its own. Impatient, it seemed, to pour forth what was needed to defeat the enemy.

"You must direct its power," Lord Moshat spoke, his voice carrying above that of the storm that raged about them. Shrieking forms leapt at them; snarling and growling as they sought an opening to reach their quarry. Gabriel reared back as something lunged at him, narrowly missing him as Chera leapt high, her aim true; the big wolf shuddered involuntarily as the stench of anger and desperation grew, but now there was a new scent being carried through the air. Fear.

Gabriel growled softly as Chera, her muzzle stained red, joined him, while above them the air swirled; no longer warm, icy tendrils reaching out to caress.

Lord Moshat shivered as the Old One, her aged body reacting in kind to the sudden change reached out to Jerome, the forest warrior lending his strength now to that of the others. Thoughts poured forth between the companions as abilities fused.

Gifts lent, acknowledged, and strengthened by the wisdom given by the elders of Skye.

Orith blinked against the brilliant light as his body shuddered from the power coursing through it.

Before him, before them all, Nickolous changed as the light from the staff engulfed him, slowly spreading out from his fingertips to embrace those who gathered about him; their one thought to protect him.

"*No*. Do not try to speak." It was the elder from the hidden place who spoke, the words riding softly above the swirling light.

"Ride with it, but do not let it overpower you. In unity lies strength. Understand it. Share it…"

The sudden calm wasn't nearly as nerve shattering as the screams from Lord Nhon's chosen.

§ § § § §

The warrior beckoned to the circle where six others waited; the sweet scent of the burning grass reaching upward and out, permeating the air about him.

Understanding, he still stood in that place with the others, as well as here, with the Seven—Nickolous entered the circle. The mists frothing and swirling about him to take him back—

Back to when it had begun.

Here, the world was just beginning. The earth rose and fell beneath his feet. Her heartbeat strong and pulsing with hope. Nickolous closed his eyes. *Emotions. So many.* They rose up from within as he was filled with memories of what it was like when there was nothing but perfection and the trees grew straight and tall. Flowering with a beauty not seen in a millennium of conscious thought.

Time passed, and the world changed about him as he stood within its center. Now he watched as if from a great distance as the world darkened. Mists rose and swirled yet again as things changed. The two-legged—not four-legged—now held dominion over the rest.

And the darkness grew.

Within the center, where the young warrior stood, a sorrowing sigh arose as something stirred. The stench of decay creeping upward and out, clinging with a cloying sweetness that was suffocating as Nickolous struggled against the fear of the unknown. The wisdom of the Seven, a comfort as words, whispered in the ancient dialect of the ones who had been there since the world had begun, showed him what must be done.

§ § § § §

Such sorrow. The Flame flickered against its prison as the Earth dwellers frantically pushed against the invisible wall that held it. From his place of knowing, Nickolous watched, helpless as first one, then another of the earth dwellers fell, crushed by the creature Lord Nhon had brought forth. But still they came—the little ones, the heartbeat of the earth; unafraid of what lay ahead.

Aided by the elders within the sacred circle, Nickolous felt the power rising as the knowledge, given to many, yet understood by only a few, flowed through him; into the others.

§ § § § § §

Lord Moshat drew on the powers of Skye. The guardian from the hidden forest lending strength to the powers of the elders beyond that realm where the veil had thinned; allowing Nickolous safe passage, and them, a glimpse of what before had been a mere telling; a confirmation within of what they, and their forbears had always known. Beside them, the Old One gasped as she also recognized within herself the things she had always known.

But even with the knowing, there had always been the merest flicker of doubt. The seed within them all that caused indecision when they refused to listen with their hearts.

The howling above their heads intensified as the staff hummed; the white-blue light emanating from its center swirling around the one who held it, until he himself was held within the center of the light— protected by the Ancient Ones from beyond the realms of knowing.

§ § § § § §

Lord Nhon moved wraithlike along the narrow passageways, certain of the outcome of the battle; confident in the powers of the shadow being that he, himself, had brought forth from the dark realms. He didn't bother to pause when the first tremors beneath the ground began. Behind him, unseen, A-Sharoon stopped, her nostrils flaring as she let the sensations flow through her. Beneath her robes, the amulet stirred, the stone within its center awakening, seeking.

"Have a care, sister."

The honeyed words washed over her as she drew in her breath sharply.

"Don't interfere now!" The words were hissed as she searched the hidden places about her; but no, he wasn't there. She shrugged in the darkness. "Stay where you are. In your own place; in your own time..." The words were whispered; even so, the answer echoed.

"There are many realms of darkness and light, dear sister. Have a care that you are not displaced out of yours."

A-Sharoon clutched the amulet tightly, soothing it as she closed her mind to her brothers' presence; willing the veil of the unseen to close between them.

"Owen. There. Above you." The Old One flung the lifeless body aside to face yet another as Jerome, swinging his war club, cut a deadly swath toward Orith; the old warrior holding his own despite being wounded. Above him, Owen battled as Gabriel, and Chera fought off a changeling intent on reaching the bearer of the staff.

It was the changeling's dying screams that carried through the passageways to Lord Nhon. The Fallen One quickening his pace until he was running; the incantations uttered as he burst around the corner of the cavern to face Lord Moshat and the warrior from the hidden place. With a roar that was heard above and below in the realms beyond realms, Lord Nhon flung himself at his old mentor. The cries of battle deafening as light and darkness met.

For turnings beyond remembering, Lord Moshat had known this time would come. As the fiery ball arched toward him, increasing in speed so that it was nearly a blur, he met it with an increased power of his own; the frozen shards splintering as they fell about those who scurried hurriedly out of the way. Time was temporarily suspended as the companions, caught within a vortex of spinning light, watched; helpless to interfere as the embodiment of all they had ever admired or feared, met.

The watcher from the hidden place reached out to Nickolous, pulling him back from the sacred circle. His call to the elders, the seven, heard. Whispers carried upon the wind that swirled silently above them had carried the message to the cavern where none dared walk unless invited.

Nickolous felt himself being pulled through the misty places. The faces of the elders fading as the veil closed behind him.

§ § § § §

"*Die.*"

The words were hissed as Lord Moshat narrowly avoided the flying shards that shattered about him. Twisting around, blue-white light flowed through his body to meet the challenge thrown out by Lord Nhon. As the two energies met, voices, long passed into a time distant beyond remembering awakened, and the Fallen One paused as something buried deep within him stirred in answer. His body went rigid as he brushed the fleeting emotion aside as the voices stilled; no longer seeking for the answer had been given. As Lord Nhon straightened, his hood fell back, revealing a face that was terrible. Lord Moshat, seeing what had passed from the other, grieved, knowing that any humanity that had existed within the twisted features of the one who had once been known as Lord Nhon was now gone forever.

Lord Nhon regretted nothing and was beyond thought of anything rational save ridding himself of those who opposed him. His hatred blinding him to everything save the young man who stood before him, protected by the powers of the circle elders. Blood-red eyes, their black centers mere slits narrowed as the veil that protected Nickolous slowly dissolved; the contact broken. His focus now on the one before him, he cast a rune spell to hold the others back, his intent to destroy this half-son of Skye.

"*To me.*" Nickolous held the staff in front of him, the humming sound reverberating off the rocks around him, the blue-white light flowing up and out of the polished wood as the power of the Ancients poured forth. Their memories flowing through Nickolous as their combined thoughts summoned the winds from the four corners; even as the darkness threatened to overwhelm his senses. Words, unbidden, rose from within and were spoken softly as the Fallen One strode purposefully toward him; his hooded cloak flowing behind him as he raised his arms; the power coursing through him as he loosened the dark fury within himself against the one who held the staff aloft…

…Its own power racing through the ancient wood that had lived before them all.

Lord Moshat and the elder from the hidden forest were thrown aside; the explosion ripping through the cavern. Jerome, as massive as he was, barely withstood the force of the blast; nonetheless, he was able to shield the Old One and Orith with his body, his massive girth saving them from serious harm.

Owen plummeted toward the Fallen, talons reaching out to grasp the robed figure. Dodging the outreached arms, he struck. Hard. The blow was returned in kind. Winded, the snowy owl fell; the darkness washing over him. As if from a great distance, he heard Nickolous calling and the strength offered was accepted as the great wings unfurled, the upward rush of air scented with power as Owen once again struck out at the Fallen One.

"*Orith.* Go to him." The Old One struggled against the wind that clutched at her, embracing her with a stubborn tenacity to match her own. Turning about, she sought out a place between the crevices, and bracing herself against the fury of the unnatural wind made her way slowly toward it. Orith, seeing what she was doing, and knowing that she was safe, struggled toward Nickolous as Gabriel and Chera fought the dark ones who poured forth from unknown places.

"Owen!" The words were drowned out against the rush of sound as the Fallen One roared in rage.

A thousand turnings he had waited for this moment to face the elder whom he had once called friend and now the Halfling who dared think he could ever be a true son of Skye. As the Old One watched in horrified fascination, he began to change—

To grow...

Recognizing what the Fallen One was becoming, the Old One averted her eyes as she drew deep within herself, preparing; while the unnatural wind raged about her, intensifying; the elders of Skye and Nickolous turned as one to face Lord Nhon's wrath.

§ § § § §

A-Sharoon inhaled sharply, her senses tingling as the fury of the battle permeated her senses. One hand went instinctively to the amulet that burned at her throat; the other silencing those who stood behind her. The urge to interfere, to sway the battle so that things would be as they were before, was nearly uncontrollable as she watched the Fallen and the half son of Skye prepare to do battle. Ancient murmurings stirring within them both as the Old Ones awakened.

The Flame called to her. A-Sharoon started forward, the incantation already cast from bloodless lips. The Fallen sensing her even as the half-son of Skye raised the staff high above his head, summoning the warrior's vision within the living wood to guide him. What started as a soft growl became a roar as Gabriel leapt upward only to be swept aside by a force that reeked of untold turnings of dark magic.

The Daughter born to the darkness of the *before* time paused; the Flame calling to the stone nestled within the palm of her hand.

Forged at the time of the awakening of awareness, what were opposite now became kindred—seeking to find a balance. As the burning sensation became nearly unbearable, the stone threatened to ignite within her grasp.

"*So, you would think to challenge me.*" The words echoed within her mind as the force of the first fire ball bounced off her, her nostrils flaring as she ripped the stone from its chain, releasing it from the gilded backing that had held it prisoner for millennia.

§ § § § §

Within the confines of its tiny prison, the Flame reached out; no longer tentatively seeking, it began to grow in size. On the other side of the prison, the earth dwellers drew closer, as the unseen wind began to move faster and faster in the small tunnel, fanning the stale air until it crept through the fissure nearly invisible in the rock.

§ § § § § §

Like a moth drawn to a light, the Flame and the wind sought each other out.

§ § § § § §

"Nickolous, protect yourself."

The shouted words were lost amidst the cries of the injured and dying as A-Sharoon moved to block the Fallen's path. Seeing his chance, Nickolous released the power locked within the staff, the blue-white light fanning out away from the wood and the one who held it; wraithlike tendrils wrapped around the heavily robed form who roared a challenge.

Striking out at what he could not see, fear and hope overtaking all thought, the lost son of Skye released all that was within himself—

Even as the Daughter of Darkness released the power that lie within the center of the stone; hers alone to command.

§ § § § § §

The power washed over him, nearly taking him, as the staff warmed in his hands, the armlet reacting to the ebb and flow of the pulsating power that threatened to consume his senses. Reaching out, Nickolous sought the unspoken help offered by Lord Moshat and the elder from the hidden forest as the first wave of darkness rolled over him. White Light surrounded him, creating a shield of power as Gabriel placed himself in front of Nickolous, only to be pushed gently aside.

"Hold." A-Sharoon spoke, her voice rising as she stepped in front of them, her long, black hair streaming behind her, her robes fanning out so that she seemed to be rising off the earthen floor. Nickolous stepped back, pulling the big wolf with him. Within him the still small voice whispered. *"Not yet..."*

"You dare to interfere!" The red eyes flashed, their pupils narrowed until they were mere slits. "You! Have you forgotten who and what you are?" Laughter, dark and grating burst forth from bloodless lips.

A-Sharoon stepped closer, black eyes blazing. "No. I have not forgotten who I *Am,* for I have always *Been.* Into the darkness was I brought forth. I and others like me. We are everywhere. It is you who do not belong. *How dare I?"* Long white fingers relaxed their grip on the stone that struggled to be free.

Moving closer, A-Sharoon rose to her full height. *"How dare I?"* Even as she spoke, the stone's full power was released amidst the faintly whispered words.

"How dare you!"

Icy cold tendrils wrapped themselves around the companions; seeking... Nickolous remained where he was, the throbbing of the staff he held reaching out to meet the pulsing power of the stone.

27

Power, ancient and forbidding to those found unworthy; drawing the very breath from the hidden watchers as the Flame burst forth from its prison, consuming those who sought to reach it through the earth dwellers. So swiftly that those who had stood guard barely felt its passage amongst them the Flame stretched out—lengthening—blending into the cold gray rock that concealed its passing.

Behind it, the tiny dwellers of rock and earth gratefully accepted the long-forgotten gift of warmth left within its wake.

§ § § § §

Nickolous swayed beneath the rush of power that flowed through the staff to him. In front of him, A-Sharoon, arms raised above her head, commanded the force of the stone as the Fallen raged at them all. Nearly unrecognizable, he had grown. Changing as the change-lings had; towering over them, his face, or what once had been his face, a mass of darkness as the evil, uncontained, burst forth. At the same time, the staff flew from Nickolous's grasp, while the roar of the wind as it merged with the Flame carried it to the stone that fell from A-Sharoon's nerveless fingers.

As A-Sharoon, Daughter to the Night, turned to shield herself, Nickolous braced himself to accept the power of The Three.

Strength lent by the grandfathers from before the dark time; the stone opened itself to the purity of the fire. Memories, whispered upon the endless winds that blew, fanned the hot breath of the Flame while the living stone, commanded by the woman to do what it must chose the way of Fire and Wind. From somewhere deep within the earth an answering cry echoed as the dwellers of rock and earth surged upward, their thoughts linked to the watchers above.

The warriors of Skye.

Nickolous blinked against the brilliant light as the cavern dissolved in an explosion of shattering rock that shifted outward and away, the voices of the elders guiding him as the silver glowed incandescent against his skin. Words, unbidden, spoken against the storm's wrath as he drew the Old One and Orith to him while Gabriel and Chera fought to keep their balance.

Beneath them the earth heaved upward, spewing debris as a large crack opened—slowly widening as the rush of heat overwhelmed those closest to it.

A-Sharoon straightened slowly, her ability to call the darkness failing her as she looked upward into the face of death. Knowledge, buried deep within memories from the before time were sought, and found as the Fallen towered over her. Even as the power of The Three combined against him, he sought to destroy the Daughter of Darkness for her betrayal.

Nickolous drew in his breath, letting it out slowly, calming himself as he aligned himself with the others. Lord Moshat flanked him on one side, while the watcher from the hidden forest flanked him on the other. The Flame grew, pushed by the wind that blew endlessly, the stone commanding that of its kind to no longer shelter a fallen warrior of Skye. Protected by powers that were beyond comprehending, the companions could only watch as A-Sharoon and the Fallen faced each other.

"Know this Fallen One and remember well these words," A-Sharoon hissed the words as the wind and Flame embraced her, the words trailing off to a whisper as she felt their soft caress against her skin. Her eyes widened as she spoke the words that were not her own but that of the Flame as it used her voice to speak—

A gift of understanding between it and the woman it had briefly touched while encased within its prison.

"Son, born of light, the choice was always yours and yours alone to make. From the beginning I knew you; touched you even though you never knew it, even as I touched all things living deep within that well where all thought exists. In the before time; even from the beginning, I was; as were all things born of darkness and light."

A-Sharoon trembled as the force of the Flame gripped her, its bright orange tendrils cooled by the wind that steadied it. Black eyes

widened as the power of the stone swept back to its mistress amidst
the swirling light, while behind her, Nickolous steadied the flow of
power that raced through his body as the silver armband tightened
against his skin.

Caught within the circle of power, the words spoken in the tongue
of the Ancients silenced Lord Nhon's retort as the darkness swirled
around him, trying to smother the golden glow that surrounded the
Daughter to the Night.

"*Now.*" Nickolous released the power gifted from the circle
elders...The strength of the watchers, the earth dwellers, the little
ones, rising upward to join the elemental powers that battled the darkness that struggled against the Flame.

Both borne into the beginning of understanding. This, the moment
of truth.

Lord Nhon, now beyond any resemblance of a warrior of Skye,
opened his mouth to speak but could not. Tendrils of burning flame
engulfed him as the wind sighed about him, fanning the heat that
seemed to affect him alone as A-Sharoon stumbled backward. Caught
off balance by the Flame's sudden release, the stone clutched tightly
within her hand, red droplets spattering the ground as she drew back
within herself. Back to her center—

To touch and be touched by that which had been from the beginning—then to come back to what she was; left her drained. She
glanced at the companions; at the half son of Skye. Feeling the power
surging back to herself, knowing that she would return to whom she
was, yet at the same time wondering if the memories left by the Flame
would ever recede into the void she felt within herself.

Gabriel snarled a warning to his mate as the fire roared about them,
the changelings shrieking their protest as they turned to ash. Jerome
shielded the Old One and Orith as the wall of Flame rose up before
them. Horrifying and beautiful at the same time, its translucent tendrils wreaking devastation, yet at the same time giving new life as the
earth beneath their feet opened to receive the fallen one of Skye.

§ § § § §

Owen blinked against the light that assailed him as the dust rose
upward to be steadied by the cooling winds. Carried to the four corners; sifted through. To be dispersed by the winds so that nothing of
the darkness that had been here would remain to gather ever again.
They were no longer surrounded by rock and earthen floor. Warmth

flooded the clearing they now found themselves in; the grass beneath their feet soft and comforting as they breathed deeply of the fresh air.

"A-Sharoon?"

"Gone back to her home in the dark forest," Nickolous answered the great wolf that stood beside him.

"And the *Fallen?*" Gabriel turned to look up at the young man who but a few short turnings ago had been but a mere youth. Seeking answers to questions that most would have pondered but never dared ask.

"Into the darkness another has fallen. Having failed to destroy those who seek the light, he will wander endlessly, seeking revenge." Nickolous murmured the words softly as he bent to pick up something that lie half buried in the grass.

It was the amulet that had slipped from Lord Nhon's grasp as he had been consumed by the very darkness that he had served. Wordlessly, he handed it to Lord Moshat, the elder accepting what was once his. The power within the stone had settled, back to its center. It was where it belonged. Lord Moshat glanced up; his gaze meeting that of the elder from the hidden place. Thoughts passed between them in the ancient way of the warriors; the elder from the hidden place nodded his head in assent.

Nickolous accepted the amulet that the winged warrior pressed into his hand as the others watched—their silence their approval of the warrior who had taken his place amongst them.

"Will Lord Nhon find a way to come back?" Timothy asked, helping the Old One as she sat down carefully, her body only now reacting to the stress it had been under.

"The gatekeepers will keep watch." Nickolous held Lord Moshat's gaze as the knowledge of the Ancients, unspoken, once again passed between them. The watcher from the hidden place clasped Nickolous's forearm in a tight grip of friendship, the call of the hidden valley pulling at him. He had been gone too long, and he still had much to do.

A series of high-pitched whistles sounded. Jerome, visibly relieved, replied to his warriors as the rest of the companions gathered about Nickolous, hardly daring to believe it was over. Orith moved slowly, aching in every part of his body, only now missing the staff on which he had leaned so heavily. The Old One patted him gently as he lowered himself beside her, their thoughts as one. The hidden knowledge that had been revealed deep within them—their destiny was now that of teaching others, so that those who chose to would grow; the cycle of growing within oneself a continuing thing.

Around them new life stirred, even as the earth mourned those who had fallen beneath the darkness. Gone was the Flame, carried by the wind back to its sacred place, guarded by the eldest of the forest warriors; the entrance hidden to all but the ones who could see the *unseen.*

Chera and Gabriel, now released from their pledge to guard Nickolous, were free to return to their pack; to the moonlit nights of the chase. The primordial stirrings were strong within them both as that which had commanded them at the beginning to protect; now released them from that oath.

"Warrior of Skye; Son of two worlds—it is time to make a choice."

Nickolous looked down at the speaker, for it was the Old One who had spoken. Black eyes looked up at him as they had so many times before, but this time there was sadness deep within their depths as she waited for his answer. He looked around at those who had journeyed with him and knew he would not, could not, return to that other place where the beginning had been forgotten—displaced by scientific explanations for events unexplained.

He drew in his breath then let it out slowly, the answer given. The Old One stroked his face gently, the touch gentle as she smiled, relieved.

"Was there ever any doubt?" Nickolous spoke within her mind, blocking off the other companions' ability to hear his conversation. As long as his journey between the two worlds had been, the Old One, with her wisdom, had always been with him. He knew that now. Knew that he had been borne to this world; had struggled in the other to understand things that he could not speak of. Had lain awake nights listening to the whisperings of the elders as they reached out to him across an endless void filled with darkened thoughts that intercepted and distorted their true meaning. He let out his breathy slowly. And yet…he was here.

He turned to Lord Moshat, the elder's gaze on his as he nodded his assent.

§ § § § §

Owen soared above the trees, wing tips brushing against the topmost branches as he followed the companions' slow journey out of the deep valley; for that is what remained of the dark caverns after the battle. Hidden were the sacred places; once again new life flourished in their stead, the little ones of the earth the caretakers once again. Beneath him walked the new hope—a half son of Skye. Warrior now, no doubt he would seek out his sister. Gabriel and Chera choosing to walk by his side for a time while Liege, with the other wolves sank back into the depths of the forest, unseen; their wraith-like forms a part of the shadows that are always at the side of one's vision; to be determined as friend or foe, depending upon the heart within.

The Old One moved a little more slowly, more cautiously, while Orith walked close by.

Watching them, Owen doubted if they would ever separate now. Two companions bound by knowledge from a deeper time. It was their time now. Timothy hurried ahead, no doubt eager to get back to Sarah.

The great Owl sighed deeply. He, too, wished to get back to what he had once known. Dipping low, he soared over Jerome, the warrior acknowledging him as he followed behind the others, while Lord Moshat and the elder from the hidden place walked with Nickolous, their voices low, indistinct even for his hearing.

Beyond the towering mountains was home. Owen felt a great restlessness within as the great Eagle soared above him. The need to return to the hunt of the night riding strong within him as he acknowledged the Eagle's right to the light.

§ § § § §

The woman ran her hands over the runes, listening to the stone beneath as the cavern glowed with an unnatural light. Whispers, carried upon the wind that snaked its way through the endless tunnels; heat, intense then cool caressed her skin as the sighing passed over head. Tilting her head to one side, listening with her heart, she spoke the words written within the stone.

Protected by the grandmothers from the beginning, she did not look up when the Flame passed overhead. Its passage marked by a warm breeze as the wind guided it to the sacred place. The woman brushed her hair back from her face as the chanting began, the sweet smell assaulting her senses as the fragrant scent of burning grass filled the air.

She straightened up. It was time to find her son...A warrior of Skye.

Beneath her, deep within the caverns of the living rock that sheltered them, the circle elders increased their chanting; their voices rising. Carried by the wind through crevice and stone, echoing through the passageways, resonating until the earth dwellers raised their voice carrying the message to those who walked above.

The Flame was home.

Looking back, Nickolous bid a silent farewell to the watcher. The valley would remain hidden; guarded by those who dwelt within. The Eagle's cry rang in the early morning air, and Nickolous responded; amazed once again at the feeling of belonging that swept over him. Around him his friends gathered. They would all share the return path.

Where they would go when that journey was completed would have to wait until they got there—to that place—

Grasping his staff to him, he felt the warmth of the wood as it responded to his emotions. It, too, was in a new beginning, and as the youth turned warrior paused at the top of the rise the great Eagle dipped low, its golden eyes mirroring the new days dawning.

Epilogue

Leah crouched in the shadows. Her senses tingling, her breathing ragged. The storm had came out of nowhere, the thunder and lightning hitting so fast that she hadn't had time to seek shelter. She blinked as the rain swirled about her, blinding her as the cold crept upward, while her body, numbed by the intense cold, reacted instinctively to the need to survive as she crept forward; out from behind the copse of red pine trees into the open. Shocked at what she saw, she could only stand there; her eyes seeing what her heart denied—chaos all about her. Slowly she moved forward. Cautiously, trying to make no sound, she skirted the edge of the clearing, the knowledge layered deep within that her world, as she knew it, had changed yet again.

Gone were the caverns with their long, winding tunnels and stale, musty air. Gone were the small ones, those of the earth diggers; the clans who lived beneath, they who listened in the darkened places so that they could warn the clans who walked above.

All gone.

Leah covered her face with her hands and sank to her knees upon the sodden earth, while the tears mingled with the cold rain.

§ § § § §

Not bothering to spare a backward glance for the figure huddled in the driving rain, the *Other* moved forward, his long strides taking him away. Away from the destruction his coming had brought. Away from the young woman who had not been there but mere moments before, but somehow had followed him when the cavern had collapsed inward upon itself from that other place where the Clans of the earth and sky warred with those like and unlike himself. Looking up into the grey sky where even darker clouds swirled—shadows within that turned endlessly upon themselves, the man breathed a sigh of relief. *Good.* His world had not changed in the short interval he had been gone. Sparing a backward glance toward the female who still huddled on the ground a short distance away, he dismissed her presence with the knowledge that his sentries would do what was necessary.

§ § § § § §

Leah tensed as the sensations washed over her. *"Danger,"* the voice whispered as she knelt in the mud, the chill creeping upward not from the dampness but from something else. She remained where she was, her body language not betraying what she saw within her mind, as dark eyes swept the wooded area in front of her for a place to hide from the unseen ones who watched. She knew she was unprotected, here, in this place. She also knew that she wasn't in that other place; the place where winged warriors guarded from distant realms—

Drawing in a deep breath, she let it out slowly, centering herself; turning inward to that other place she and her brother, Nickolous, sometimes shared when one needed the other. Thoughts guarded, reached out…seeking.

Leah pulled back, her mind reeling at what she sensed rather than saw; darkness so total, so complete…she drew in her breath sharply as the realization hit her that the connection to her brother—to that other place—was gone. She glanced around, the knowing within that she was in danger and defenseless nearly overwhelming. Carefully she started to rise, to stand. Her attention drawn to the heavily forested area in front of her, she didn't see the shadowy form watching her from beneath the overhanging branches of the hemlock tree, nor did she notice the low lying clouds that were centered slightly above her, their shape ever changing as the air about her became electrified; grey smoke like tendrils curling down to embrace her tightly within their grasp.